PROLOGUE
232 BC: RAJAGRIHA, MAGADHA

Despite its imposing size, his room in the palace was rather spartan. The ancient city of Rajagriha literally meant, 'Home of the King'. The Emperor Ashoka's empire stretched from Persia to Bengal, but of all the great cities where his writ ran large, this was his favourite. Nearby stood the finest university in the world—Nalanda. The city itself had been there for eons. Legend has it that the chariot tracks consisting of two parallel furrows cutting deep into the rock for about thirty feet, were burnt into the rock by the power and speed of Lord Krishna's chariot when he entered the city with Bhima and Arjuna to defeat the then king of Magadha, Jarasandha. Also present in the city was Venuvana, a gift to the Buddha himself from King Bimbisara (r. 543-491 BC), which became the site of the world's first Buddhist monastery where the Buddha rested and gave discourse. The Saptaparni Cave, where the first Buddhist Council met under the auspices of Maha Kassappa was not too far. The city had seen more bloodshed and political intrigue than most ancient cities, and it was at the cusp of another history-defining development.

He knew he only had a few days to live, a fate to which he reconciled without much despair. Glancing at his own reflection, that of a tired old man, he shuddered to think back about his bloodthirsty youth. Was he the same person? Had he done enough so that his good deeds outweighed his sins now? He wouldn't know in this lifetime for sure. He did know that if he could have, he would have done much, much more.

In the first years of his reign, Emperor Ashoka wreaked havoc around the world and built an empire the size of which was much greater than any other country had witnessed so far. From Persia to Bengal, the sight of his magnificent army sent shivers down the spine of other rulers. It wasn't merely the size, but the sheer speed and technology with which his army traversed that cowed down the enemy. Opposing troops swore that they did not even remember surrendering. Some who survived Ashoka's onslaught claimed that his troops came down from the sky or created such a storm that entire battalions were wiped out in the blink of an eye. Then he clashed with Kalinga and his life changed completely.

Kalinga was the final piece of the jigsaw which would complete his empire. It was a proud and small kingdom which refused to become a vassal of Ashoka. Given its small size, the thought that such a tiny kingdom could defy the Ashokan Empire infuriated Ashoka no end. He decided to wipe out the entire kingdom with every weapon at his disposal.

After the victory, Ashoka was going about the countryside filled with glee act his newly acquired prize. Suddenly, he felt the sting of a mosquito bite on his back. And then he felt a few more. He turned around to realize that they were not mosquitoes, but pebbles hurled at him by a child no more than six. His delight of conquest turned into agony and horror. Not a single able-bodied man survived in Kalinga. All he saw were rotting corpses, wailing women and orphaned children throughout the province. The dead bodies of boys as young as 12 with spears still in their hands created an unbearable odour throughout the land. They hadn't even had the opportunity to put up a fight.

Victory had been achieved, but to what effect? The empire was his, as were the curses of the people. After all this time, what exactly had he achieved at the end of his conquests?

Now, Ashoka summoned the nine men and women he had chosen and addressed them more like a friend than as an emperor.

'Many, if not all of you, must have wondered what brought about the change in me all those years ago after we captured Kalinga. I renounced violence and became a Buddhist. As I lie dying, none of my children are at my side. I thoroughly deserve this fate given the legions of children that I orphaned, the legions of old parents whose sons I slaughtered in my younger days. My suffering is nothing compared to that. My wives and children have been sent to the four corners of the empire to spread the message of non-violence and love through the teachings of the Buddha. May they succeed.

'Today, there is no war in any of my lands. The people of this empire love me. As I sit on the verge of entering into the next life, I wonder if I have done enough to wash my past sins. Before I renounce this world, there is a secret which I must share with you. Many years ago, as a young man, I would spend hours at the royal library to quench my thirst to learn more about warfare. In a dusty corner of the library, seldom if ever visited, I came across nine books.'

October 5, 1938: Sportpalast, Berlin, Nazi Germany

Addressing the crowd which was full of adulation, the Fuhrer roared above the din, 'Six years ago I took over the leadership of the Reich. On that day, one of our so-called "statesmen" said: "Now this man has taken the decisive step. Till now, he has been popular because he has been in opposition. Now he must govern and we shall see in six or eight weeks how his popularity goes!" Six years—not six weeks—have passed and I believe that they have been the most decisive years for German history. What I have achieved in these six years was possible only because I had the German people standing behind me. No single man could solve the problems which faced us unaided; only when he could speak and act in the name of the whole German people, could he master these questions....'

The middle-aged Indian man posing as a journalist was listening intently and gauging the reaction of the crowd. This was uncanny—could it be possible? As Hitler spoke on, his audience appeared to be in a trance. The speech ended with, 'In the history of our people, the year 1938 will be a great, incomparable, proud year. Later historians will show that the German nation found its way back to its position as a great nation—that our history once more became a worthy history.' The crowd was delirious. The Indian made up his mind—someone would have to go to Nalanda and double-check. He prayed that there hadn't been a leak.

March 19, 1939: Berlin, Nazi Germany

'Heil Hitler!'

'Save the theatrics, Major Heidler. What about the rest of the books?'

'They are scattered all across Asia. It's not going to be easy to get them. We don't even know if all of them still exist.'

'No one said it was going to be easy. This is precisely why you were chosen to locate and acquire them. You know how important these books are to the Fuhrer. Do whatever it takes. I want a weekly report on your progress. Dismissed!'

Major Josef Heidler stepped out of the building. '*Scheisse*,' he nervously muttered, as he took out a red cardboard cigarette pack from his jacket which read 'Sulima Zigretten—Sondermichung'. He lit a cigarette to calm his frayed nerves. He wondered if he would ever know the name of the *beamter*, the bureaucratic drone, he had just spoken to. He did know one thing though—he had to deliver the goods. He was a reluctant member of the Nazi Party and didn't attach too much importance to the Nazi ideology. The Nazis were saying what the people wanted to hear and Hitler was giving them something important after the embarrassment at Versailles and the misery caused by the hyperinflation in the Weimar Republic—self-belief and hope. Austria was now part of Nazi Germany and the British-French alliance had ceded the Sudetenland province of Czechoslovakia to the Nazis. Hitler's high-handedness apart, he could not deny the progress he saw around him. Germany was rising from the ashes of the Great War and there was optimism in the air. Who would have imagined this ten years ago? The ignominy of Versailles was history. A new Germany beckoned. If these books were important to the Fatherland, he would use his skills to acquire them.

He got into his newly acquired Opel Olympia, an all-steel bodied roadster, which definitely turned heads and was a testament to German engineering and craftsmanship. He admired its interior. How could a nation which built such machines have lost the Great War? More determined to find those books, he decided to drive straight to work.

March 19, 1939: Bombay, British India

At about the same time, a morose Prithvi Rathore was fixing the flat tyre on his Austin 7 in the members' parking lot at the Cricket Club of India as his friend Geoffrey Townsend was helping him lift the chassis with a rusted jack, its green colour peeling off in parts.

Bombay, unlike the other great cities of India which are ancient, has been built from nothing by both the Indians and the British. This unheralded fusion gave it a surfeit of unique characteristics. In 1665, when Bombay passed into British hands from the Portuguese as part of the dowry of Catherine of Braganza, the king's advisor displayed unbelievable geographical ignorance and told the king with utter conviction, 'Your dowry—Bombay—is within a very little distance from Brazil.' On the other hand, displaying remarkable prescience, the Portuguese Governor of Goa implored the king of Portugal in a letter not to give away Bombay, reasoning, 'India will be lost to Portugal on the same day on which the English nation is settled in Bombay.'

With no distinct natural advantage other than an unrivalled harbour on a coastline bereft of havens, Bombay, with over a million inhabitants, has grown to be the second city of the British Empire, strangling Goa, Surat and Ormuz to become the Gateway of India. But transcending the natural advantage that geography afforded it, its people had grown to become its greatest asset. Caste, class and creed divided India into unbreakable compartments. In the rest of India's cities, manufacturing remained firmly in English and Scottish hands while trade had been monopolized by the ardent Marwari trading community. The Anglo-Portuguese wedding had given birth in Bombay to the Parsis from Persia, the Banias from Gujarat, the Bhatias from Kutch, the Konkani Muslims from the south and a smidgen of Baghdadi Jews. These were amongst the keenest trading races in the world and made Bombay far too speculative rather than ultra-conservative which was the besetting sin of most of India. In most parts of India, the delineation between the Englishman and the Indian were clear and in some it was possible for an Englishman to spend his entire life without knowing an Indian gentleman intimately; in Bombay this demarcation was all but a footnote of history.

The Bengali of Calcutta was undoubtedly more cultured and a better orator in the English language, the South Indian from Madras had found his Mecca in the educational machinery and produced better administrators, scientists and mathematicians which helped the British administer India. However, Bombay guided India in forming a metropolitan, commercial outlook which comes only from business, voyage and the influence of assets. Nowhere was this clear cosmopolitanism more apparent than in the great cricket clubs of Bombay where the upper crust Indians wore the cricketing whites with the English on the field and shared a Byculla Cocktail off it in the club bar.

'Three ducks in a row, old chap. You are walking on thin ice. You may not be in the XI soon. What happened to those supple Asian wrists of yours?' posed Townsend.

Prithvi replied, 'I have no idea. In all fairness, Tennyson was bowling extremely fast on a green pitch. The overcast conditions were conducive to swing too.'

'Excuses, excuses!' exclaimed Townsend

'There! It is fucking fixed. I hope nothing else breaks down today in this epitome of British engineering. Do you want to grab a bite at the Taj?'

Townsend let out a sigh. 'I sure would. Ask your dad to call up Mr Gandhi and call off the strike. Don't you read the news? Everything is shut as a sign of protest. And it is an English car, not British. We Scots would have built a better car.'

'Sure you would have if you managed to get out of the bar. You are probably the only Scot who actually loves cricket. What's the protest against?' asked Prithvi.

Townsend laughed, 'Who is the bloody Indian in this car? It's a new law in the United Provinces which places restrictions on the newspapers and radio. Sedition is in the air!'

'And how is keeping the coffee shop and restaurants at the Taj shut going to help prevent sedition?'

Townsend replied, 'I'd be damned if I know! Seriously though, don't these protests, these movements to get rid of the British affect you at all?'

'No. I have more important things on my mind.'

'Really? Like what?' asked Townsend.

Prithvi quipped, 'Like my complete lack of batting form at the moment.'

'Don't you want India's "independence"? Surely, you must have some kind of political views.'

Prithvi replied, 'Do I? Well, I think that Gandhi is an impressive man and one can't argue with his logic. But I believe you English are a stabilizing force in an extremely diverse nation. There is as much in common between a Kashmiri and a Tamil as is between a Greek and an Englishman. The only unifying force seems to be the Union Jack at the moment.'

'For God's sake man, I am Scottish!' Townsend shouted. 'And you existed as a very developed society in ancient times. Didn't you study archaeology at Oxford? Surely, I need not point out the Indus Valley Civilization to you.'

Prithvi quietly replied, 'That is ancient history. It is irrelevant for the future.'

After dropping Geoffrey off, Prithvi reflected on the conversation. His father was decidedly pro-British. The old man only wore bespoke suits from Savile Row, almost all of which were from Gieves & Hawkes. The rest were from Norton & Sons. And Gandhi's call to boycott British goods was met with an expression of genuine shock, 'He wants to help me get freedom by burning my clothes? No thank you sir, I'd rather be clothed than be *that* free!' As far as Prithvi was concerned, the pendulum of the father-son relationship swung from frosty to lukewarm. His father was a kind, large-hearted man whose life revolved around making money. He expected his son to take over one day and had made all the right moves that a brown sahib could. Prithvi had been sent to Winchester College, where he fell in love with cricket. His pedigree also got him into Oxford, despite his Winchester grades, where he studied archaeology. His father had played every conceivable card to make sure his son turned out to be as much of a sahib as him. But then, he hadn't accounted for Prithvi's closeness to his grandfather.

Prithvi's mother had passed away when he was three. The earliest memory Prithvi had was of his grandfather lifting him up, to help him light the pyre on which his dead mother lay. The rest of the family and friends were urging him not to cry, little realizing that Prithvi wasn't crying at all. His tears were caused by the fumes and smoke of the pyre. Only his grandfather realized that his eyes were burning and took him away. Prithvi was too young to comprehend the death of his mother but was old enough to realize that the only person who seemed to understand him was his grandfather.

He often wondered if his closeness to his grandfather was a result of that unfortunate happenstance. It was a question which often kept him awake at night during his adolescent and early teenage years. Given a choice, he would definitely want his mother alive. Whenever another kid would show off a sweater knit by his mother or talk of a meal cooked by her, Prithvi felt a glut of emotions within a matter of instants— envy, betrayal, guilt followed by a sense of hollowness, finally ending with a desire to experience a mother, however stern or cruel she might be. Sometimes he would assure himself that she had merely gone away somewhere because of something bad he had done as a child. And that there was light at the end of the tunnel and that she would soon come back and forgive him and take him away someplace. She never did.

The absence of a mother and the distance from his father drew him all the more closer to his grandfather; his Dada who taught him everything he loved—reading, riding and of course, cricket. As a child, Prithvi would hide his grandfather's umbrella which doubled as a walking cane at times, till his Dada agreed to play a game of cricket. In all these years, he had only one major showdown with his grandfather, which was just before he left for Oxford. Thinking of his grandfather's demand, the smile was replaced by a frown as he pulled his Austin 7 into the driveway of his Malabar Hill apartment.

March 29, 1939: Office of the Under-Secretary of State for India, London

Richard Austen Butler, Baron Butler of Saffron Walden, looking much older than a man at thirty-four should, served as the Under-Secretary of State for India and was known in official circles as Rab. That's because he signed the umpteen documents, which were not considered important enough for the Secretary, with merely his initials.

Butler was born in Attock Serai, in British India, into a family of Cambridge dons and Indian governors. He had injured his right arm in a riding accident there and hence did never have a firm handshake. Else, he would probably have been the Secretary and not the Under-Secretary. His perpetual stoop did not help either. He was, however, a scholar in his own right. He was educated at Marlborough College and Pembroke College, Cambridge, where he served as President of the Cambridge Union Society in his third year in 1924. While at Cambridge he read French, German and, in his fourth year, history and international relations, in which he obtained one of the highest Firsts in the University.

Today, Butler was not necessarily in the best of moods. The Nazi regime had requested another 'cultural exchange', through which more German archaeologists would visit India. Looking up at a startled Major Hewitt, he demanded, 'For a gent who talks so much about the German future, Hitler seems far too interested in digging up India's past. Why is that?'

Hewitt apologetically said, 'I don't know, sir.'

Butler continued, 'Precisely old boy—no one does. I have checked with other departments. When they do send mountaineering expeditions all over the world, to prove that no summit is too high for the perfect race, that is understandable. But why archaeology and why India? They are not sending archaeology teams to any other part of the world at this rate. This is the fourth request in the last eight months. What are they digging for? Are they looking for something we should be aware of?'

Slightly embarrassed Hewitt said, 'I don't know, sir.'

'I know you don't. It was a rhetorical question, Major. But you need to find out. Here are the names of the chaps who are or have been members of expeditions to India. There happen to be seven of them. But one name is common to all but the first expedition: Josef Heidler. Within the next 48 hours, I want a thorough dossier on this man and as much information about these expeditions as possible. Collect information about other members too. Anything that sticks out like the proverbial sore thumb must be brought to my attention. Your entire department must burn the midnight oil if it has to.'

'Yes sir.'

'And Hewitt, put me in touch with our man handling German counter-intelligence in New Delhi. I want him to keep a tab on these archaeologists. By the way, who is handling German counter-intelligence in India at the moment?'

Hewitt thought for a moment, 'Youdale is.'

The Under-Secretary's reaction was an uncharacteristic, 'That Yorkshire man? Oh, fuck!'

April 2, 1939: Office of Major Josef Heidler, Berlin, Nazi Germany

Josef Heidler entered his office to find his two main aides bent over a fairly large model of British India, so immersed in work that they did not seem to notice him at all. Heidler cleared his throat to make his presence felt. Simultaneously, they looked up at Heidler and smiled, not bothering with the Nazi salute.

Max Kahn was the older of the two, aged 55. He had spent five years studying the Vedas in Benares and was considered one of Europe's premier Indologists. He often gave guest lectures at German universities on Hinduism and on India. He had been specifically identified by Heidler as a critical cog in this quest. While there were quite a few India specialists in Britain, they were hard to come by on mainland Europe.

Karl Lewerenz was a good two decades younger than Kahn and was considered a leading name in the emerging field of experimental archaeology, not only in Europe but all over the world. Experimental archaeology employs a number of different methods, techniques, analyses and approaches in order to generate and test hypotheses or an interpretation, based upon archaeological source material, like ancient structures or artifacts.

'So has there been any progress at all?' asked Heidler impatiently.

Karl looked quizzically at Max, awaiting a response from the older man.

Kahn stroked his stubble and replied, 'Josef, Josef, you have to be patient.'

Heidler replied, 'Patience and time are not luxuries we have.'

Kahn continued, 'We aren't talking about something a few hundred years old. The book we found was thanks to some excellent work by young Karl here and if I may say, a fair bit of luck. How useful was the first book to the State?'

'The answer is visible. The book was priceless. Now the Fuhrer wants them all as soon as possible.'

'Of course he does. What about our Indian travel permits, are they ready?'

Heidler confidently said, 'They should arrive soon.'

Lewerenz cut in, 'Get ready to leave for India then. We will try to narrow down the location by the end of the week.'

A slightly annoyed Heidler asked, 'Sometimes I wonder who is running this show: you or I?'

Kahn defused the tension by saying, 'Of course you are running it, Josef. But there would be no show without me now, would there?' Max then looked at Karl and added, 'Well, and there would be no show without him either.'

April 14, 1939: Mahabaleshwar, Bombay, British India

Richard Youdale was ironing his jodhpurs for the next day's polo match when he received a telegram to report to Bombay immediately.

In British Raj parlance, Youdale was a Yorkshire man who had gone 'native'. Unlike a lot of the British officers in India, he wasn't from Eton or Winchester College or even the local equivalent, Sherwood or Mayo. He was the elder of two siblings and had joined the Indian Civil Service more for the money than the prestige. There was an obvious class difference between him and most of the other British officers; this enabled him to empathize with a lot of the Indians.

A major tiff with a British landlord over working conditions for Indian workers in the Bengal province resulted in the landlord being heavily penalized and forced to rectify his manner of operation. It also resulted in a 'routine transfer' of Youdale to the dour Foreign Desk in charge of Germany and Scandinavia and he was moved to Bombay. The message was clear: Youdale had gone native and his actions could embarrass British citizens and hinder British business interests. It was best to move him to an office where he wouldn't be a problem.

Initially, the arrival of the Nazis created a buzz in his office. Rapid German industrialization and militarization had already raised the alarm bells in the UK, but India was a world far removed from continental Europe and the buzz died down soon enough. His work usually entailed helping German and

Scandinavian citizens with transport, permits and keeping them out of trouble.

Youdale was curious about what his next assignment would be. Despite the minor annoyance of missing out on the polo match, he looked forward to getting some real work done for a change.

April 20, 1939: The Rathore Residence, Malabar Hill, Bombay, British India

Prithvi frowned. He had recently been asked to study archaeology by his grandfather. Like British food, archaeology too was an acquired taste.

The old gardener Babu almost threw the water hose at Prithvi as he ran the Austin 7 over a bed of flowers arranged by the gardener. Smiling sheepishly at Babu, Prithvi then entered the house, unaware of the mud on his cricket shoes leaving a trail on the gleaming marble flooring. Another dirty look was a followed by an even wider sheepish grin.

'Babu, where is Dada?'

'Remove your shoes before you spoil the rest of the house. I cannot sit and clean all day,' replied Babu as he busily rolled a bidi with his hands, whilst his eyes stayed fixated on Prithvi's shoes. Satisfied that Prithvi had taken the shoes off, he continued, 'Dada left for Calcutta in a hurry after Chatterjee sahib came with some telegram. He looked very agitated. I've never seen him like that before. Now, sahib is in London, while big sahib is in Calcutta. So, you are the master of the house.'

Babu had spent close to 50 years in the household. Over the years he had become the self-appointed head among the domestic help in the family home. While he was unfailingly polite to Prithvi's grandfather and almost grudgingly polite to his father, he still thought of Prithvi as the child of the house. It annoyed Prithvi a touch—but then again, Babu had bought him his first cricket bat from the market when Prithvi was five, sparking a passion for the game unlike any other. Anything was forgivable for that!

'Something must have come up at our jute mill in Calcutta. He usually doesn't go without informing me. It must be really urgent. Has he left me a letter?'

'Yes, as a matter of fact, he has.' Babu lifted his tunic and removed a piece of paper, which was neatly tucked into the waist of his pyjamas.

> Dear Prithvi,
>
> Things are not right. I've had to go to Calcutta on some urgent business. Your life might be in danger. Under my mattress is a revolver. Carry it with you at all times. If push comes to shove, do not hesitate to pull the trigger. Be very careful and do not socialize with new people. If something untoward happens, Calcutta is the place you should come to.
>
> Love,
> Dada

This was truly bizarre! His grandfather was a rational, logical man. This letter went against the spirit of his genial nature. However, from the tone of the letter, it was obvious that he was dead serious. And he certainly had no clue where in Calcutta was he supposed to go to in case 'something untoward' happened. How abstract 'something untoward' was, anyway! Much to Babu's chagrin, Prithvi absent-mindedly put his shoes back on and headed straight to his grandfather's room.

His grandfather's room hadn't changed in years. The room had a high ceiling and all the walls were lined with ceiling-high bookshelves. There was a ladder on a rail for easy accessibility to all the books located at a good height. It was one of Prithvi's favourite contraptions as a child. Located in the centre of the room was a sturdy teakwood bed with a mosquito net around it. Prithvi lifted the mattress to find a cardboard box. On top of the cardboard box was a poem handwritten by his grandfather—

> Oh brother,
> Do you know where heaven is?
> It has no beginning, it has no end,
> Nor is it any country. ...
> In my heart
> Heaven finds her home,
> And in my songs
> Her melodies ...

The poem did seem familiar. The box revealed a Kongsberg Colt revolver and boxes of cartridges. The left side of the slide was stamped '11.25 m/m Aut. Pistol M/1914'. It was a variation of the .45ACP caliber semi-automatic American Colt M/1911 pistol made under license in Norway by the Kongsberg Vaapenfabrikk.

Paying heed to his grandfather's advice, he loaded it and decided to keep it with him at all times. Although he had been to hunt a few times, he hardly considered himself a good shot. As he headed to his room to take a shower, he felt tense holding the pistol and hoped he would not have to use it.

April 27, 1939: Office of the Under-Secretary of State for India, London

Butler had just finished reading the thin dossier whilst sipping tea. He put the cup down and looked up at Hewitt. His look was a mixture of puzzlement and sheer disdain.

Butler said, 'Hewitt, this report states that they are on a trail and that they are digging at sites of ancient Hindu temples and asking locals questions about books.'

Hewitt crisply replied with a smile, 'Indeed, sir.'

Butler rolled his eyes and said, 'Hewitt—that is what all archaeologists do. The other people who dig are called miners. I am sure the Germans are not looking for coal.'

'Indeed, indeed.' Hewitt felt blood rushing on to his cheeks.

'Do we know what books these are?'

Hewitt weakly said, 'Probably some religious texts.'

Butler mockingly arched his eyebrows and asked, 'Really? Near temple ruins? I would never have guessed. What kind of books, Hewitt?'

'We do not know, sir,' Hewitt said, looking stricken.

Butler said, 'The work permits have not been dispatched to Germany. Give them a ten-day permit. If they ask for an extension, tell them something about some random native festival that must not be disturbed. With travelling, that should amount to five days of archaeology which is too short for such an operation. If they still come, we will know that they are really desperate. Put Youdale on their trail to gather information from them and about them. And then I want a real report.'

May 1, 1939: Calcutta, British India

All nine of them were finally seated, waiting for someone to break the silence. Finally, the youngest man in the room whom everyone here addressed as Mahindra removed his reading glasses, pressed the ridge of his nose and cleared his throat to speak.

'We do know that they have found one of the books. Has this council been compromised?'

The oldest man in the room firmly said, 'Not a chance.'

'Then how did this happen?' asked another.

The old man continued, 'There are clues. The Germans seemed to have found the trail which has not been unearthed for centuries.'

'So what do we do now?' asked a third.

The old man patiently replied, 'We could unearth the trail too. Thankfully, the back-ups are safe. We do have the advantage of the knowledge of the sequence. They most certainly don't. On the other hand, they have a lot more manual resources.'

The third man continued, 'No man in this room is younger than 65. We are too old to follow the trail. I don't recollect the last time all nine of us met—we have been reduced to a coffee club. The knowledge of sequence is probably useless in the quest. I never believed that it would come down to this—at least not in my lifetime.'

Finally the old man said, 'We shall have to recruit someone outside the council. Before any of you raise an objection, let me say that I know this has never been done before. But these times are extraordinary. My grandson Prithvi has been groomed to take over my position when I die. He will just have an initiation earlier than expected. Does anyone have any objections?'

Prithvi's grandfather waited patiently for a minute. Since no objection was forthcoming he said, 'It is settled then! As convener of the Nine Unknowns, I formally adjourn this meeting. However, all of us need to remain in the vicinity lest we need to meet at short notice.'

May 10, 1939: Patna, British India

Despite spending most of his adult life in India, Youdale mused that he would certainly never get used to the heat in Central India. Unlike Bombay, there wasn't much humidity here, which meant the heat pricked a lot more and you sweated a lot less. What has obsessed the Germans to agree to a ten-day trip? To their credit, they had not wasted a single day. They would be arriving shortly and Youdale would be their 'British liaison'. He had to admit, this was a lot more fun. And in all his years of stay in India, he had never heard of Nalanda. After going through the archives, he was quite excited by the prospect of visiting the ruins.

Nalanda's story was quintessentially the story of India. It represented everything India once was, what India could potentially have become and what India today had become. It was one of the oldest, if not the oldest university in the world. Founded in AD 427 by Kumaragupta I, its name translated in Sanskrit, meant 'Giver of Knowledge'. And that is precisely what it did for over seven centuries. In its halcyon days it housed 10,000 students and 2,000 faculty members from India, Sri Lanka, Korea, Japan, China, Tibet, Indonesia, Persia and Turkey who lived in dormitories in the campus itself. The campus also housed a nine-storied library, meditation halls, temples and classrooms and was set amidst picturesque parks and lakes. Education was free as taxes from 100 neighbouring villages secured the finances of the university. Unlike other ancient universities, the studies and research at Nalanda were not religion-centric. Besides Buddhism-based theology, subjects taught included astronomy, medicine, mathematics, linguistics, logic and grammar. Despite suffering serious damage during wars, Nalanda was rebuilt and upgraded by King Purugupta and King Harshavardhana. However, this great centre of learning couldn't take a third blow when the invading Muslim armies of Bakhtiyar Khilji laid Nalanda waste, by massacring faculty and students and burning what they saw as 'infidel texts'.

Today, Nalanda was a ruin, ninety per cent of which remained unexcavated. That was a lot of digging, even for the "racially superior" Germans given that they had only ten days, mused Youdale.

Less than five kilometres from Youdale, the German archaeology team was having a heated discussion.

Josef Heidler, 'But how can you be sure?'

Karl Lewerenz looked at him as if Heidler was an ignorant fool. 'We can't be sure. I am done explaining. Max, you try.' Lewerenz stormed out.

Max Kahn spoke in a much milder tone. 'Major Heidler, the discovery of the first book was a sheer accident. From the first book, we found out about the existence of the others and unearthed what could be a potential trail. The first book spoke of the need to procure nine bricks to build an edifice. We interpreted it as a reference to nine books based on other historical and mythological data. Experimental archaeology is a relatively new and unproven technique. Young Karl is probably the best experimental archaeologist in the world but I have been strictly instructed not to divulge all data to him. We couldn't just go to Nalanda and start digging. So given the current state of the ruins, we recreated a model of the entire university in Germany. This model was based on Vedic architectural layouts and techniques. We have estimated what would be ideal locations to hide valuable artifacts from a Hindu or Buddhist mindset and current practices. However, on the flip side, we are trying to second guess extremely smart men. They were working with advanced astronomy and mathematics while the Europeans were slightly better than cave-dwellers. We don't even know what we are looking for. It could be the remaining eight books. It could be just one of them. It could be a clue leading to the books. It could be in Sanskrit or it could be in Pali. And lastly, but most importantly, we could have picked the wrong university. These could also be in either Vikramashila or in Taxila, not to forget minor ones like Odantapuri. But Nalanda is the best bet.'

'Best bet? These are not horses! I understand your point, but I don't know if the Fuhrer will.'

'Ten days is too less to mount an archaeology expedition.'

'I know. But we had to take this chance. The British seem to be getting suspicious. Next time, they might decline our request for permits. They have even given us a British 'liaison' this time. He is supposed to assist us with local culture and tradition and drive us to Nalanda. As if we are on a goodwill tour in this damn country to mingle with the local idiots. He is a spy. Make sure we speak in German at all times. The English never bother to learn anything else. It's time to go meet this "liaison".'

May 16, 1939: Cricket Club of India, Bombay, British India

This was an important cricket match. Not necessarily for Prithvi's club, but for him to retain a position in the playing XI. He had worked hard to break into the regular first XI, after being the twelfth man for close to two seasons. But what was he supposed to do with the Colt revolver? He pictured himself walking onto the pitch with pads, gloves, a bat and a holster. That would surely make Tennyson think twice about bowling bouncers and beamers. He decided to keep his gun in the kit near his legs, whilst he waited his turn in the pavilion. He usually went in at number five or six depending on the situation. That meant that on most occasions there would be a wait of a couple hours before he took his guard at the crease. He tried to put the thoughts of his grandfather's letter behind him and concentrate on the game. The pitch looked flat enough, but there was a wind blowing and the cloud cover meant that a good bowler could swing the ball. And the visiting XI from Australia had some very good pace bowlers.

The first ball was short pitched and Townsend caught it right in the ribcage. Townsend was his best mate and Prithvi's mind was already off the letter. The second ball was a bouncer and hit Townsend either on the throat or the jaw—it was too quick to know for sure. Off the third ball, Yardley the Aussie quickly ended Townsend's misery with a toe-crunching yorker that disturbed the furniture. Actually, the leg stump was shattered and a new one had to be called in.

The captain said, 'Prithvi, you're in.'

'But I usually go in at five or six. Never batted at three.'

'Stop being a sissy. Grow a backbone. You've been scoring ducks all season at five or six. Might as well baptize you with fire. Now go!'

While Prithvi crossed Townsend on the way to the crease, Townsend, still rubbing his sore jaw whispered, 'The bastard is fast and the ball's swinging. Watch it.'

Prithvi ducked to avoid the first ball, able to hear it whiz past his ear. 'That was a Goddamn understatement, Townsend!' The second ball was a short, fast outswinger and Prithvi faintly nicked it to the wicket-keeper. Thankfully, the umpire turned down the vociferous appeals. Well, he wasn't about to be a gentleman and walk off either. Prithvi wondered if the bowler had a three-card trick—two short ones, followed by a yorker. Not wanting to be bullied, he took his chances—stepped out of the crease, converted the yorker into a low full-toss and whipped it toward the leg side for a boundary. He could hear the cheers on the balcony of his dressing room and smiled.

He had always been a stoic, studious and dour batsman—right out of the English school of batting. Today, he threw caution to the wind and used his wrists to great effect, with not a whiff of concern for his technique. The Aussies just did not know what to bowl. At lunch he was 48 not out, and the team score was 61/2. By tea the score was 141/4 and he was on 93 and a touch nervous. At tea, his captain told him of a telegram waiting for him at the reception. Prithvi decided the telegram could wait for a couple hours. After tea, two wickets fell in succession and he was left with the tail. Not wanting to miss out on a century, he once again defied tradition and lifted the opposing off-spinner for two straight sixes to bring up his century. The wickets continued to fall at the one end, and Prithvi kept blasting fours and sixes at the other. It was as if he was playing a different match on a different pitch from the rest of his team mates. Finally the innings wrapped up at 339; Prithvi remaining unbeaten on 207, his first double century and a record for runs made in a single day's play on this ground. As he walked back to the dressing room, the Aussie players gave him a polite round of applause and many spectators gave him a standing ovation. He wished his grandfather were here. The rest of the team members whistled as he returned—all except the captain. The captain came over, patted his back and muttered, 'I am sorry, son.' He handed Prithvi a telegram which bluntly informed him that his father had died in an plane crash in the Alps.

May 18, 1939: Patna, British India

Youdale greeted the wiry bespectacled Indian Sergeant flashing a broad grin. 'They didn't get too suspicious, did they, Pandey?'

Pandey replied, 'Not at all. They were very careful when they saw British officers and held their tongue. They were quite carefree around the Indians.'

Youdale smiled and said, 'What a bunch of arrogant fools. You probably speak better German than anyone else on the German desk, including the Brits.'

'Not quite, but I did eavesdrop at times and heard most of their conversation.' Taking note of the questioning look in Youdale's eyes, he said, 'Well, they are after a series of ancient books which belong to the Nine Unknowns.'

'The who?' Youdale looked at him quizzically.

Immediately and almost without batting an eyelid Pandey repeated, 'The Nine Unknowns.'

A confused Youdale posed, 'Tell me Pandey, is that a translation goof-up?'

Shaking his head Pandey assuredly said, 'No. I am sure.'

His forehead creasing into a frown, Youdale said, 'Well, I better go find out more and file my report for London.'

May 25, 1939: Bombay, British India

Outwardly, it appeared that Prithvi took the news of his father's death with admirable equanimity. In reality, he was too shell-shocked to react. The match was forgotten; how irrelevant cricket now seemed.

Once he reached home, he knew that it was time to go to Calcutta. But where in Calcutta was his grandfather? He immediately went back to the poem to look for a clue—

> Oh brother,
> Do you know where heaven is?
> It has no beginning, it has no end,
> Nor is it any country. ...
> In my heart
> Heaven finds her home,
> And in my songs
> Her melodies ....

Of course! The verse was by Rabindranath Tagore. He proceeded to his grandfather's room and found the Tagore book, *Balaka* (Flight of Swans). Scribbled on the last page were the words 'Come to Shantiniketan'. His grandfather was in Shantiniketan, the university town near Calcutta founded by Tagore! He had to get there fast—a train ride could take a week. He decided to make a call. He dialled the required three digits.

'Hello Jeh. How are you?' asked Prithvi.

The accent which replied was a curious mix of Indian and French, 'Hello, Prithvi. I am doing fine. Nice of you to ask. Is this a courtesy call? The urgency in your voice doesn't seem to signify so.'

Prithvi said, 'I really don't have the time to explain but I do need a favour. I need to fly to Calcutta right now.'

The voice at the other end replied, 'Aha. You are in luck then. Just go to the Juhu Aerodrome and ask for my pilot Neville Vincent. I shall make the arrangements but the ride might not be very comfortable. You will also have to stop at Nagpur and Jamshedpur on the way.'

Prithvi heaved a sigh of relief and stated, 'Thanks. Comfort is not a priority. What do I tell Mr Vincent?'

'Just give him my name.'

Prithvi asked, 'Just tell him Jeh sent me?'

The reply from the end was—'No old friend, but I am not going to burden you with telling him my whole name either. Just tell him—JRD Tata.'

At the Juhu Aerodrome, all the arrangements had been made. Prithvi realized that Jeh had typically underplayed the 'uncomfortable' bit. He had to travel in a de Havilland Fox Moth biplane sitting on top of a lot of airmail. But he reached Calcutta later in the day and made his way to Shantiniketan.

He was expecting his grandfather to say something about his father's death and give him a hug. No such gesture was forthcoming; not even a greeting or a smile. The only words said were, 'Have you heard of The Nine Unknowns?'

232 BC: RAJAGRIHA, MAGADHA

Emperor Ashoka raised his hand to silence the group of people who had began murmuring.

'In that corner of the library, I found nine books.

'Book One: *Nītivistāram evam Manastātvik Yudhavigraham* (Propaganda and Psychological Warfare)—how to convince a nation to go to war and how to control the population of a newly acquired land; Book Two: *Yudhavigraham Sārīravrittim* (Physiology in Warfare)—how a person can kill a fellow human with merely a touch; Book Three: *Jīvanuvijnānam* (Microbiology)—how tiny organisms can be used to wreak havoc upon entire masses of people; Book Four: *Samyogam* (Communication)—how to communicate with troops and generals thousands of miles away without the need of a messenger; Book Five: *Āloka* (Light)—how to build a weapon of mass destruction which can cause the death of millions by splitting the tiniest of particles; Book Six: *Aparasāyanaśāstram* (Alchemy)—how to alter the state of metals; thus giving the owner of the knowledge an unlimited supply of money and weaponry during war; Book Seven: *Mādhyākarṣaṇam evam Abhikṣepaśāstram* (Gravitation and Rocketry)—how to travel through space and build planes, rockets and missiles to be used in war; Book Eight: *Sriṣṭitattvam* (Cosmology)—how to use the speed of light, thereby making interstellar travel possible and give futher impetus to develop advanced weaponry and aircraft; Book Nine: *Samājavijñānam* (Sociology)—how to study societies, their evolution and predict their downfall.

'The origin of these books is unknown. However, I do believe them to be at least a few thousand years old and written after the war of Kurukshetra between the Pandavas and the Kauravas—a war which almost rendered this land devoid of all human life. Think about it. The Brahmastra is the weapon of mass destruction used by Arjuna. The book is replete with tales of *vimanas*. However, I was still not convinced. So I decided to build them myself. And I was successful. Who could defeat an army which could fly, communicate from thousands of miles away and destroy the enemy with merely one weapon? Which is why, Book Nine is far more important than it looks. Societies and civilizations will always seek to control other societies and civilizations. It is in the nature of Man to control his fellow humans. I could have used the knowledge I gathered from this book for the good of humanity, but I chose to conquer the world. All I did was cause death and destruction. It left me with a sense of emptiness, of meaninglessness. I then decided to dedicate my life to Buddhism and be a good human being. An emperor is truly an emperor only if he uses all means at his disposal for the upliftment his people. After the Kalinga war, that is all I have done.

'But today, I have made a difficult decision. I had planned to destroy these books when the time came. However, this knowledge can be used for the benefit of humanity. I have decided that I shall entrust one book to each one of you. Each of these books will be passed onto your successor who may or may not be your progeny. A sturdy tree may not necessarily bear a sweet fruit. Hence, the successor has to be approved by the majority of the nine chosen ones. There may come a time when it may not be safe for individuals to keep books. If a collective decision to hide the books needs to be taken, then the Nine Unknowns must do everything within their power to ensure the safety of the books.

'Borders change, kingdoms, empires and even entire civilizations rise and fall. You will see the entire history of humanity as a tapestry and not be wavered by the prevalent political scenario, no matter how bleak it is. You will never pledge your loyalties to any kingdom or empire. Your loyalties will always lie with humanity and you must always use this knowledge for the greater good and never for personal or political gain. The greed inherent in every human being will tempt you to do otherwise, but the presence of the other eight will help keep you in check. You have been chosen because I believe you to be the finest men and women of my empire.

'Finally, you shall never reveal your existence to the outside world. You shall call yourselves "The Nine Unknowns".'

May 25, 1939: Office of Under-Secretary for India Rab Butler, London

Butler had just finished reading the report. After checking with a few reliable sources, he realized that this wasn't the report of a stark, mad Yorkshire man gone native.

Turning to Hewitt Butler said, 'Hewitt, you will increase the stay of the German archaeologists as a "gesture of goodwill". We must not let them know that we know what they know.'

A slightly confused Hewitt asked, 'Excuse me, sir?'

Butler chuckled and stated, 'You are thick, aren't you Hewitt? You didn't bother reading the report, did you?'

Hewitt shook his head and replied, 'Well, no sir.'

Butler said, 'I am glad you didn't. Else you would have in your infinite wisdom thought it was the report of a lunatic and not passed it along to me.'

Hewitt managed to mutter, 'Well …'

Butler interrupted him, 'Tell me, Hewitt. Have you heard of the Nine Unknowns?'

May 25, 1939: Nalanda Ruins, Nalanda, British India

Heidler was getting exasperated with Karl Lewerenz's attitude. While the kid was bright, even brilliant, he simply did not understand the importance of the books for the Fatherland. Lewerenz had been curious and had questioned Kahn and Heidler about it. But they deemed it prudent that he did not necessarily need the information. However, given the urgency of the situation, Heidler took a decision.

He said to Kahn, 'Max, I think it is time we tell Karl everything about the books. He needs to understand the importance and urgency.'

Kahn replied, 'I've been saying that for a while. But it is your call.'

Lewerenz's interest was piqued, 'I've wanted to know about the books for while. What's the fuss all about?'

Kahn smiled at him and asked, 'Tell me, Karl. Have you heard of the Nine Unknowns?'

May 26, 1939: Shantiniketan, West Bengal, British India

Prithvi wondered if his grandfather had gone senile overnight. He asked his grandfather, 'You know Dada I've always thought of you as a rational man. But you really expect me to believe this fantastic tale of the Nine Unknowns?'

His grandfather nonchalantly replied, 'No, I don't expect you to believe it. I wouldn't believe it if I were you. However, perhaps you would give me a few logical explanations since you are so rational.'

Prithvi arched his brow at his grandfather knowing that this was a game he had to play. 'Sure.'

His grandfather asked, 'The iron pillar at the Qutub Minar in Delhi—it is 2000 years old—made by the great Chandragupta Vikramaditya ...'

Prithvi continued, '...Yes, during the Gupta dynasty. Well, the Jain temple that surrounded it was destroyed by Qutub-ud-din-Aibak. The building material collected from the rubble was used to build the Qutub Minar. I know the history, Dada—what about it?'

His grandfather snapped, 'Very good. I know you've studied it. I paid for that damn education of yours. A work of art and a testament of its era. But tell me lad, why ... hasn't ... it ... rusted?' The old man looked at his grandson triumphantly.

Prithvi hesitantly replied, 'Well, uh, I am sure there is a logical explanation.'

The old man quipped, 'Then give it to me.'

Mildly irritated at being stumped Prithvi said, 'Surely, you don't expect me to buy this story because of a pillar that has resisted rusting!'

The amused old man asked, 'You're not wriggling out so easily. Do you have a logical, rational explanation?'

Prithvi drily replied, 'No.'

'Next—there is more gold in India than any other country on the planet. In times of famines and droughts, the temples have been flooded with gold.'

Prithvi replied with his own question, 'So?'

His grandfather emphatically asked, 'Where do you think the gold mines are?'

Prithvi weakly said, 'Uh, I don't know.'

'No gold rush either. It's been there for eons with just one gold mine?'

Pausing for dramatic effect, the old man continued, 'And there are so many holy rivers in India. What is the significance of people dipping almost exclusively in the Ganges?'

A stumped Prithvi said softly, 'I don't know.'

His grandfather said, 'From time to time, chemicals have been added to the river to cure ailments. Of course, this stopped a while ago but old habits die hard. Now let's speak of warfare.'

'Warfare?' posed Prithvi.

His grandfather continued, 'Yes. In the battles that Tipu Sultan waged against the English, he used rockets. This was in 1799. The English began a rocket programme in 1801 after defeating Tipu. Where would Tipu Sultan get the know-how to make rockets? And how would a tiny Indian state have more advanced weaponry than any European power?'

'You gave him the technology?'

The old man replied, 'Not directly, but through channels. He never knew of our existence. No one does.'

'But why help him when your mandate was not to take sides?' A curious Prithvi continued with his questions.

His grandfather explained, 'Our mandate to help humanity overrides any other mandate. When the British came, the Marathas had lost the battle of Panipat. There was a power vacuum in India. If pushed by nationalist fervour, we would have assisted any of the small Indian rulers; we would have fragmented this country even more. Ashoka wanted to create a strong, unified Indian nation which would be a beacon for all of humanity. We decided not to intervene with the European powers because we saw that it was only an outsider who could unify this nation. However, Tipu was an exception. In him, we saw a ray of hope to build an empire that would rival Ashoka's empire, if not in size than at least in grandeur and vision. He also had the right ideas—he was not overtly religious, in fact, he was very secular—a tolerant and moderate ruler. These are ideals we seek as we hope to rebuild a great nation.'

'So Tipu is the only one you've backed since Ashoka?' quizzed Prithvi

'No, son. There have been others. We did back Akbar. He was one of the finest rulers India has had since Ashoka. When the Mughal Empire spawned Aurangzeb, we knew the reign of that empire had to be cut short. So we decided to back Shivaji and it was the Maratha Empire which became the predominant force.'

'Then how and why were the Marathas defeated at Panipat?' asked Prithvi

The old man continued, 'You do realize that we have to strike a balance on the kind of information that we release. We usually release enough to win wars, not take over the planet. Human greed and ambition are intoxicating. Just imagine, if we had released information on devices which could kill millions of people to Akbar, who was astute enough not to use it, how could he possibly have prevented his bloodthirsty descendant Aurangzeb from using it? The British have been here for 200 years and they have helped create a certain class of people who believe that democracy is the way forward—power to the people. Someone like Ashoka would have loved the idea. But, those like the British have also exploited this land no end. The end of British rule in India is imminent.'

A surprised Prithvi exclaimed, 'You are joking! They are not going to leave easily!'

The old man smiled. 'Oh, one thing I have always credited the British for is common sense. They won't even put up a fight. They will just pack their bags and leave.'

'I don't think so. But why on earth are you telling me all this?' asked Prithvi.

'I do so because we've lost one of the books to the Nazis. Of course, the back-ups are safe with us.'

'What? How did that happen?'

His grandfather counter questioned him, 'So you believe me now? Ashoka had asked the Nine Unknowns to keep the books safe at all costs. The Ashokan Empire collapsed within 100 years of the death of Ashoka. When an empire collapses, you have a lot of nobility jousting to carve up the empire. There were numerous wars—ranging from minor skirmishes to major battles. Given the instability of the region, the Unknowns took a decision in about AD 50 to hide the books in various parts of the Ashokan Empire and the places where he wanted to spread Buddhism and peace. Back-up copies of the books were to be maintained in a safe in the most stable kingdom in India. After the British became the predominant power in India, the backups were shifted from Poona in the Maratha Empire to Bengal, as Calcutta was the British capital till recently. The Nazis came across the one on propaganda and psychological warfare. We believe they discovered it by chance during an archaeological excavation at Nalanda. The Nine Unknowns knew that the first book is in Nalanda.'

Prithvi interrupted and asked, 'So how did you know the book was stolen?'

'They've used it well to convince the German people about some absurd Nazi beliefs. They even have a Ministry for Propaganda. The first book deals with propaganda and brainwashing the general population about the need to go to war—that is how we were alerted; it was too much of a coincidence. So I went to Nalanda and discovered that the spot where the first book is kept had been excavated. Now they will soon be looking for the rest—they will go to Nalanda and try to look for a clue to the second book. Can you imagine the havoc that those cretins can wreak on the planet if they get their hands on such literally explosive knowledge?'

'How do you know that they know of the remaining books? They probably don't.'

Prithvi's grandfather sighed and said, 'We certainly hoped they didn't know. But our sources tell us that they have applied for permits to do some more archaeology work. We certainly can't take chances. Besides, the first book mentions the need for nine bricks to build an edifice. They will put two and two together and they will certainly return to Nalanda. This would be a catastrophe.'

'And what am I supposed to do?' asked Prithvi.

'You, of course, are supposed to get them for us before the Nazis get their hands on them,' his grandfather said as if he was assigning him a simple enough task.

Prithvi was flabbergasted. 'What? Firstly, I don't know which order they will seek the books. Secondly, I am an amateur cricketer who pretty much whiles away his time. What makes you think I am equipped to take on the Nazis?!?'

His grandfather took a deep breath before saying, 'To answer your first point, they will have to acquire the books in chronological order. The ruins of Nalanda housed the first book. A clue pinpointing the exact location of the second book is located in the vicinity of the first; the exact location of the third book is pinpointed in the vicinity of the second and so on. Without these, they would be looking for the proverbial needle in a haystack. The Nine Unknowns too do not know the exact location, to avoid a situation where a single bad apple decides to make do with all the books or is captured in one of the wars and tortured to reveal all information. We are required to physically go to each location. The back-ups are kept in a safe which requires at least five keys to open. Each Unknown is in possession of one key.'

Prithvi said, 'If they found the first book, they have the location of the second one which I don't. And once again, I am not equipped to take on the bloody Nazis!'

His grandfather said, 'What do you think I was doing in Nalanda, young man—taking a stroll, perhaps? The clue for the second book is: "I am cursed not be worshipped; I am below the moon and Vishnu". And as far as your second point is concerned, you are at best an average cricketer, but I did see some other qualities in you. You can differentiate between right and wrong and you can see two sides of an argument. It is difficult to persuade you with emotion; only reason matters to you. And I have always groomed you rather than your father to take over my place in the council. Why do you think I had to force you to take up archaeology in England?'

The reality of Prithvi's father's death suddenly dawned upon him. 'Did the Nazis kill Pa?'

His grandfather looked at Prithvi almost apologetically. 'That's ridiculous. He is well and alive. I had to send you that telegram so that you would get here soon enough.'

Prithvi was shocked. 'That is just cruel and wrong! You could have made some other excuse. You had no right to do something like that!'

'I am well aware of what I was doing. Now get cracking on the second clue.' Clearly, this was no time for sentiment or apologies. Prithvi realised he had no choice in the matter.

'Dada, do you know where the second clue leads to?'

'Do you think I would wait for you to come to acquire the second book if I knew where it was?'

June 2, 1939: Bombay, British India

'One more cup of tea, please!' Youdale shouted at his orderly as he considered the journey he was about to embark upon.

Bombay was a far cry from the non-descript village of Kilnhurst in southern Yorkshire. Everyone in the village depended on the booming mining industry that fuelled the empire. Coal was the new gold and the British could not mine enough of it. New seams were routinely being sunk in Yorkshire and Scotland to mine more coal. The Thrybergh Hall Colliery sustained the livelihood of the village known as Kilnhurst. The Barnsley seam was sunk in 1858 and as recently as 1917 the Swallow Wood had been sunk. As a young boy of six, Youdale remembered his father's funeral. The chair lowering about forty men into the pit overturned and all of them fell 200 yards into the abyss. None of them survived. His mother received 10 pounds as compensation and she started a small bakery near the mine in order to raise him and his brother. The mine was like the Almighty in the village—it provided the means to live and, quite bizarrely, took lives away when it deemed fit. But the empire had to be powered; the loss of inconsequential lives was a small price to pay for powering the ships and trains which helped Britannia rule the world. He distinctly remembered the moment his father's casket was being lowered. His mother had whispered in his ear, 'You will never go down that mine.'

He had faced a lot of monetary and social roadblocks on his way from Kilnhurst to London and then to Calcutta. He was the rank and token outsider, whose elevation to a successful post in the empire enabled a lot of the fellows from Eton and Winchester give themselves a proud pat on their respective backs for their liberal views of emancipation and equality. His face-off with the British landlord in the tea-estate in Darjeeling in Bengal had caused a few frowns but his transfer to the desk in Bombay had taken care of that small problem. After all he had 'kicked up a storm' about the workers of the tea-estate, hence he had to be put in line and to placate the increasingly vocal Indian political class that something had to be done about the estate. Denied food and water for hours on end and made to pick leaves in godforsaken weather, the workers were dying a slow, painful death. Only about three of five born babies on the estate survived and those who did were acutely malnourished. The landlord claimed this was how the natives had lived for generations and Youdale did not know how to conduct business in the Empire. 'Everyone in England enjoys their daily cup of Darjeeling tea, why do you care how I get it there?' What Youdale did know was what it was like to grow up without a father and what it was like to sleep hungry. He didn't regret bringing the arrogant landlord to task; what he did resent was that although the conditions of the workers improved dramatically, the landlord got away with just a fine.

Now he had been ordered to put his life on the line to acquire those books for the benefit of the Empire. He knew of enough men who would do so without hesitation—'Anything for the Empire'. But did he owe that kind of allegiance to the Empire? After all, the Empire had swallowed his father in the mine. He had seen the lives of the Indian masses struggling to feed their children, seen signs around clubs and hotels which said, 'Europeans only' or worse, 'Dogs and Indians not allowed'. It was on this hypocrisy of equality and emancipation that the mighty edifice called the Empire stood. How long before it crumpled? On the other side of the fence, the books falling into Nazi hands was not a trivial matter. At least the British made the right noises about equality and justice. The Nazis were a totally different breed altogether. He decided that the books would be safer in the hands of the hypocrites.

June 14, 1939: Bangkok, Siam

Heidler looked at the construction of the Anusawari Prachathipatai, or the Democracy Monument and couldn't help but smile at the irony of a monument celebrating democracy being commissioned to commemorate a military coup d'état. It was supposed to be a symbol of a westernized Bangkok; an endeavour to shake off its Indic heritage to embrace the West. On June 23, the country would officially be renamed Thailand, a more western-sounding name than the prevalent Siam. His thoughts were interrupted by the voice of Max Kahn.

'When are we getting our travel permits? We should get there as soon as possible.'

'It hasn't been too long since we found the clue to the second book in Nalanda. In fact, it has only been three days. If we knew beforehand that the trail would lead us to Indo-China, we might have arranged for the permits. Besides, considering this is our first foray into French Indo-China, it shouldn't take too long. However, there is no love lost between the Thai and the French and the German relationship with France can charitably be described as "icy". So I suggest we enjoy the relative civility of this place while we can. I have no idea what Siem Reap is going to be like.'

Sergeant Pandey had been following them from India and eavesdropping from time to time. Let alone be bothered, the Germans have not even realized that I exist, thought Pandey.

He allowed himself a quiet smile of satisfaction as soon as he heard the words 'Siem Reap'. He realized where the Germans were heading to and sent a simple telegram to Youdale. It read 'SIEM REAP. STOP. IN 4 DAYS. STOP'.

June 14, 1939: Calcutta, British India

The British and the French had decided to carve up Asia between themselves. Small pockets of colonial France existed in India and the British were accommodating enough to let the French run those parts without much fuss. Things became bitter in 1893 when the Thai and the French went to war. Despite being in a position to play a decisive role in favour of the Thai, the British asked the king to make peace on whatever terms the French offered. It was a European 'you watch my back and I'll watch yours' approach. Asia was big enough for two European powers but the rise of a major Asian power could wreck havoc as nationalist feelings could then sweep the lands.

Youdale had been waiting in Calcutta for three days hoping to hear from Pandey soon, the Germans having left Calcutta toward Siam. Wiry, short and bespectacled Pandey was the perfect plebian foil for the pompous Germans. As soon as he received the telegram, he packed only the bare necessities to make his way toward Siem Reap. However, he faced a quandary. The people he was competing with were trained archaeologists, while he was at best a smart soldier. Even if he reached the location before they did, he had no idea where to look. He would have to take the book from them after they had acquired it. So it was imperative that he reached the location before they did and make the necessary arrangements.

June 18, 1939: Grand Hotel d'Angkor, Siem Reap, French Indo-China

Siem Reap literally translated to 'Defeat of Thailand', Siem being a bastardization of the ancient 'Siam' and referred to a centuries-old war between the two empires. A sleepy town till a few years ago, Siem Reap was now the closest town to the ancient Hindu and Buddhist ruins of Angkor Wat where tourists had incrementally started trickling in. This is where the second book lay.

The Grand Hotel d'Angkor itself was the most grandiose and opulent hotel in all of Indo-China although patrons of the Hotel Le Royal in Phnom Penh would disagree. As Youdale was checking into one of the sixty rooms, he was handed a red and black English brochure of the Angkor Wat ruins titled 'Angkor—fascinating city of the ancient Khmer monuments'. On the other side was a picture of one of the temples in Angkor in the background with a local man dressed as a French chef, offering a bowl of fruits in the foreground, with the title 'Les Hotels de Indo-Chine'. Carefully placing the brochure in his pocket, Youdale handed a bill of a 100 Piastres to the bellboy (courtesy the British government) and asked, 'Has any German entourage checked in?'

Quietly pocketing the bill the boy crisply replied in a French accent, 'The management does not permit us to reveal details about other guests.'

Youdale smiled and flicked two more 100 Piastres bills between his thumb and forefinger. 'Are you sure about that?'

The boy returned the smile, pocketed the bills and replied, 'No Germans have come in yet. But an entourage is scheduled to arrive later this evening.'

Another 100 Piastres were handed as Youdale closed in and said, 'We never had this conversation. If the Germans ask about me, do not tell. If you want more Piastres, they will be coming your way. His Majesty can definitely afford it.'

The boy replied, 'Don't worry, sir. I don't like Germans too much.'

'And the English?'

The boy beamed back, 'To be honest, I don't like them too much either.'

Youdale couldn't resist a chuckle and said, 'Ha! I don't blame you. Now please direct me to the restaurant.'

As Youdale was waiting for his meal and going through his brochure, he noticed an impeccably dressed Indian gentleman entering the restaurant. The semi-filled restaurant went quiet all of a sudden as the European patrons all glanced at the young Indian. It obviously wasn't common to see a coloured person in an upscale restaurant in Indo-China; certainly not as common as it would be in Bombay or Calcutta or even London. But the young man seemed to be used to being stared at, and politely nodded at each staring table as he made his way to his own. Obviously Indian aristocracy or from one of the premier Indian business families, thought Youdale. Youdale was meant to keep a low profile but at the spur of the moment got up, walked to the young man and said, 'Would you like to join me at my table? I could surely use some company from back home. I work in Bombay.' The young man accepted the invitation and joined Youdale at his table. Youdale held out his hand. 'Richard Youdale.'

Prithvi replied, 'Thanks for inviting me to your table. I am Prithvi. Prithvi Rathore.'

'Whereabouts in India are you from?'

'I am from Bombay too.'

Youdale exclaimed, 'Aha! Fancy meeting a fellow Bombayite in Indo-China.'

Prithvi politely smiled and shrugged, 'Small world I guess.'

Nodding his head, Youdale said, 'Indeed. So what brings you here? Business?'

'Pleasure. Just came to see the ruins.'

Youdale queried, 'Ah—a history student?'

Prithvi retorted, 'No, just a cricketer who needs to get away from the pitch for some time.'

Youdale glanced around the room to see people still staring at the young Indian. 'You seem to take the staring in your stride. Are you used to it?'

Prithvi considered his answer. 'Well. I used to get the stares in England too. The stares seem more resentful here. But it doesn't bother me anymore. What about you—what brings you here?'

Youdale gave him a non-committal neutral reply, 'Official business.' Prithvi nodded in reply as if he understood.

Quickly deciding to change the topic Youdale said, 'Cricket eh? Are you a batsman or a bowler?'

Prithvi broke into a smile at the opportunity to discuss cricket. 'Primarily a batsman, although I do occasionally do bowl leg spin. What about you, do you play cricket?'

'I am from Yorkshire, lad. The best English fast bowlers come out of our coal mines.'

'And yet they don't seem fast enough to stop a certain rampaging little Aussie named Bradman,' quipped Prithvi.

Youdale rolled his eyes. 'That little bastard is otherworldly. But do look at the brighter side of things—we always win against the Indians.'

Prithvi smiled wryly. 'Your grip on the game is as strong as it is on your Empire. We shall see how long either lasts.'

'I took you for an Empire man to be honest. Are you one of those Indians who want to ruin India themselves without us meddling?'

Once again Prithvi was at a loss to answer. He decided to turn the question around, 'Do you think the Empire is good for India?'

Youdale considered his reply. Should he give the politically correct answer or just be brutally honest? To hell with it, he thought. 'I work for the Empire and I do love what I do. But often I ask myself—what interests does the king of England have in a land so far away?'

Prithvi answered back in a dead-pan manner, 'Commercial, I suspect. India provides a massive market for the industrial goods manufactured in Britain.'

'That may well be true. But India's political aspirations and interests might get in the way of Britain's sooner rather than later. People like me will then become redundant.'

Prithvi laughed, 'A fast bowler never becomes redundant—you need one in every team.'

As they made small talk, both men seemed to enjoy each other's company and decided to get in touch when in Bombay. Prithvi invited him to the Cricket Club to repay the invite.

As Youdale made his way to his room, he bumped into the bellboy and promptly asked, 'I have one more question for you. Do you like Indians?'

The bellboy said, 'Don't know any. But I like them.'

'Why?'

The bellboy quipped, 'If no Indians, no Angkor Wat. If no Angkor Wat, then no hotel. If no hotel, then how would you tip me so generously?'

Youdale smiled. You couldn't argue with that logic!

June 20, 1939: Angkor Wat Temple Ruins, French Indo-China

The massive Angkor Wat complex spread over an area of 500 acres only appeared to get bigger as the German team got nearer. As soon as the central structure became more visible Kahn excitedly told Heidler, 'You see those three rectangular galleries, one over the other?'

'Yes, I do. What about them?'

Brahma is the Hindu God who was cursed not to be worshipped. Very few temples dedicated to him exist. The lowest gallery houses a Brahma temple, the one above houses the moon and …'

Heidler cut in, 'The one on top houses Vishnu.' He repeated the clue they had unearthed at their second sojourn in Nalanda to a beaming Kahn: 'I am cursed not be worshipped; I am below the moon and Vishnu.'

Built by Suryavarman II, it was initially dedicated exclusively to the Hindu God Vishnu and later to the Buddha. Its architecture reflected the Hindu view of the cosmos. At the centre is the quincunx of towers representing the five peaks of Mount Meru, the mythical abode of gods in the Hindu pantheon. The entire complex is surrounded by a moat representing the oceans of the planet and the outer walls in lieu of the other mountain ranges.

The intricately carved bas-reliefs narrated episodes from the Hindu epics of the *Ramayana* and the *Mahabharata* in a linear manner, culminating in the battles of Lanka and Kurukshetra respectively. An awe-inspiring scene depicted the Churning of the Sea of Milk when ninety-two Asuras (demons) and eighty-eight Devtas (gods) got together to unearth elixir from the depths of the ocean using the serpent Vasuki to churn the waters. However, there wasn't enough elixir for everyone and the gods intoxicated the demons, drank the elixir and thus became immortal.

Uncharacteristically, Kahn let out a small laugh. He turned to his alarmed entourage and stated, 'You know it was always thought to be a mistake.'

'What mistake?' asked Heidler.

Kahn replied, 'In mythology it was ninety-two Asuras who were involved in the churning. However, there are ninety-one depicted here. It was thought to be a mistake but there was never any real logical explanation. But that is the clue for the third book.'

'How so?' posed Heidler

Kahn countered 'Don't you see? Ashoka thought of himself as an Asura—a demon for his past sins. He isn't here—instead there will be a clue to the exact location of the next book. Look around till you find a stanza or verse in Sanskrit. It will probably be on the side of the wall where the demons are churning. Pass me the flame, porter.'

The porter masquerading as a Khmer was Pandey. He hesitated, then quickly regained his composure and did not hand the flame to Kahn who had barked the order in German. Kahn realized his mistake and asked for the flame in French and Pandey acquiesced. Was he being tested?

Neglecting him, Max Kahn passed the flame on the wall that depicted the demons and sure enough, between the demons was an inscription in Sanskrit:

I am one among fifty one

In this land of Gold

A proud father to a valiant warrior who

Chose friendship over family

And Death over an Empire.

Heidler stated, 'The warrior, of course, is Ganesha. Shiva killed his son Ganesha in a fit of rage when Ganesha did not let him enter his abode on the orders of his mother. It would make sense. Kumbhakonam has a Shiva Temple. Now we can get the second book.'

Max Kahn replied, 'No. But it was a good guess. The valiant warrior is Karna, the illegitimate son of Surya—the Sun God. He chose to fight against his brothers in the Mahabharata, choosing to be with his friend Duryodhana who gave him the chance to live with dignity and honour. His mother offered him the chance to rule the empire if he switched sides, but he chose an honourable death at the hands of his brother Arjuna, preferring to die for friendship. Thus, the book is where the Sun deity is located in Kumbhakonam.'

'Perfect. Can we now get the book?' asked Lewerenz.

As they moved toward the scene depicting the final Battle of Lanka, Max tried to loosen the ten heads of the demon king Ravana one by one. The seventh head finally gave way and a chamber revealed a small box. Just as Max was about to open the box, the surroundings were illuminated and a voice boomed out.

'Well, gentlemen. You have done an excellent job locating a treasure which belongs to the Government of French Indo-China. You are surrounded by soldiers. Please hand over the box.' Youdale stepped out from the shadows.

'Ah! The British liaison. Your hospitality obviously knows no geographical boundary. But how do you represent the French Government?' Kahn asked.

Youdale replied, 'I most certainly don't. But Officer Masson here does. Hand it over.'

Kahn proceeded to open the box first and laughed aloud as he handed it to Youdale.

Youdale asked, 'What can possibly be so funny under the circumstances?' Then he saw for himself. The box was empty except for a small note in neat handwritten English.

> Greetings Nazis,
> Did you really think we would let another one fall into your hands? I suggest you head back home.
> Regards
> The Nine Unknowns

Kahn beamed at Youdale and said, 'I guess you can't keep us for retrieving an empty box. But all of us know now that this is now a three-horse race. Have a good day.'

July 5, 1939: Calcutta, British India

Despite being the Under-Secretary for India, Rab Butler wasn't exactly overjoyed to be in India at the moment. Not bothering with niceties he immediately got to the point and addressed Youdale. 'Major Youdale, are you telling me that these Nine Unknowns acquired the books before either we or the Germans could reach them? The only positive thing to emerge is that the German entourage will be detained for questioning for about a month. But they will get away pretty soon. The Germans have already annexed the rest of Czechoslovakia and that foolish Prime Minister of ours thinks he can still avoid war with Germany. There is talk that Poland is next on Hitler's agenda. I certainly hope for the sake of His Majesty that you are the bearer of some good news!'

Youdale replied, 'I hope there is no war, it will cause misery all around. I have a fair inkling about the identity of the Indian who acquired the books. Actually, we had a meal together.'

Butler barked, 'You what?'

Youdale evenly said, 'At that time, neither I nor he was aware of the other's intention. He still is not aware that the British too are after the books.'

Butler queried, 'The same name you mentioned in the telegram—Prithvi Rathore?'

Youdale nodded. 'He seemed cool and composed and very sure of himself. He claimed he was there to check out the ruins—Angkor Wat is not exactly a playground of the upper class of India. They are much more at home in Mayfair. But I had no reason to disbelieve him.'

Butler stated, 'The dossier states that he belongs to one of the premier Indian business families. His father has been shortlisted for an OBE, although he still hasn't received one. He has never shown any mutinous or nationalistic tendencies. He has never even attended a Congress meeting as far as we know. He plays cricket for a predominantly English team. His best friend is a Scotsman named Townsend. So we can't pin any charge on him. Even if we made up some minor charge, we possibly couldn't use force or third degree measures on him to get revealing information—his family is just too well connected. His grandfather has golfed with the Viceroy! At the moment he is simply untouchable.'

Butler paused for what seemed an eternity. He then got up from his chair, and reached into his pocket for a Butz-Choquin pipe, a family heirloom. It was from the first series of pipes released way back in 1858 with a flat bottom hearth, elongated by an albatross bone and held together by a series of silver rings. He finally lit it and turned toward both Youdale and Pandey. 'With the limited resources at your disposal you have done an excellent job, Youdale. We would like you to continue this operation. Any assistance you require in the field of archaeology will be provided directly from Oxford and Cambridge. But before that there is another matter that we need to resolve.'

'What matter?' asked Youdale.

Butler replied, 'Although he has done a commendable job so far, Pandey must be off this assignment.'

Pandey who had been quiet so far spoke out of turn, 'But why? I have put my life and limb in line for the British.'

Butler continued, 'That may well be so. And we certainly do appreciate that. However, the current political climate is charged and sedition is in the air. While it is possible to trust a native sepoy if this race was against the Germans only, now that the Indians are involved too, we do not need a case of divided loyalties. Youdale will go to Kumbhakonam alone. The Germans will not be given a permit to enter India so your race is against these Nine Unknowns only. However, Hitler has Chamberlain by the balls. And he is squeezing them. Unrestricted travel access might just be a sop thrown at the Nazis. The priority of His Majesty's government is to prevent a war in Europe. Europe is on a keg of gunpowder, all that is needed to set it alight is a spark. Besides this, the young Mr Rathore arrived yesterday to India and went straight to his home. We are keeping a watch on him. We are unsure if he deciphered the next clue. Perhaps he is working on that. Thanks to the excellent work by Pandey, we know where the next book is located. So I suggest you get on your way right now.'

'Sir, I strongly disagree with removing Pandey. Considering he is a native, he can be a lot more inconspicuous. I strongly implore you to reconsider,' Youdale pleaded as he watched Pandey leave the room.

'I shall do that, but as of now he is off this assignment and will resume his regular duties in His Majesty's service.' Still not sure if Pandey was out of earshot, Butler whispered, 'As it is, the name Pandey does not inspire much confidence.'

August 12, 1939: The Rathore Residence, Malabar Hill, Bombay, British India

Babu, the gardener, opened the door to the tiny man dressed in unassuming clothes. As was his wont, Babu was characteristically rude. 'What do you want?' he snapped.

Babu hated being disturbed when there was no one else in the house. He used the couches he was normally not allowed to sit on and listened to the radio at leisure; sometimes he even took a short nap. The bespectacled man had just interrupted his afternoon siesta. The rest of the domestic help in the house did not dare to disturb him unless absolutely necessary.

Pandey replied, 'I am here to see Mr Prithvi Rathore. My name is Pandey.'

The gardener replied, 'Baba is not at home. He has probably gone to play that godforsaken English game of his.'

Pandey asked, 'It is of utmost urgency that I speak to him. When is he expected?'

Babu replied with a tinge of sarcasm. 'I am but a humble servant. I don't ask the masters about their schedule.'

'I can wait for him,' replied a mildly amused Pandey.

Every word of Babu dripped with sarcasm. 'You are more than welcome. Guests are like God in this house. You can wait in the living room and listen to the radio.'

Pandey politely said, 'Thank you.'

As Pandey sat waiting in the living room, he considered the course of action he had chosen to take. His thoughts went back to a long time ago, when he was still a young man of 19 and had followed his father in joining the British Indian Army. The year was 1914 and what was then known as the Great War (World War I) began in the summer of 1914. Like most Indians, both military and civilian, Pandey too supported the British cause in the hope that Indian support to the British war effort would result in Indian self-governance like that in Australia and Canada. He was looking forward to joining his regiment in the Middle East but one day he was summoned to see the 'General Sahib'.

The General sized up the diminutive bespectacled Indian who offered him a smart salute and stood at attention. The General said, 'At ease, soldier. Pull up a chair. We need to have a conversation.'

Pandey complied with a touch of surprise; it was not very conventional for a General to offer a seat to a mere foot soldier. Nervously, he wondered if he had done something wrong and was about to get a reprimand or worse. Noticing his uneasiness, the General said, 'Take it easy, soldier Pandey. You have done nothing wrong but what I am about to say to you is highly confidential. Forget your regiment; no one in your family can be privy to this discussion. Do you understand?'

Still not comfortable speaking to the General, Pandey merely nodded his head and managed to murmur, 'Yes, Sahib.'

The General took a deep breath before continuing, 'Is it true that both your father and your grandfather were also soldiers in the British Indian Army?'

Pandey replied, 'Sir, my father is a Lance Naik but my grandfather was not a soldier, he was a water-bearer and later a batman to a commissioned British officer.'

The General smiled and said, 'Reminds me of Kipling's Gunga Din from *The Barrack-Room Ballads*.' The General took a moment before triumphantly reciting, 'Tho' I've belted you and flayed you,/By the livin' Gawd that made you,/ You're a better man than I am, Gunga Din!'

Pandey tried his best not to look confused, wondering why the General was reciting poetry to him.

The General continued, 'The assignment to which you are to be deputed is fraught with risk. We need someone extremely loyal to the British and ready to be the direct cause of the incarceration of some mutinous troops and anti-British elements. How loyal are you to the British, Soldier Pandey?'

What exactly does he expect me to say under the circumstances? thought Pandey. He replied, 'I think my lineage speaks for itself.'

The General nodded in agreement and asked, 'Tell me Pandey, have you heard of the Ghadar Party?'

Pandey replied, 'No sir, I can't say I have.'

The General said, 'That is what I thought. Till recently they were a minor irritation and a source of amusement—the people running the Ghadar Party. But things have taken a more serious turn now. Some young Indian immigrants and students in the US formed the Ghadar Party with the rather fantastic aim of overthrowing the British in India. As stated, we have scoffed at and ignored their newspapers and activities till now but British counter-intelligence now knows that they are being aided by the Germans.'

The General slid a poster to Pandey and said, 'This was published at the University of California at Berkeley.' He then proceeded to show him another pamphlet in Hindi. It read:

Today there begins in foreign lands, but in our country's tongue, a war against the British Raj.

What is our name? Revolution
What is our work? Revolution
Where will be the revolution? In India
The time will soon come when rifles and blood
will take the place of pens and ink.

*Cover page of
a pamphlet of
Ghadarite poems
published in 1923.*

After waiting for Pandey to finish reading it the General continued, 'Needless to say *ghadar* means "revolution" in Urdu. The counter-intelligence report states that with German and even Ottoman Turk aid these people are planning something really big—along the lines of the Mutiny of 1857.' Looking at the shocked expression on Pandey's face the General said, 'I hope you now appreciate the gravity of the task that is to be assigned to you and the need for absolute secrecy. If word gets out to the common man in India—do you realize the secessionist movement can gain some serious momentum? And this is not 1857—we might not be able to win so easily.'

For the first time, Pandey spoke openly. 'Why don't you ask the Americans to force this party to stop their activities?'

The General chuckled and said, 'That is the obvious solution. Don't you think we would have tried? The general consensus among Americans is that fighting colonialism is a noble aim—after all they too fought the British and dare I say, won. Moreover, the Americans are neutral in this war and they maintain cordial relations with the Germans. The Germans are using their consulate in San Francisco to supply weapons and monetary aid to the Indian revolutionaries. Now do you know what am I going to ask of you?'

Pandey considered his reply, 'I don't, but I would do anything to help the British.'

The General was growing fond of this young man. 'We will help you infiltrate this Ghadar Party in California. We need someone young to pose as a student who has transferred to California from the German speaking region of Switzerland. For the next six months, you will be coached extensively in German. In fact, that is the only language you will speak. If I wake you up at four in the morning and ask you the time, you will look at your watch and reply to me in German. You will also be coached to start thinking like one of them—their ideals, their beliefs and their sense of ethics. Do you now realize why it is important that we have someone there whose loyalty to the British is unimpeachable?'

Pandey looked up at the General who it seems was sizing him up again and replied, 'Yes sir, I do.'

For the next six months, Pandey was whisked off to Shimla and put up in a safe house. British counter-intelligence did not allow him to venture outside and he was spoken to and had to converse only in German. While he was unable to lose his thick Central Indian accent, the need for communication made him rapidly adapt to the German language. At the end of six months, he spoke German as well as an Indian possibly could.

Upon his arrival in California, with British help he enrolled at Stanford University. Given the small Indian population in California at the time, he quickly infiltrated into the Party. His fluency in the German language soon had him interacting with officials at the German consulate in San Francisco representing the Ghadar Party. The scale of the conspiracy left him dumbfounded and he wondered if his cover was blown and if the Germans were sending him on a wild goose chase. Nonetheless, he passed on the information to the British officials in the US. Not only was material and financial support being given by the Germans but even the Irish Republican movement was offering their support to the Indian cause. While he had become quite friendly with some of the Indians in the Party, he did not lose focus of his objective and stayed loyal to the British cause.

Finally, in April 1917 Woodrow Wilson made up his mind and the US styled itself an 'Associated Power' and declared war on Germany. No longer neutral and now staunchly allied to the British, the Americans rounded up and imprisoned all Ghadar Party members including Pandey. It was only on the intervention of the British Embassy in Washington that Pandey was released and made a State witness in the trial that ensued.

Known as the Hindu German Conspiracy Trial, it was then the most expensive trial conducted in American history. Eight Indian nationalists were indicted on a charge of conspiracy to form a military enterprise against Great Britain.

During the course of the trial, Pandey wore his British Indian Army military uniform and revealed the scale of the Ghadar conspiracy. The Indian nationalists had managed to convince, arm and finance mutiny amongst Indian troops in Singapore, Lahore, Rawalpindi and Fort William in Calcutta and included plans to raid the military arsenal at various places in India and stage a simultaneous pan-India mutiny. The Baluch regiment stationed in Rangoon in Burma was to mutiny next and the troops from Punjab would move toward capturing Lahore and then march onto Delhi. Given the paucity of British soldiers, it could have very much heralded the end of British rule in India. Thanks to Pandey's inputs from California, the British were able to foil most of the plans except the Singapore mutiny which resulted in the death of various civilians and military personnel and was brought under control only after the Japanese, French and Russian ships brought in reinforcements.

While there had been other British infiltrators across the globe, Pandey's foray into the Ghadar Party was considered the most successful since he had breached the upper echelons of the Party. The trial in the US was eventful with the American courts—to British chagrin—acquitting the Indian nationalists on the basis of America's own history of throwing off the British yoke, its anti-colonialism ideals and public opinion favouring the Indians.

Irrespective of the outcome of the trial, Pandey remembered two instances. One, the British Ambassador to the US attending the trial and inviting him for tea; and two, the look of sheer disgust on the faces of his erstwhile friends in the Party. But in his mind, he was only furthering India's cause for self-governance by aiding the British. He had done his duty as a soldier but had he done his duty as an Indian too? Suddenly his thoughts were interrupted by a voice. 'You know sir, I have been staring at you for the past few minutes and you seem to be in a trance. I did not wish to interrupt you but I definitely want to buy the stuff that you are smoking. I am Prithvi Rathore by the way and I believe you are here to see me. I assume Babu was his usual obnoxious self so please accept my deepest apologies.'

Pandey looked up to see a young man with his arm in a sling smiling at him.

Pandey smiled back and replied, 'Yes sir, my name is Suryakant Pandey.'

Prithvi continued, 'Okay, Mr Pandey. What can I possibly do for you? Ah, but before that I would really like to know what it is that you were thinking about?'

'Please call me Surya. I was deputed to tail the German entourage in Indo-China.' Pandey then went on to narrate the happenings at the Angkor Wat ruins.

Prithvi stroked his faint stubble and asked, 'So why are you narrating this to me?'

Pandey said, 'I wish to assist the Nine Unknowns.'

Prithvi tried not to show shock on his face. 'Well—I don't know what you are talking about—perhaps you have the wrong information.'

'Let's not play games, shall we, Mr Rathore? The gentleman you shared a meal with at the Grand Hotel d'Angkor is a British intelligence officer named Youdale. Of course, at that time neither of you knew that the other too was chasing the same book.'

Prithvi rubbed his fingers against his forehead and said, 'And so I gave him my real name—how stupid of me.'

Pandey retorted, 'To be fair you are not an intelligence officer. Imagine the music he has had to face. And you can't be that stupid since you managed to acquire the second book.'

Prithvi exclaimed, 'But why are you telling me all this? Are you not a British soldier? Aren't you loyal to the British? Why would you ever want to help me? Is this a ploy to arrest me?'

Pandey went on to narrate the incident at Butler's office. 'So you see sir, I don't think I have been treated fairly by him after all that I have done for them. I never in my wildest dreams imagined that my loyalty would ever be questioned. Do you know how painful it is for a soldier to have his loyalty questioned?'

Prithvi mused, 'After all that you did for them? Tailing a bunch of power-hungry Nazis does not amount to much.'

Pandey patiently replied, 'It is just not that. Why do you think I was deputed to them in the first place? How do you think I was taught fluent German by the British?' He then proceeded to narrate his saga during the Great War.

Prithvi said, 'Let me get this straight. This Ghadar Party thing is something I am completely unaware of. But let us safely assume that the events you narrate did take place. So you realistically expect me to trust someone who worked as a British infiltrator against Indian patriots? Just look at it from my perspective.'

Pandey retorted. 'Look at it from *my* perspective. Do you know how difficult it was for me to sit in that courtroom and be looked at with contempt and disgust by people who used to think of me as their friend? Like most Indians I believed that helping the British during the Great War would lead to India gaining dominion status like Australia and Canada. Time and again, I have risked my life and limb for the British—and now some British bureaucrat questions my loyalty! You are right. It is difficult for you to believe. But what can I possibly do to make you believe me?'

Prithvi considered Pandey's offer. It would be handy to have someone on his side who spoke German fluently but a British officer—could he trust him? He did think that the British too were trying to prevent the Nazis from acquiring those books. His mandate was to acquire those books and prevent the Nazis from acquiring them too. If the British think they could use Prithvi—should he use the British too? If Pandey was a British agent—he could get rid of him if things went awry. But then ... what would his grandfather think? However, this was his show and it was Prithvi who needed to employ all means available to complete his mission. He took a decision.

Prithvi said, 'I don't trust you right now. So you will never carry a firearm or weapon when you are with me till you win my trust. Even if I get a whiff that you are a British agent , we will part ways. If you are a British agent, I assume I am more important to you alive than dead so you will not kill me. But I can't gauge your intentions right now. Are we clear on this?'

Pandey replied, 'Crystal. I can win your trust by helping you acquire the third book!'

Prithvi asked with a touch of mild amusement in his voice. 'Really? Where is it?'

Pandey sounded irritated. 'Are you testing me? Surely you have the clue as well. It is in the Kumbhakonam Temple. Or perhaps it was there and now the British have acquired it since the Germans are indisposed in Indo-China.' Pandey then went on to explain how Max deciphered the clue from the missing demon and how Youdale had been deployed to acquire it.

Prithvi continued, 'Excellent. And you said you were there dressed as a Khmer and were eavesdropping?'

'Yes, I was.'

Prithvi asked, 'And now Youdale has probably acquired it from the Kumbhakonam Temple?'

'Indeed sir.'

Prithvi retorted, 'Well Surya, I must say, you are very lucky to be alive.'

A surprised Pandey exclaimed, 'Excuse me sir?'

'You heard me. Even with some brilliant disguise work, you would hardly look like a resident of Indo-China—a regular Khmer. An inconspicuous Indian—you can pull off that one with the Germans I imagine. But they would have seen through it when an Indian tries to pass himself off as a Khmer. You see, they led you on and now you've led Youdale on. He ended up in a small town in the Madras Presidency, when he was supposed to be somewhere else. Did you ever get the feeling that they knew?'

Pandey recalled the moment he had flinched when asked for the torch in German. 'For an instant, I did have the inkling that they did. So from where do we acquire the third book then? Or have you already acquired it?'

'We haven't. I came back empty-handed from Ceylon. The clue said "One among fifty-one in the land of gold". The land of gold is Swarna Dweep, the ancient name for Ceylon, bastardized later to Serendip from which we get the word serendipity.' He then pointed to the sling in which his arm lay and smiled, 'Better empty-handed than with no hand at all.'

Two weeks earlier: Dambulla, Sri Lanka

Karl Lewerenz was growing impatient. 'You were cocksure that we had shaken off the British swine. So what are we waiting for now?'

If the boy was not such a good archaeologist, Heidler wouldn't have had second thoughts about emptying all the bullets in his magazine into the head of this upstart. He tried to remain calm. Lewerenz was an excellent archaeologist and his work was critical for this mission. But given his age and rank and himself being an unknown quantity on the field, Heidler and Kahn had taken a collective decision to feed him information on a need-to-know basis. But at every juncture he questioned Heidler. While he understood that Lewerenz was merely a civilian, Heidler was not used to having his authority challenged and questioned every now and then by a brash subordinate. He did not like the idea of working with civilians—give him a soldier from Bavaria any day—those kids knew how to follow orders and respect authority. 'We have shaken off the Brits for the time being. However, Ceylon too is a British colony. Considering that Siem Reap was under the French, we were released after a month as the British would be averse to releasing too much information to the French. However, if we are captured on a British colony we may never see the Fatherland again. Even if we did, the British would have acquired all the books by then and the Fuhrer would have us killed. So we came here on forged Swedish passports. We've taken a huge risk here and all I am trying to do is to mitigate any risk of our exposure.'

Lewerenz asked, 'What if the Nine Unknowns get the book before we do?'

Heidler brusquely replied, 'If they get it, there is nothing we can do about it. They may have already swooped all the books. You know in order to throw off the British Indian solider masquerading as a Khmer, Max did exactly as he was told. The British must think we are incredibly stupid. Did they believe we can't tell the difference between a regular Khmer and an Indian with a disguise? But we can certainly use their arrogance to our advantage. The only reason I did not involve you is that you ask too many questions. This is not a field trip but a military operation. It is imperative that you do not question my moves.'

Lewerenz continued, 'Oh please! Without me you wouldn't be able to mount this operation.'

Heidler responded, 'I know that and that is also the primary reason that you are alive.'

Lewerenz challenged, 'Is that a threat?'

Heidler nonchalantly replied, 'It's merely a fact, Karl.'

Kahn had had enough and decided to intervene. 'Gentlemen! We need cool heads. We are on the same side. Josef, you are the one leading this operation—none of us doubt that for a minute. But you need to realize that Karl is a scholar and an intellectual who feels that his wings are clipped by the military nature of this operation. At the end of it, we are archaeologists and not soldiers.'

Turning toward Lewerenz he continued, 'On the other hand Karl, Major Heidler is correct when he says that this is a military operation and not a mere archaeological one. We need to trust his military instinct. Our lives could be at risk from both the British and the Nine Unknowns. The first book that we acquired quite by chance was on propaganda. The Fuhrer has used it to great effect; you've seen the sense of nationalism that is currently sweeping our lands.'

Heidler softened up and interjected, 'Karl, perhaps I was too harsh with you. However, the successful completion of this mission is a requirement specified by the Fuhrer himself; consider the pressure I operate under. Think of the Nazi flag—nationalism is represented by the colour white, socialism is represented by the color red and finally the Aryan Race is represented by the swastika, an ancient Hindu-Buddhist symbol. Do you think that is a coincidence? The way the Fuhrer wants to shape Germany is dependent on the acquisition of these books. And we've already lost one of them.'

Lewerenz said, 'My only problem is that we have sent the British on a wild goose chase. They are bound to realize this sooner or later. We need to get that book as soon as possible. Will you at least tell me when do you plan to acquire it?'

Kahn stood up and said, 'Tonight, young Karl. During the day let's enjoy our time as Swedish tourists.'

The landscape of Dambulla is what India would have looked like if not for the Muslim invasions. While a typical Hindu religious city had mosques often built by the victorious Muslim armies or a sizeable look population which adhered to Islam—sometimes converted by force, sometimes a remnant of the conquering hordes—Sri Lanka had been left untouched by the orgy of medieval violence. The Portuguese more than made up for it in the later years, but many parts of Sri Lanka still remained unscathed.

Nestled between pristine green hills, Dambulla had everything—people, monkeys and elephants. Tiny fishing boats in the lagoon completed the picture-postcard beauty of the place. From certain vantage points Sigiriya, the ruined rock fortress, jutted majestically, often leading the viewer to question whether it was naturally formed or man-made. Of course, what stood out most and what the town revolved around was something else—the ancient cave temples.

The rock hosting the eighty odd caves towered 160 metres above the surrounding plains. Each of these caves contained mainly Buddhist paintings, murals and statues while some of them had a sprinkling of Hindu deities in them, almost as if they were an afterthought. After all, Ceylon, known locally as Lanka, was predominantly Buddhist, unlike its giant neighbour to the north. The three main caves were called Cave of the Divine King, Cave of the Great Kings and the Great New Monastery. Prithvi zeroed in on the Cave of the Divine King assuming it was a reference to Ashoka.

After spending the better part of the day combing each artifact twice, Prithvi could not find anything to do with the Sun God, nor could he find a clue pinpointing the location of the next book. Ashoka wasn't given to illusions of self-grandeur; Prithvi decided that he was probably looking in the wrong cave.

Ashoka had thought of himself as nothing but a disciple of Buddha and hence Prithvi decided to concentrate on the Great New Monastery which was the smallest of the three and had many statues of Lord Buddha which were a replica of each other excepting an odd one amongst them all. It was the statue of the Sun God. Prithvi counted the statues of Buddha then; there were exactly fifty. Prithvi smiled as he remembered, 'I am one among fifty-one!' Prithvi reached for his magnifying glass and began to look at some kind of clue to pinpoint the location of the next book. He almost missed it and brought back the magnifying glass to the location he had just skimmed. Almost incomprehensible but undeniably present were two words in Sanskrit: 'Drepung Kalmykia'. That didn't make any sense to him so he double checked. Yes, that's what it said. He quickly memorized it. His work in Ceylon was certainly not done yet. The next item on his agenda in Ceylon—he had to acquire the third book; the one on microbiology.

The next day, three Germans entered the Great New Monastery when Heidler stopped the other two in their tracks as he saw a faint light in the distance.

'Well gentlemen, looks like we have company. Don't put on any lights,' he whispered.

While the others were not armed, Heidler cocked the exposed hammer of his Walther PPK and tiptoed toward the noise. He did not know how many of them would be there and did not wish to take any chances. He was partially relieved when he saw just one person bent over a statute of the Sun God with a box in his hand. The man did not have a holster nor did any of his pockets bulge with the silhouette of a firearm but Heidler was not about to take any chances.

Heidler ordered sharply, 'Put your hands up and turn around. My pistol is pointed straight at your head and I am a crack shot.'

Prithvi slowly turned around, the box holding the book still in his hand.

'Ah, you are an Indian.' Heidler relaxed his grip on the pistol not expecting to be overcome by an Indian after all. 'So are you here acquiring this book for the British Government?'

Prithvi felt the heat-induced beads of sweat on his brow multiply, 'Yes I am.'

Heidler said, 'You lie. The British would never trust an Indian to acquire this book and we sent the British to Kumbhakonam. You are one of the Unknowns or perhaps you are here at their direction.'

If this was bait for him to speak, Prithvi did not take it. Ignoring him Heidler continued, 'I will obviously take the book. Perhaps you can give me a good reason not to kill you?'

There was only one way out of the cave and Heidler and his cronies were blocking it.

'I guess you will not speak. Crouch and throw the book in our direction.'

Prithvi did exactly as he was told. All three Germans looked down at the box as Lewerenz bent down to pick it up. Still crouched and noticing that none of the Germans were looking at him, Prithvi pulled the knob on the paraffin lamp creating total darkness in the cave. He then reached into his right sock, pulled out his Colt and began firing shots in the general direction of the Germans as he ran toward the exit. He heard a thud as he went past the Germans and seconds later felt an excruciating pain just above his right elbow as one of Heidler's bullets hit him. He ran even harder.

Kahn looked straight at Heidler who was looking for a pulse on Lewerenz's neck. 'Karl is dead—no pulse.'

'What about the book?' asked Heidler.

'It's under him. He was one of the smartest minds in Germany. I hope that your bullet makes that Indian die a slow and painful death.'

Heidler replied, 'I doubt it. If it had hit a major organ, he would not have continued running.'

A fuming Kahn spat out, 'If we see him in town, do me a favour and kill the bastard.'

Heidler calmly retorted, 'I doubt he will be moving around in town anymore. And even if we saw him, we can't do anything to him. Ceylon is British territory and he is one of their subjects. We are travelling on forged papers. On the bright side, he can't do much to us either. He can't go to the police or the local authorities, else he might find himself in prison for stealing a national artifact. What matters is that we have the book. But his death poses a problem. We now have to ascertain the location of the fourth book ourselves without the assistance of Karl.'

Ignoring him Kahn said, 'We must make arrangement for his body to be taken back to Germany.'

'Unfortunately, we can't. We have to bury him in the caves.'

A fuming Kahn shouted, 'What? You can't be serious. He is one of us. We can't just bury him in an unmarked grave like an unwanted vagabond.'

'We can't take a bullet ridden dead body with forged papers back to Germany. There will be too many questions. He will be buried here. I am sorry.' Heidler was firm.

August 9, 1939: Madras, British India

His arm in a sling, Prithvi was in a fairly foul mood at having lost the third book from within his grasp. After having acquired the second book from Angkor Wat and handing it over to his grandfather, he had felt fairly confident of sidestepping the Nazis. He was not so sure anymore. He had convinced the doctor in Colombo that he had been hit by a stray bullet while hunting deer in Dambulla. He had sent a telegram to his grandfather from Colombo that the third book was in Nazi hands. Once again, a call to Mr Tata had ensured that he would be able to fly from Madras to Bombay on a stack of airmail from the aerodrome at the Mount Golf Club near the St Thomas Mount. With a few hours to kill before he flew, Prithvi headed for the Madras Gymkhana to have a drink.

At the reception he presented his member card from the Cricket Club of India. 'My club is affiliated to this Gymkhana. I would like to use the bar to get some scotch.'

The turbaned receptionist looked perplexed and stated, 'I will be right back, sir.'

After what seemed like an eternity the receptionist returned followed by a portly, middle-aged Englishman. The Englishman came up to Prithvi.

'My name is Colonel Hawthorne and I am the club secretary. I believe we have a problem, young man.'

A surprised Prithvi asked, 'What's the problem?' He thought it must be the dress code issue.

Hawthorne said, 'While it is true that members of CCI in Bombay are allowed to use the facilities here, I am afraid this is a European only club.'

Prithvi frowned and said, 'But surely as an affiliate member I should be able to use the facilities.'

'You do look like a respectable WOG but…'

Prithvi interrupted him and posed, 'A respectable what?'

Hawthorne continued, 'I said WOG—Worthy Oriental Gentleman. You are right about us being an affiliate but rules are sacrosanct here and under our agreement terms affiliate clubs must respect each other's laws. If CCI in Bombay allows members to bring in their dogs, we certainly can't allow that. Catch my drift?'

Prithvi could not believe what he had just heard. He smiled at Hawthorne, 'Do you see that my arm is in a sling?' He held up his arm for Hawthorne to get a good look.

Hawthorne leaned in to take a closer look at his arm and spoke with what seemed like genuine concern, 'That would not be reason …'

Before he could complete his sentence Prithvi clenched his left fist and thrust it straight into the startled face of the Colonel. 'I still have a fairly strong left arm you pompous fuck. Lest you forget, this is my country, not yours!'

Putting a handkerchief to his bleeding nose the Colonel shouted, 'Call the police. Stop this man!'

No one called the police and no one stopped Prithvi. Some were too stunned to react, others, perhaps, were secretly thrilled; they had never seen an Indian hit a Brit, least of all the Club Secretary himself!

August 10, 1939: Madras-Bombay Flight, British India

As Prithvi sat uncomfortably on another stack of airmail, he mulled over the incident at the Madras Gymkhana. He had often seen the British treat their Indian domestic help shabbily. To be fair he had seen Indians treat their help the same way. However, he never imagined that he would ever suffer such an indignity, least of all in India itself. The cosmopolitan outlook of Bombay had been but a bubble he inhabited. The fact that Bombay was not essentially an ingredient of the Indian peninsula was no longer just a geographical verity to him. A conduit in the north did link Bombay to mainland India but had he ever actually crossed that bridge to see what the bona fide India was like?

It wasn't all black and white. Hadn't the British introduced railroads, newspapers, universities and irrigation? The Congress which was waving the flag of independence now had been founded by a British civil servant named Hume to prevent a national revolt. Prithvi thought how the quaint customs of British justice had been introduced and accepted— how ridiculous Indian barristers and judges looked in wigs and the imperial ermine. The Union Jack proudly fluttered atop all public buildings and along statues of conquering British generals astride their stallions, gazing blankly into an unfamiliar land.

Prithvi had always thought that the treatment meted out to certain Indians was a manifestation of social or economic disparity, not one of racial disparity. For the first time he realized what Gandhi must have felt when he was thrown out of a first-class compartment despite having a valid ticket and forced to travel third-class. He felt the anger of Bhagat Singh. He recollected that the gardener Babu always had his head bowed when he was addressed by any of the British visitors in the Rathore household. The gardener never felt any such compulsion when speaking to Indians, irrespective of their social standing. He was actually curt and rude to Indians in particular. Was the bowed head an acknowledgement of the singular legitimacy of the whites, or of the fact that he was not an equal before them. Was the rudeness meant to illustrate to the Indian upper classes that they had literally signed away the country and the people? A few years ago, the illiterate Babu had come running into his room with a sheaf of paper saying, 'Read this to me, it is a poem about my Jhansi.' Prithvi had obliged without giving it much thought. What were the words? He remembered the first stanza:

> *Sinhasan hil uthey raajvanshon ney bhrukuti tani thi,*
> *Budhey Bharat mein aayee phir se nayi jawani thi,*
> *Gumee huee azadi ki keemat sabney pehchani thi,*
> *Door phirangi ko karney ki sab ney man mein thani thi*
> *Chamak uthi san sattavan mein, yeh talwar purani thi,*
> *Bundeley Harbolon key munh hamney suni kahani thi,*
> *Khoob ladi mardani woh to Jhansi wali Rani thi.*

The British throne was shaken, the Indian kingdoms
had made up their minds
Old India once again regained the vigour of its youth
The forgotten worth of freedom was realized

All decided to throw off the foreign yoke
The old swords glittered once again in 1857
We've heard it from the ballad singers
She fought like a man, this Queen of Jhansi.

Babu's reaction on hearing the poem was, 'It's true! I've heard—she fought like a man. She strapped her six month old baby on her back and fought the British. What valour!'

1857 had been the year of what was known as the Sepoy Mutiny. As recently as 1909, Veer Savarkar had reinterpreted it as 'The Indian War of Independence' and published a book on it. He had been rewarded with a 50-year life sentence for sedition, part of which was served in the notorious Cellular Jail in the Andaman Islands. Prithvi was always told that it was nothing more than a mutiny, just some wayward soldiers challenging the might of the noble and just British. But what would lead a 21-year-old Queen to strap her baby on her back and ride on to the battlefield? Surely, it had to be more than just savagery. Had Prithvi always looked at the Raj through rose-tinted glasses?

The life he had embraced of clubs, cricket, scotch, British private schools and Oxford now appeared like a temporary pass into British bastions where he was a guest. The life he had never thought about—the *sadhus* on the banks of rivers, the *fakirs* and the snake charmers, the puppet shows, the vermilion and the ballads of yore, the adroitness of Shivaji and the unwavering spirit of Maharana Pratap—he felt sentimental about them now. These were the facets of India he should have related to all along. Sushruta invented cataract and plastic surgery, Aryabhatta invented modern mathematics, Buddha espoused tolerance and non-violence, Ashoka carried forward that torch. The great legacy to protect and nurture all things

Indian was being challenged by 'modern' education. British institutions and actions were changing the landscape and gradually eroding a rich and varied heritage, creating pseudo-Englishmen like him.

Why had he been taught Latin when Sanskrit was the language he should have inherited? In his book *Mein Kampf*, Adolf Hitler had clearly stated that the blueprint for the German Empire was the British Raj. The superiority of race—did he get that idea from the British Raj? How could Prithvi have been indifferent to the plight of his fellow countrymen? Did he really need a pompous club secretary to highlight this reality to him? There were many good Britishers in India and he counted some of them as his closest friends. But the Raj stood for something else; it was a testament to the fact that all Indians were living like second-class citizens in their own land. Some of these Indians like him were better off than the others because of their wealth and social stature. But could either of these ever be substitutes for self-respect? Shouldn't the gardener hold his head high? His grandfather was right. The British were surely on their last legs in India.

August 14, 1939: Shantiniketan, West Bengal, British India

Conscious of the reality that could not be hidden, Prithvi's grandfather addressed the remaining eight people in the room without a quiver, but the sweat on his brow could not belie his nervousness. 'We have lost the third book to the Germans. Some of you are already aware of this recent development and some are not.'

One of them asked, 'What about the fourth book? That is the one on communication.'

The old man said, 'Prithvi is on his way to acquire it. He took a bullet from the Germans and was lucky to survive.'

'Perhaps he is just not competent enough,' one of the other men said gently.

The old man considered his reply before saying, 'He killed one German. But you are right—perhaps he is incompetent. Do you have a better replacement?'

The man continued, 'No. I don't. But perhaps we should have a backup plan.'

Prithvi's grandfather said, 'Yes. Over the years our confidence at not being discovered has resulted in complacency. Let's be honest—we have largely become a coffee club who meet at regular intervals. None of us foresaw something of this magnitude happening. We can just hope that Prithvi gets the remaining books. But we have to be realistic. We may not get all the books back. Prithvi's brief has been to acquire as many as possible, but he is competing against two empires with merely a Colt revolver. As the oldest member of this generation's Nine Unknowns, it is my duty to assume responsibility of these meetings and of the mission. If the remaining members want, I shall take the unprecedented step of resigning.'

There were murmurs before one of the others replied, 'No sir. We trust you and we trust your grandson. All of us are to blame equally. We must be one as we always have been.'

August 18, 1939: Moscow, Soviet Union

There was something inherently depressing about Russia which was surprising, given the abundance of architectural marvels and its fascinating history. Prithvi decided it was the combination of dreadful weather and his inability to communicate to the locals in Russian that depressed him the most. Getting to Moscow hadn't been easy. It had taken him a month to get here from Bombay to London by steamer, then onward to Scandinavia. The last leg of his journey had been by automobile from Finland to Moscow on dreadful roads; if indeed they could be called roads. He was exhausted. And the journey was still incomplete.

Thankfully the staff at The Savoy spoke fluent English. Prithvi was amused to see that the hotel stood for everything that Russia did not. It was ostentatious in every respect; the elevators, the artwork, even the hotel talisman, a salamander, a mythological small lizard living in a flame, reeked of affluence and class and its chief patrons were the spoilt children of Communist Party officials. So much for egalitarianism; not that Prithvi was complaining one bit. The hotel doctor was finally able to remove his cast and that made him less glum.

Prithvi certainly did not have time to head into the city and sight-see. He intended to finish the job in the Soviet Union and head back to Bombay as soon as possible. He approached the Russian girl at the help desk. She was wearing a name tag which gave her name as 'Olga'.

Olga asked politely, 'Yes sir? How can I help you?'

'I need to rent an automobile for a week.'

'And where would you be going?'

Prithvi replied, 'Elista.'

'And that is in Russia?' she sounded confused.

Prithvi laughed and said, 'It sure is. Would you like to check the map?'

Looking visibly embarrassed, she said, 'I am so sorry. Usually tourists like to go to Leningrad or Stalingrad. At what time should I keep the chauffeur and car ready? You will be provided with the latest Gaz, a Soviet car.'

Prithvi wasn't too happy with this prospect. 'Yes, well...can I get a British or American car? I don't mind paying a premium.'

Olga had a flair for the dramatic and put on her best aghast impression. Prithvi wondered if this was part of the training—it certainly looked like it. 'We only have Soviet cars. Let me assure our esteemed guest that Soviet cars are the best in the world. You can have a self-drive if you do not need a chauffeur and you can test for yourself how good our Soviet cars are.'

Prithvi quickly said, 'No thanks. I shall take your word for it. I don't understand the signs here and neither do I speak the language. I would very much prefer the chauffeur.'

'Would tomorrow 9 am be a convenient time to leave?'

Prithvi said, 'No. I would prefer to leave right away, or at least within the hour if possible.'

Olga queried, 'How long is the journey?'

Prithvi consulted his book before stating, 'It is an 18-hour journey by road.'

Once again Olga was taken aback. '18-hours? We will have to give him petrol. There might not be a petrol station on the way. And it might take a few days to reach there; surely you can't drive 18 hours non-stop. And we would not like our esteemed guest to be stuck. Bet let me assure you, Soviet people are friendly and warm to all strangers, irrespective of their nationality or skin colour.'

Clearly dealing with non-Caucasian guests had not been part of the training, he mused. 'Great, that is very heartening to know. I want to rent the automobile for a week. When will the car be ready?'

Olga said, 'I will arrange it. It may take a couple hours. You can wait in the lounge, or in your room if you like, sir. '

'I shall wait in my room.' Prithvi looked at Olga again. She was extremely beautiful; a far cry from the weather-beaten peasant look he had seen so far in Moscow. Making up his mind, he slid a 20-pound note on her desk but still covered half of it with his palm. 'Would you like to join me in my room once you have given the instructions?'

'Oh I have a lot of work and it won't be wise of me to leave my desk, sir...' Her eyes remained fixated on the smiling face of the British monarch on the note.

'Are you sure?' Prithvi asked again, as he now flicked two 20-pound notes between his forefinger and thumb.

'I can always get Dinara to cover for me in 20 minutes' time.' She smiled at him coyly.

Prithvi returned the smile and headed back to his room. Russia did not seem all that bad anymore.

August 18, 1939: Berlin, Nazi Germany

Max Kahn was seething. 'What do the authorities mean we can't go to Russia? We are already here in Germany. Do we just forgo the book? And how do we get the next clue? I am tired of these imbecile bureaucrats!'

For a change, it was Heidler who was trying to be reasonable. 'There is no love lost between us and the Communists. However, we are on the verge of signing an important document with the Russians. This document would make the Soviets virtually our allies. Till it is finalized, we do not wish to raise red flags, ha, *red* flags, for the British or the French. Our request to go to Russia has been shot down by the very highest authority in the Fatherland. It goes without saying that we would usually have not been privy to such information. But our Government wishes to avoid any political embarrassment so this information has filtered down to us.'

Kahn asked, 'So what do we do now? How do we get the next clue? That Indian must already be in Russia.'

Heidler replied, 'Yes, he had a head start on us. It took us a while to figure out about Kalmykia. In all probability he will have the book by the end of this week. As soon as he leaves Russia, we can start trailing him and see to it that he leads us to the next one. The other option at our disposal is to look for the next clue ourselves once the deal is signed between us and the Russians. Either way, we must resign ourselves to the actuality that the fourth book is lost.'

August 18, 1939: Office of Under-Secretary for India Rab Butler, London

Butler sat on his desk with his head in his hands and each of his thumbs massaging the two sides of his throbbing temples. He looked up at Youdale and said in a soft voice, 'My head's about to explode. You were digging around in a place which did not have the book?'

Youdale said, 'Yes sir.'

'And wasn't it that Pandey chap who screwed things up? The Germans sent you on a wild goose chase to a remote corner of India because of the sheer incompetence of Pandey. Do ensure I don't see him. I might just strangle him. And what about your Indian cricketer friend? Where is he?'

Youdale said, 'I got a telegram that Mr Rathore was on his way to Russia and that I should return to Bombay. That is when I was asked to report to you in London. The British Embassy in Moscow informs us that he has been enquiring about Kalmykia.'

Butler barked, 'And now we have lost the trail of the books. As if the Germans were not enough, now I have to deal with a nation of peasants and vodka drinkers. You go to Russia and accost Mr Rathore there. Moscow is not Bombay—he is not an immune there.'

Youdale turned to leave when he was interrupted.

'Wait! Perhaps I should tell you. I had a chat with Irwin.'

'Lord Irwin, the former Viceroy of India?'

'A man more commonly known in certain circles of London as Irwin the idiot; probably the dumbest man in the UK holding one of the highest offices possible.'

Youdale said, 'Yes. Of course I know of him. I just never heard anyone refer to him in first person.'

Butler continued, 'While you merely know of him I have had the misfortune of dealing with that buffoon several times. We sent him as the Viceroy of India, the highest representative of the King in India, to negotiate with Gandhi. You know what he did?' Not waiting for a response, Butler continued, 'He ignored Gandhi for 19 months! Then he threw Gandhi in jail along with the rest of Indian leadership. He appointed the Simon Commission to look into India's demand and capability of self-government and did not include a single Indian! He sent Bhagat Singh to the gallows making him a martyr there and the non-violent protestors were about to get very violent. We literally had to force him to sit down with Gandhi and ink a pact which brought relative calm. Once the deal was signed, he was immediately replaced.'

Youdale quietly said, 'I know all about him, Lord Butler.'

Butler enthusiastically continued, 'But it gets better! As Germany began re-arming itself, the German Air Force chief Hermann Göring invited Irwin for a hunting expedition. We had been using Irwin for back channel diplomacy and he was briefed that he might be meeting Adolf Hitler. Do you know what happened there?'

Youdale stated, 'No sir, in all honesty, I don't.'

Butler looked mighty pleased as he continued, 'Adolf Hitler, the Fuhrer of Germany opened the door to greet Irwin and Irwin the idiot mistook him for the doorman and handed him his coat and hat! I know that Irwin had not met Hitler before. But apparently he doesn't see newspaper pictures either. Even a child today knows that the diminutive man with a funny moustache and exaggerated side-parting with looks eerily similar to those of Charlie Chaplin is the Chancellor of Germany! It goes without saying that Hitler was not amused, but to his credit he took it in his stride. Then the two men spoke at length. Can you guess about what?'

Youdale ventured, 'Umm... Germany's impending take-over of Czechoslovakia?'

Butler said, 'Not quite. Hitler enquired a great deal about India. I met Irwin yesterday and this is what he told me. Hitler wanted to know quite a bit more about Hinduism, about the lives of Indians, about their heritage, customs and their temple ruins! Of course, Irwin did not have a clue about any of these questions given that he buried his head like a proverbial ostrich once he went to India. But look at the intent! I am sure Hitler's fascination with India is somehow connected to the Nine Unknowns!'

'Well sir, if we had been forewarned...'

Butler interrupted, 'None of us had a clue. But now it can be insinuated that Hitler's fascination with India is not just limited to the swastika or merely academic purposes. Youdale, I guess you can go once you answer one last question which has been pestering me for a while.'

Youdale nodded his head and asked, 'Yes sir?'

Butler pounded his hand on his desk and counter questioned, 'What the fuck is Kalmykia?'

August 18, 1939: Moscow, Soviet Union

His new found admiration for Russia was reflected in the smirk plastered across Prithvi's face. As he watched Olga button her blouse, he considered spending a few more hours with her. Perhaps he could leave in the morning. The ring of his service telephone interrupted his thoughts. It was to inform him that his car and chauffeur were ready.

He said, 'Well, my car is ready. I shall be back soon.'

'I hope so.'

The Gaz-M1, known locally as the 'Emka' and the pride of Soviet engineering turned out to be a bit of an anti-climax. It was nothing but a 1933 Ford Model B manufactured under license with the M standing for the Russian Foreign Minister who signed the deal with Ford—Molotov. Prithvi would hear the name once again very soon, albeit in a different context.

The chauffeur was a heavy set man named Petrov and greeted Prithvi politely. Fifteen minutes into the drive, he sighed and stated, 'Long drive ahead.' He opened a box on the passenger seat and held up a bottle, 'I have eight of them for the long journey. It might take a few days with some rest stops. You think it is enough for you and me?'

Prithvi laughed aloud as he was handed the bottle of Stolichnaya vodka with its traditional red and gold label. It was 80 proof. Russia was certainly filled with pleasant surprises!

August 20, 1939: Shantiniketan, West Bengal, British India

As Prithvi's telegram to his grandfather was passed around the room, one of the Nine asked, 'Why is he in Russia? Do we have a book there? The information that we have says nothing about a book being located in Russia!'

His grandfather replied, 'Technically, it is within the Russian border, but it is in Kalmykia and not in Russia. And you are right, we don't have that information. I do not have the faintest idea of how it got there.'

'What is Kalmykia?' interjected another.

His grandfather said, 'To be honest, I did not know about it either. It is probably the world's best kept open secret. It is the only Buddhist nation in Europe.'

There was some excited chattering amongst the Nine. Clearly, no one knew of its existence.

Prithvi's grandfather continued, 'There is another matter that needs to be dealt with. Prithvi has informed me that an Indian soldier named Pandey had been deputed by the British to tail the Nazis and that now the British too are after the books and know of our existence as well as Prithvi's mission. Pandey has apparently switched sides and offered his services to Prithvi. Prithvi has conditionally accepted them but is unsure if the British are playing some sort of game. He wants our opinion, too.'

One got up and said, 'The British are a million times better than the damn Germans. The books must be prevented from falling into the hands of either of the two. But if someone was to acquire them I would rather it be the British than the Nazis. At the end of the day, Prithvi is fighting a lone battle. Any help should be welcome.'

The grandfather got up and asked the remaining Unknowns, 'Does anyone have a contrary opinion?'

No one did.

1194 AD: LHASA, TIBET

The old monk addressed the gathering of his disciples, some 1,500 of them who lived in the monastery itself. The left half of his body was badly burnt and the combination of age and rotting skin meant that he had to make a great effort to speak clearly to the gathering.

'My children, many of you wonder what happened to me. I had gone hale and hearty two years ago and came back a completely broken man, both physically and mentally. As some of you know, I had gone to Nalanda to teach. What I saw there last year is unspeakable. The Islamic invaders, led, by Bakhtiyar Khilji, burnt Nalanda to the ground. I have never seen such barbarity and I hope none of you ever do. Eyes were gouged out, embers were placed on mouths, women were raped and children were burnt alive. It was my karma to get out of Nalanda alive. I wish I had died—the pain was unbearable. I was lucky to escape and flee. As I hid in the nearby forest, I was accosted by another man. He was about the same age as me and was one of the teachers at Nalanda. He taught in a different department so although we had seen each other before, we had never really spoken, except for exchanging the odd pleasantry. While I taught religion, if my memory serves me right, he taught communication. His classes were very popular amongst the students. When I saw him that fateful night in the forest, he was a shadow of his former radiant self. The invaders had pulled out the nails from his hands. His hands were then tied behind his back and he was suspended in the air by means of a rope attached to his wrists. The idea was to dislocate both his arms. To add to the pain, bricks from the burnt university were tied to his feet to increase the body weight borne by the arms and thus increase the agony. To complete the humiliation, the holy cows kept in the university cow-shed were slaughtered and their fat was smeared on the soles of his feet and they were slowly roasted. It must be through sheer willpower that he survived. They finally set him free convinced that he would die in a few hours. In his last few hours he met me in the forest. I let out a small yelp, as I thought it was an animal that was crawling toward me. He couldn't move his arms, so with his eyes he pointed to a pocket in his cloak. I reached for it and came across a book. He then asked me to bring my ear close to his mouth.

'He proceeded to give me a set of instructions and took a solemn vow that I shall carry them out. He pleaded with me to put him out of misery and to end his life. I am a Buddhist and it is expressly forbidden to take the life of any living being, least of all a human life. But looking at the state of that man, I decided that the more honourable thing would be to carry out his dying wish. No living being deserves to suffer either. Perhaps I shall have to pay for my sins in the after-life. But I took him to a nearby lake and made him drink some water. He nodded at me and then I pushed him into that lake so that he could drown; that would put an end to his misery. The image etched in my mind is that of his head disappearing into the lake—he smiled at me and shut his eyes as if he were relieved.

'I brought the book with me here and have kept it with me at all times. The teacher asked me not to open it and I have kept my word. However, I know I will not live too long either. That is why you must bear the responsibility of keeping this book safe with you and never open it. This book is now the property of the monastery and does not belong to any one person. It is my wish that once I die all of you will go as far away from Tibet as you can and take this book with you. I wish that it is hidden in a place where no one understands or speaks Sanskrit at all. That was one of the promises I made to the teacher.

'Once you have moved to such a place, two of you—Dorje and Chogyal—must go to the Great New Monastery in Dambulla in Sri Lanka. There, on the base of one of the fifty Vishnu statues, is the name of a location. You must replace that name with the name of the place where you finally keep this book. Finally, each of you has to memorize this little stanza and you must pass it on to future generations. It is critical that this is done:

> Wife-elopement here is a custom
>
> So tell me dear Rustom
>
> Do you want to pay double
>
> For a wife who causes so much trouble?'

The same week, the old man died. The 1,500 disciples decided to carry out the wishes of their guru and after much discussion and debate headed westwards. Finally convinced that no one spoke or even knew anything relatively close to Sanskrit there, the Buddhist tribe set up their homes on both sides of the lower Volga River. Adapting to local customs, the Buddhists built and lived in yurts, transportable wooden trellis-framed dwelling structures, while resisting outside influences. The two men assigned to carry out the task of putting in the clue travelled all the way back to Sri Lanka and carried out the instructions of their master. The book was placed in another yurt, and it was called the Drepung Temple named after one of the 'great three' Gelukpa University monasteries in Tibet, located at the foot of Mount Gephel, close to Lhasa. In Tibet it was also known as 'The Nalanda of Tibet' and the chosen name was a silent nod to this fact. It served to remind the disciples about their Tibetan heritage and Indian connection through the years.

As the population grew and the Tibetans prospered, continuous raids by various nomadic tribesmen made the Tibetans embrace a militaristic lifestyle violating some of the basic tenets of their religion. But it was survival of the fittest out there; their mandate was to protect the book at all costs and after much soul searching, violence too became a part of their culture.

Three hundred years down the line, the people and nation came to be known as Kalmykia. Keeping the evolving political and economic scenario in mind and to reduce the number of ever-increasing raids from nomads, the Kalmyks decided to become subjects of the Russian Czar. They promised to protect Russia's southern borders along with Russian soldiers in exchange of an annual allowance and access to Russian border markets to sell their goods and services. Despite friction with the Czarist Russia which chipped away a lot of Kalmyk autonomy, the Kalmyks prospered and the yurts were gradually replaced by fixed settlements and temples except one. The Drepung Temple yurt housing the book remained and was constantly moved. In 1865 Elista, the capital city of Kalmykia, was built and the Tibetans finally had a permanent home away from home. But an event turned the relatively peaceful world of the Kalmyks upside down in 1917—the Russian Revolution.

Having supported the Czar and having fought the Red Army, the Kalmyks feared the worst. A lot of them who fought with Czarist forces fled to Turkey and Serbia fearing reprisals. But Lenin, ever mindful of pleasing the Asian world where Buddhism was revered decided to go soft on the Kalmyks and they were allowed to retain their autonomy. His nephew Stalin was not so kind. In 1931, determined to Sovietize the Kalmyks, priests and large cattle owners were shipped to Siberia; Cyrillic script replaced the traditional vertical Todo Bichig Kalmyk script; monasteries were shut down, many religious texts were burnt and the 'voluntary' collectivization of agriculture was thrust onto the Kalmyks. In order to save the one book they really cared about, the tiny yurt holding the precious book was constantly moved around and the Soviets did not even know of its existence.

From 1931-33, 60,000 Kalmyks perished because of the policies of Stalin. It was in the midst of this social, financial and cultural disaster that Prithvi landed in Kalmykia.

August 22, 1939: Elista, Kalmykia, Soviet Union

Soldiers of the Red Army posted to maintain order in Kalmykia usually were 18 or 19-year olds from the Urals. Few of them had seen a private automobile. So when the polished Emka ferrying Prithvi snaked its way through the lanes of the Kalmyk capital, it was assumed by the soldiers on duty that it was a dignitary from Moscow doing the rounds. Much to his amusement, Prithvi's car was even saluted.

Noticing a group of young Asian looking men playing chess in a square, Prithvi decided to get out of the car. Surprised at seeing a foreigner, he was immediately accosted by three young Soviet soldiers. They barked something in Russian at him and Prithvi was at a loss on how to communicate with them. Petrov got out of the car; seeing his crisp chauffeur uniform the soldiers were a bit taken aback. He barked right back at the soldiers and the only word that Prithvi caught in the rapid conversation was 'Savoy'. After an intense five-minute conversation, the soldiers' demeanour became less aggressive and the tone a lot less hostile. They smiled at Prithvi. Prithvi motioned to Petrov to hurry back to the car.

'Petrov, what was that conversation all about?' he asked.

Petrov replied, 'They don't like foreigners here. But old Petrov sort them out.'

'What did you tell them?'

Petrov said, 'Stupid peasants. I told them that you were the half-Indian son of the British Ambassador to the USSR, and are staying at the Savoy as you are on a vacation from India. You wanted to visit Buddhist sites of Kalmykia because of your Indian background. I also told them that yesterday I had the privilege of driving you to the Kremlin where you had tea with Stalin! I invited them to take both of us into custody right away and we would see which of us would be shipped to Siberia.'

Prithvi tried to keep a straight face but was unable to do so. 'And they bought the story?'

Petrov said, 'Of course they did. They are children yet and you don't really wish to pick a fight with someone who comes in a chauffeur-driven automobile. In the land of equality, the ones who own autos are more equal than the others.'

'How many vodka bottles do we have left?'

A disappointed Petrov replied, 'Three of them are left. You are a light drinker.'

Prithvi reached for one of the bottles, stepped out of the vehicle and walked to the soldiers. He did not say anything but handed the bottle to one of them and instantly realized that he had made new Russian friends. In the Emka, Petrov shook his head in disgust at watching such expensive vodka being wasted on peasants and spat on the road. The soldiers shook Prithvi's hand vigorously and one of them did a little Russian jig for him while another pointed to the group of chess playing men inviting Prithvi to go speak to them.

The chess players had stopped their various games as they watched the proceedings between the Russian soldiers and the foreign looking man in the fancy car, with a mixture of curiosity and fear. Given the language incompatibility, Prithvi decided to keep it simple and said, 'I am looking for Drepung.'

The young men were in a state of flux, looking at each other uneasily and rapidly exchanging words with one word standing out—'Drepung'. One of them pointed to an older man smoking hand-rolled tobacco in the corner who nodded his head vigorously toward Prithvi saying something in the local language. The old man too was taken aback on hearing the word 'Drepung' but instead of blabbering in a tongue Prithvi would not understand he quizzically raised his eyebrows and asked, 'India? Indian?'

On getting an affirmative nod, he grabbed Prithvi's just healed arm and marched him off to a well maintained home two kilometres from the chess square. Outside the home, the old man let go of Prithvi's arm finally and held up his palm indicating that Prithvi should wait here. After about ten minutes a short, pleasant looking middle-aged woman stepped out of the house and said to him in peculiarly accented Hindi, 'Hindustan *se aaye ho*? India *se*?' (You come from Hindustan—India?)

Prithvi was taken aback, but responded in Hindi.

She invited him into her home which was sparingly but tastefully furnished. She offered him some goat milk, which he politely sipped. She finally sat down on the only chair in the room and gestured to him to sit as well on one of the stools.

Frowning at him, she looked him directly in the eye and continued in Hindi, 'So tell me Indian, from where did you find out about Drepung?'

He said, 'In Ceylon, perhaps you know it as Lanka.'

She shot back, 'Where in Ceylon?'

He once again replied honestly, 'In the Great New Monastery in Dambulla. Why do you ask?'

'I shall ask the questions, Indian.' Forgoing the frown, she smiled at him now. 'You know, I haven't gotten a chance to speak in Hindi since my mother passed away some 30 years ago. And what do you expect to find in the Drepung? What is it that you seek?'

'I am seeking a very important book of Indian heritage.'

She posed, 'And why would I give it to you?'

'Well for starters, the Nazis are after it and so are the British. I just want to return them to their rightful owners in India.'

She then took a deep breath and said, 'This is difficult. For generations, women of my family have been taught Sanskrit and Hindi as we are keepers of the book. It was decided that the women would be keepers as usually even invaders and murderers spare the women and children. Initially, we were only taught Sanskrit but then some 100 years ago my great grandmother decided to learn Hindi as well, as Sanskrit was disappearing from India and Hindi was becoming the lingua franca. I don't have a daughter so when I reach the age of 45 in three years' time, I am supposed to select a girl from the community and pass on the knowledge.

'People here know what Drepung is but very few are privy to the information of what the Drepung holds. The Russians have destroyed our culture and our monasteries under Stalin, so we are reluctant to trust anyone. Come to the terrace with me.'

The yurt stood in the terrace. She pointed to it and said, 'This is the Drepung! Not quite what you were expecting, is it? It had to be mobile because we were nomadic and were constantly moved back in the old days. And we might just need to move again. People here think of it as a holy relic of our Tibetan heritage. You know what Kalmyk means?'

He said, 'No, I don't.'

She softly said, 'It means "those who remained"—those who remained in an alien land to carry out their duties and to keep their word.' She proceeded to the back of the yurt and of the sides removed a huge painting held in a frame. ...icture in it depicted the Buddha in the lotus position. ...slid open the frame and removed a tightly wrapped brown package. 'Here is your book.'

Prithvi quickly opened the package and sure enough he had the fourth book, on Communication. He could barely contain his excitement. 'You don't know what this means to me and to our people. I must go now.' He proceeded to leave, stopped and turned around. The woman was smiling, 'Aren't you forgetting something?'

He looked at the painting and the container, thoroughly confused. She continued smiling and said, 'It's a clue isn't it? How many such books are there?'

'Yes, but where is it? And there are a lot of books. This is the fourth one.'

'I never knew it was a clue and actually thought it was a silly rhyme which made no sense at all. I was taught to say it to the one who sought the book. This is how it goes:

> Wife-elopement here is a custom
> So tell me dear Rustom
> Do you want to pay double
> For a wife who causes so much trouble?'

Prithvi repeated it and the woman excitedly asked him, 'What does it mean?'

A completely confused Prithvi memorized it, repeated it once again and finally said, 'Damned if I know!'

August 25, 1939: Residence of Under-Secretary for India Rab Butler, London

As the Baron awoke, he picked up the tiny silver bell kept next to his bedside and rang it vigorously. That usually implied that one of the domestic workers in the house was supposed to bring in hot tea and the morning newspaper. This time, just the servant rushed in. Butler was cross; he was not a new servant.

'Where is my tea and newspaper?' he snapped.

'Sir, you are wanted at your office right away.'

Butler fumed with impatience, 'I run my office as I please, when I please. Now please go and bring my tea and newspaper! Now!'

Within a minute a tray holding a cup, sugar, a kettle and the morning edition of *The Times* was presented to the Baron. The helper stood by the bedside awaiting further instructions.

Pouring himself a cup and adding one teaspoon of sugar, the Baron opened the newspaper. On reading the headlines, Butler spilled the tea on himself.

There was a cartoon of Hitler and Stalin walking down the road with cheering supporters on either side. One of their arms was around the other's neck while the other was firmly at the back, each of them holding a pistol. The headlines read:

LONDON STAGGERED; Nazi-Soviet Pact Blow Is Received in Rage and Stupefaction; TALK OF POLAND YIELDING: British Seen Facing Hazard of a Reich Dominant in Europe-- Cabinet Will Meet Today

The deadliest high explosives could not have caused more injury in London than the information that the Nazi and Soviet Governments had signed a non-aggression pact behind the backs of the British and French military missions in Moscow.

The Pact signed between the Soviet foreign minister Vyacheslav Molotov and the German foreign minister Joachim von Ribbentrop, is an agreement officially titled the 'Treaty of Non-aggression between Germany and the Union of Soviet Socialist Republics'. It renounces war between the two countries and guarantees neutrality by either party if the other were attacked by a third party. Each signatory promised not to join any alliance of powers that was 'directly or indirectly aimed at the other party'.

Not bothering to read the rest of the article he shouted at the helper. 'Wipe that smirk off your face or I shall do it for you! So much for Chamberlain's "Peace in our times" agreement with that German warmonger! Get my clothes ready; there is no time for a bath. I will have to go to the office right away.'

August 27, 1939: Moscow, Soviet Union

As news of the Nazi-Soviet Pact reverberated across Europe and indeed the world, Prithvi wished to leave Soviet shores as soon as possible. He had returned from Kalmykia just a day earlier and had been completely cut-off from the news. It had been four days since the Pact was inked. The diplomatic relations between the United Kingdom and the Soviet Union would have hit a low ebb if not the nadir. As a citizen of a British colony, it might not be the most welcoming of places. Besides, he had on his person a book which could easily be classified a national treasure of the USSR and he could be shipped to Siberia for stealing it. He shuddered at the very thought of the stories he had read about Siberian prison camps. He would have to fly from Moscow rather than take a road trip as he had done earlier—it was not a secure route anymore. Despite being tired and sporting an unkempt, dishevelled and unshaven look, Prithvi decided to leave that very day. He walked toward the lobby to enquire about his options to fly to London commercially or if necessary to charter a flight.

Before he could approach the desk, he felt something cold in his back. 'Ah, it is our Indian friend from Ceylon.'

Prithvi recognized the Nazis he had accosted in the cave in Lanka. There were two of them; he wondered if he had fatally shot the third. As if they were reading his thoughts, the unarmed one spoke up. 'You killed a very close friend of mine. You will die a slow and painful death—you have my word.'

Cutting his colleague off, the one holding a gun to Prithvi's back got straight to the point, 'Where is the fourth book?'

Prithvi said, 'I have placed it at the reception and told them to keep it in the hotel safe for me.'

Heidler said, 'Well, then you will get the book from them with the gun held to your back. You will then lead us outside where you will get into the German Embassy car awaiting us. We will then have a nice chat about all that you did in Kalmykia, all that you know about the next book and any other books at the Embassy.'

Prithvi asked, 'And then you will kill me?'

Heidler coldly replied, 'Perhaps I will. Do you really have a choice?'

'You will shoot me in a hotel lobby?'

Heidler bluntly said, 'Yes. You are a British spy and I am a German, a Russian ally. I could get away with it.'

Prithvi considered for a moment and then lead the two Nazis to the counter. There were two girls sitting there – one was Olga who beamed when she saw Prithvi and the other was a middle aged lady named Svetlana. Prithvi spoke, 'I have a package.'

Svetlana replied, 'What package, sir?'

Prithvi thrust his right hand into his jacket pocket, then his back pocket, then various other pockets and shouted at top of his voice, 'Where is it? Just where is it?'

Svetlana said, 'Calm down sir. Where is what?'

'Ah! Now I remember.' He unzipped his trousers and flipped out his member. 'Here is the package! Would you like to take a closer look?'

A horrified Svetlana shrieked in repulsion. Prithvi continued, 'Olga really liked it. I am sure you will as well. Isn't this a service you extend to all your guests?' Olga went beet red on hearing this and mumbled something in Russian. One of the security guards rushed forward to quell the ruckus. He too was shocked to see Prithvi flashing the ladies.

He said, 'Sir, please put that err… thing in its place.'

Prithvi said, 'What thing? This is the package that Olga serviced; it needs more servicing.'

Olga of course had turned into a statue not knowing where to hide.

The security guard asked the two Germans 'Are you with this Indian lunatic?'

Before they could collect their wits Prithvi said, 'Fuck that! I don't know these bastards. I want a blowjob from Svetlana right now!'

The security guard said, 'Call the police Svetlana. This man is obviously drunk. We expect our guests to behave.'

Many other people in the lobby started gathering around in a semi-circle to watch the drama that was unfolding before their eyes.

Breaking free from the two Nazis, Prithvi ran to the little artificial pond at the centre of which the hotel talisman, the salamander, was placed with the security guard running behind him. As he relieved himself into the pond he sang at the top of voice, 'For he's a jolly good fellow, for he's a jolly good fellow… Sing along with me you idiots! For he's a jolly good fellow and so say all of us, and so say all of us… why are you not singing? Spoil sports! For he's a jolly good fellow aha, that felt nice, and so say all of us.'

As three more security guards came toward him, Prithvi zipped his fly and turned toward them. 'What are you going to do? Arrest me? Fuckin' Russian peasants!' And then he spat into the pond mimicking his chauffeur Petrov. The next thing he knew, he was on the ground held down by two Russian men, and his hands were bound. Within minutes the Russian police arrived and after a quick conversation with the security guard and the still shaken Svetlana, cuffed Prithvi and led him away. As he was being led away, Prithvi shouted at the top of his voice, 'Long live mother Russia! I love Russian women!'

Prithvi then winked at the furious Nazis as they helplessly watched him being led away.

Timeline

September 1, 1939

Nazi Germany invades Poland from the southern, northern and western boundaries after staging a 'Polish attack' on the German radio station Sender Gleiwitz in Gleiwitz, Upper Silesia, Germany.

September 3, 1939

Great Britain and France declare war on Nazi Germany along with Australia, New Zealand and Canada.

September 4, 1939: Central Jail, Moscow, Soviet Union

When Prithvi was escorted to prison the world was still at peace. In a matter of three days, there had been invasions and now the world was at war. Sharing his spartan cell was a bulky Russian named Dmitri who was apparently in the cell for breaking a vodka bottle on the head of his irritating wife. The food and hospitality was definitely not a patch on the Savoy. He had thought he would be out in one day as he had asked for someone from the British Embassy to show up. When he had given up hope, the lanky Russian guard from whom he bummed cigarettes for an exorbitant bribe announced in broken English, 'Visitor visiting you.'

A chair was placed in front of the cell and in walked Youdale with a sheaf of papers and a notepad neatly tucked under his arm. Seating himself on the wrought iron chair, Youdale removed his pen and started tapping it under his chin. After a few seconds of collecting his thoughts, he let out a wry smile and finally spoke, 'So we meet again. A far cry from our surroundings last time around in French Indo-China, no?'

Prithvi said, 'Okay. What will it take to get me out of here? Just name it.'

'As if you don't know.'

Prithvi quickly added, 'Listen, get me out of here and I shall give you what you seek.'

Youdale considered his reply, 'You are in no position to make demands.'

Prithvi said, 'I bribed the guard to send a telegram to India. I am sure something is being worked out there.'

Youdale said, 'True. You have friends in the upper echelons of Indian society. The British Embassy in Moscow got a call from the Viceroy himself. But our office is absorbing the pressure by throwing up our arms and telling him that we are trying our best. But look at your situation—you are a British subject in a prison of a country on whose ally we have formally declared war. Yours was a minor transgression; you were apparently, ahem, flashing your penis at a middle aged receptionist at an up market Moscow hotel. Bravo!'

'The Nazis were …'

Youdale quickly put a finger to his lips asking Prithvi to stop, indicating that someone might be listening. 'The Nazis were what?'

Prithvi checked himself and said, 'They were insulting His Majesty and I was a bit drunk.'

Youdale replied, 'Well, you know what we require from you. Look at these papers, sign them and we shall try our best to get you out.' Youdale slid some papers and a pen to Prithvi.

The first page said,

Tell me where the book is that you have and write down the clue of the next book and I will get you out of here.

Prithvi quickly scribbled a reply and passed it back.

The book is on me. I shall give that to you. But I shall give you the clue for the next book once we are safely in India or in the UK.

Youdale read it and as he wrote the reply he said, 'Take your time to go through the papers, no rush.'

The Germans will also want to interrogate you shortly. And they will not be scribbling notes or being nice. You better give me both the book and the clue and I will get you out of here. You have my word.

Prithvi thought for a minute and wrote back:

Your word is just not good enough. I will give whatever the Germans ask for. They might actually let me live—you just might leave me here for dead. I have information and I don't see what you have to lose. I will be in your protective custody all along. Take me to UK and torture me for information if you must.

Youdale let out a short laugh on reading it. As if he could torture the scion of an Indian family in the UK; if word got out not only would he lose his job but he might be the one who ended up in prison.

Fine. Give me the clue later. Where is the book?

Prithvi pulled up his trousers to reveal a holster which did not hold a gun anymore. He removed the package and handed it to Youdale. While Youdale could not read Sanskrit he was convinced on seeing the age and condition of the book that Prithvi was being honest. He handed another sheaf of papers to Prithvi. 'Please sign these forms. By tomorrow, if all goes well, you will be released into the protective custody of the British Embassy and you will never be allowed to enter the Savoy again.'

Prithvi said, 'I don't ever want to enter Russia again.'

Youdale smiled and said, 'And this time you owe me more than just a meal at your Cricket Club.'

September 4, 1939: Embassy of Nazi Germany, Moscow, Soviet Union

Josef Heidler and Max Kahn contemplated their next course of action. Heidler was completely embarrassed at the turn of events; how could they have let that damn Indian slip away from his grasp with such an amateur and silly gimmick?

It was Kahn who spoke, 'Why don't we go speak to him?'

Heidler responded, 'Under what pretext should we do that? He is not a German citizen. He has created a public nuisance and not committed a crime. The Russians might be our allies but they don't trust us. If they get wind of the book, they would want it for themselves. Trust me, no one wants to torture that Indian bastard more than I do. But under the circumstances our best bet is to wait for the Russians to release him and then get him to our Embassy here. Personally, I would like to take him to Berlin.'

Kahn posed, 'What if he makes a deal with the Russians? Or if the British get him out?'

Heidler said, 'One thing about this young man is that he is very resourceful. You have to admire that. I have no clue what he will do next. But we must still try and get him while he is in Moscow. If he flees to the UK or India, we will not be able to catch him. The Fuhrer was shocked when the British declared war on Germany. He did not expect that at all. After all, we are not a threat to the British by any stretch of imagination. In *Mein Kampf*, the Fuhrer openly professes his admiration for the colonies of Britain and admits wishing to model the German

Empire on the British one. Thankfully, the British have only declared war and not done anything. They might be wishing to save face by doing so. Perhaps, we can still have peace.'

'So what should be our next course of action?'

Heidler replied, 'We wait and see what he does. One of our Embassy personnel is stationed right outside the prison. As soon as the Indian steps out we will be informed. I wish I could put some pressure on the Russians by informing them that he is a British spy but that would surely raise some eyebrows here and the Russians would make our torture methods seem almost pedestrian. We have to get our hands on this man by hook or by crook.'

September 21, 1939: Fort William, Scotland, United Kingdom

Despite the circumstances, Prithvi could not take his eyes off the breathtaking view. Lakes, ski slopes and the magnificent Ben Nevis—what better view could one possibly want? It was beautiful, except for the small matter that he had been virtually a prisoner for the past thirteen days.

The release from the Moscow prison had taken longer than expected; he was not sure if that was a British ploy to make him uneasy and sing like a canary when the time came or just plain old Soviet red tape. He suspected it was the latter. But at the end of the day, Youdale had kept his end of the bargain. What was not a part of the bargain was being flown straight to Scotland, and being placed in 'protective custody' in the Scottish Highlands. The rules were clear: he could not venture out of the house and the two sentries stationed around the clock ensured it; his passport had been taken away for 'safekeeping' and while every conceivable comfort was provided to him, access to any communication tool was denied—no telephone, no telegrams, no radio and no newspapers.

Just as Prithvi was working up the shaving lather on his jaw in the restroom, he heard someone barge into his room unannounced. Stepping out with his face half-covered in shaving cream, Prithvi saw Youdale.

'How nice of you to join me Youdale,' he said sarcastically. 'I assume you are not here to offer me complimentary bagpipe lessons with my paid-for vacation at His Majesty's expense. But given that I am in Scotland, I could surely use a bottle of single malt whiskey—the ones that have been put at my disposal are all blended. Is His Majesty being curmudgeonly?'

Youdale barked back, 'Fuck off, you swine. I don't even know what curmudgeonly means, but then again, I was not born with a silver spoon stuck up my arse. How the fuck did you do it?'

Prithvi replied in a sing-song polite voice which further infuriated Youdale. 'How the fuck did I do what? And I am sure you know how to use a dictionary.'

Youdale curtly said, 'You know what I am talking about. I had told you quite clearly that once we get hold of the next book we would let you go scot-free. Then why did you do it?'

Prithvi continued the mocking. 'Let me go scot-free? And pray what crime have I committed? Even if flashing someone is a crime, I did it on Soviet soil; how does that affect His Majesty's Government?'

Youdale shot back, 'Answer me—how did you get word out in the press that we are holding you against your will?'

Prithvi smirked. 'Oh, so word *did* get out. Well, the guard at the Moscow prison had become a friend, no thanks in small measure to the exorbitant prices he charged me for the odd cigarette. Once you were dilly-dallying in getting me out of prison, I handed him three sets of envelopes and promised to give him 50 British pounds once they returned my belongings to me. He must have figured I was good for the money. The first was if the Russians released me to the Germans; the second if they shipped me off to Siberia or one of their camps and the third if I was handed over to the British. My instructions to him were simple. In any of the circumstances, he was to hand over the letter to the driver Petrov at The Savoy. In the envelope was a simple telegram that had to be sent to India informing who it was that I had been "released" to. As soon as they returned their belongings to me, I handed the guard 50 pounds because I knew you would not let me stop at any post office. I figured that the guard pocketed the 50 pounds and did not bother or perhaps Petrov did not bother to carry out my request but apparently I was wrong. So what exactly was printed?'

Youdale said, 'In the editorial of *The Times of India* it said that a scion of the prominent Rathore family was being held against his will by the British Government without committing a crime and if someone so well-connected and high up on the social pecking order is treated by the Government with such disdain, one can only imagine how the common Indian man is being treated by the imperial British.'

Prithvi queried, 'And what is the reaction?'

'Quite strong,' said Youdale. 'The Viceroy called the Foreign Office and gave the Under-Secretary of State for India quite an earful.'

Prithvi mused, 'So I assume I won't have the time for bagpipe lessons. You will have to let me go.'

Youdale smirked and said, 'Not quite. There was bigger piece of news in the UK. The Russians too invaded Poland.'

A shocked Prithvi replied, 'What? I don't believe you.'

'I knew you wouldn't. Have a look at this.' It was a copy of the London edition of *The Evening Standard* dated September 20, 1939. On the front page was a cartoon by David Low titled "Rendezvous". On the ravaged ground lay a dead Polish soldier. On either side of the dead body were Messrs Hitler and Stalin doffing their hats to each other. Hitler greeted Stalin with the line, 'The scum of the Earth, I believe?' and

Stalin returned the compliment with, 'The bloody assassin of the workers, I presume?'

Prithvi asked, 'Does that mean you British are declaring war on the Soviets as well?'

Youdale angrily muttered, '"You British"! You should say "we British", since you seem to be making more use of the Viceroy than I ever shall. No we are not declaring war on the Soviet Union although the Polish Government in-exile in Romania is asking us to do so. We have issued a condemnation of the invasion. The Russians are conveniently labelling it "The Liberation Campaign"—apparently to save ethnic Ukrainians and Belarusians in eastern Poland. Don't even get me started on that region—it is a complete mess. Despite declaring war, we have yet to do anything whatsoever. The government and world is hopeful that violence will be avoided.'

'Oh, it seems a bit of Gandhi rubbed off on you after all,' said Prithvi sarcastically.

Ignoring him Youdale said, 'And as for you Mr Rathore, I shall be escorting you to London. However, your passport seems to have been lost.'

Prithvi exclaimed, 'How convenient!'

Now it was Youdale's turn to mock, 'I can quicken the procedure of procuring a fresh passport for you; of course, that would entail you telling me everything you know about the rhyme.'

Prithvi said, 'I am afraid I don't know much. Once I gain access to a library and some material, I could probably figure it out. What have you found out?'

Youdale considered for a moment. 'Nothing as of yet but we have some people working on it. And since we managed to misplace your belongings, we will put you up at a Government guest house in London while we try to retrieve your passport and your wallet.'

Prithvi asked, 'My wallet is gone too? What a surprise!'

'It is most regretful. We are quite embarrassed by it and will of course reimburse you the sum along with the passport. Should we now proceed to the guest house? It is a fairly long drive,' Youdale said in bureaucratic mock lament.

Prithvi replied, 'Thanks for your generosity. My father happens to be in London and we have a home there. I shall neither need your services nor those of His Majesty.'

'What?' retorted a visibly shocked Youdale. Someone in the intelligence was going to get a rap on the knuckles.

'My father, that is, my progenitor, happens to maintain a home—a domicile, an abode, a dwelling—in London. Need I explain it further?'

An irritated Youdale said, 'Stop being cheeky, lad! I understood it the first time. I am not looking forward to a ten-hour drive to London with you and your caustic tongue.' Youdale shook his head as he headed toward the door.

'Can I grab a bottle of Cutty Sark for the journey?' called Prithvi after him.

September 24, 1939: Berlin, Nazi Germany

As a soldier, Heidler maintained an equilibrium which kept him unfazed even when the odds were stacked against him. Battle was a fluid situation—you never knew what was coming up next. So he was surprised that his palms were sweaty and he did not feel good. Next to him, Kahn was a nervous wreck and had just toppled over a flower vase.

A tall blond soldier entered the waiting area, 'He will see you now.'

They barely noticed the tastefully done room; their eyes were fixated on the great leader, the Fuhrer who was dressed in full military regalia. They offered the customary Nazi salute and waited for an invitation to sit. After what seemed an eternity, Hitler flicked his index fingers towards two chairs, indicating that they could indeed sit in his august presence.

Just as Kahn was about to speak the door opened once more and a heavyset man walked in, wearing a uniform with multiple medals attached to the ribbon on his chest. He did not bother with the Nazi salute. His girth belied the fact that he was a decorated World War I fighter pilot with twenty-two confirmed kills and amongst the numerous medals pinned on his chest was the coveted Pour le Merite, the Blue Max, Germany's highest military order in World War I. He now headed the Luftwaffe, the German Air Force and introduced himself to the two visitors gruffly as Herman Goring. Not that Hitler's protégé Herman Wilhelm Goring needed an introduction as such. Everyone in Germany knew him as the man who made a fortune either forcibly seizing great works of art from Jews or buying them at a pittance. Kahn—already awed by Hitler's presence, seemed to have completely lost his marbles on seeing Goring and offered him the Nazi salute with the wrong hand, seeing which the big man guffawed.

An assistant brought in coffee for everyone and Goring frowned irritably. 'Don't you have something a bit more... umm... alcoholic?'

Hitler let out a sigh and said, 'Herman it is 11 am. Can't you wait just a little longer?'

Hitler dismissed the assistant and asked Kahn and Heidler, 'How much sugar will you take?' After waiting momentarily for a reply and not seeing one forthcoming, he added a teaspoon to each of their cups and handed them over not bothering with a cup for Goring.

He then continued speaking, 'Herr Heidler, Herr Kahn, it is very kind of you to join me today.'

As if we had a choice, thought Heidler.

Hitler continued, 'You are extremely important cogs in the wheel of the German nation we wish to build. Perhaps you have not realized the importance of the books that I seek. And from the reports, I gather that you have lost the trail of the books. Is this correct?'

Heidler nodded reluctantly.

Hitler winced. He then got up from his desk and pointed to India on the world map strewn across the back of his desk. 'I still can't believe that such a hopelessly poor and backward nation holds so much treasure.' He turned around and looked directly at the two visitors. 'The first book taught us propaganda and psychological warfare. It is unbelievable how easy it is to convince a nation to go to war. All you do is whip up some emotion, deride the pacifists as being anti-national and paint yourself as historically wronged. All you then need to do is to find a villain on whom you can blame this. It all fits beautifully. The German nation has shaken off the humiliation of Versailles. Poland is ours and now we can concentrate on other countries. What I did not expect was that the British would declare war on us. This puts a spanner on our desire to acquire the rest of the books given that they might be in British colonies. I have offered a peace deal to the British and the French if they accept German dominance on continental Europe. Let us await their reaction and hope that hostilities do not commence. Now let's get back to the books. Out of the nine, we have two and either the Indian has the other two or there are one each with the Indian and the British. And now we have supposedly lost the trail of the fifth book according to your report. Am I correct so far?'

Heidler spoke softly, 'Yes, Fuhrer. But we intend to get back on the trail as soon as we can.'

Goring interjected, 'What do you think this is, hunting season for you to get back on the trail?'

Heidler looked directly at him and without blinking said, 'In a way it is a hunt! If you are not satisfied with my work or progress, I shall be willing to hand in my resignation for failure to carry out my duties satisfactorily in the service of the Reich.'

As Goring got up from his chair to give Heidler a piece of his mind, Hitler raised his left palm toward Goring, indicating that he should stop. 'Far from it—I think you have done exceptionally given the hostile terrain, the language barrier and the limited resources at your disposal. But you do realize that I can't assign a battalion to you in the interest of keeping things discreet. And you do need to get back on the track as soon as you can. What is it that you need, to get back on track?'

Emboldened by Heidler's bravado, Kahn managed to reply, 'We would need some divine intervention right now.'

Hitler smiled and said, 'Would my intervention suffice for now?' He turned to Goring and said, 'Herman, do tell them.'

Delighted at being finally given the chance to speak he said, 'The German Embassy in Moscow intercepted a telegram being sent to India by a Russian man. He turned out to be the Indian's chauffeur when he was staying at The Savoy. A rather small bribe made him lead my man in the Embassy to the Buddhist region of Kalmykia where he spoke to a woman. Thanks to our alliance with the Soviets we were allowed to interrogate the Kalmyk lady. She did not say much despite threats to ship her to Siberia. We then negotiated with the Russians and brought her to Berlin for interrogation. After some,' he grappled for words, 'persuasion, she finally caved in and gave us the next clue. It is a short verse:

> Wife-elopement here is a custom
> So tell me dear Rustom
> Do you want to pay double
> For a wife who causes so much trouble?

Does it mean anything to you?'

After a prolonged silence, Kahn finally said, 'Not yet.'

OCTOBER 1896: KAMDESH, KAFIRISTAN

Unknown to most of the world, Afghanistan was not always a war ravaged apocalyptic nightmare. It used to be a predominantly Buddhist nation. For centuries the Bamiyan Buddhas were a testament to this heritage. Just like in India, Afghanistan too was invaded by the Islamic hordes and quite unlike India, the forced conversion of people to Islam was far more successful here. The ploy was simple—ask a Buddhist or Hindu to convert; if he or she refuses, chop his or her head off. The amount of Buddhist and Hindu blood spilled here led to the mountains around the area to be renamed from Pariyatra Parvat to Hindu-Kush, that is, from Mountain Abode of Angels to Hindu-Killing Mountains. Just like the people, the monasteries and religious texts too did not survive the carnage—all except one that managed to withstand through centuries. Earlier known as Kapiśa Janapada, named after the Buddhist Kapiśa dynasty which held sway over it, the region was now called Kafiristan literally translating to land of the infidels by the surrounding Muslim kingdoms. In 1896, it was finally renamed Nuristan as the final bastion of Buddhism in Afghanistan fell to Islam. But one tiny region managed to survive, paradoxically, thanks to the British.

The three tribal chiefs representing the four regions of Kafiristan sat at an intentionally designed round table. There was no one to head this meeting—all decisions could only be taken by consensus. However, the conversation was always dominated by two of them. The third hardly ever spoke, but when he did, it was usually something very important.

The first said, 'So it has finally happened. The king of Afghanistan, flush with British arms and ammunition has given us an ultimatum: acquiesce or perish.'

The second asked, 'We have been Buddhists for centuries; we cannot just ask our subjects to convert to Islam overnight!'

They continued to argue about the merits and demerits of accepting the Afghan king's ultimatum for twenty minutes. Finally, the third one spoke.

'Let us be realistic. If he invades, we will not be able to stop him. Centuries ago you know what happened to the other Buddhists here. To avoid such a fate and to prevent our children being orphaned and the rape of our women, we must comply. Besides, we can't live in isolation. A future king might just invade and kill all 60,000 of us. At least this one has offered us the chance to live.'

The first said, 'He says we will now be known as Nuristanis—the Enlightened Ones. Don't you find that patronizing?'

The second said, 'I do. But I would rather feel patronized than dead. Besides, the Buddha too was the Enlightened One.

The first continued, 'Let us assume we agree to comply with his wishes; we still have the problem of the book. What do we do? We are meant to protect it—do we just hand it over to the king? Even if we don't, the next generation might think of it as an infidel book and burn it. Or perhaps they would sell it to the highest bidder. After all, we have been the protectors of the book for centuries.'

The second one interjected, 'We have a policy in place. The book is rotated between the three of us every six months. We have to ensure its protection through the ages.'

A miser with words, the third one simply stated, 'The Durand Line.'

After two wars with the Afghans in 1839-42 and 1878-80 which ended in stalemate, the British decided to cut their losses and make peace with the king of Afghanistan, Emir Abdur Rahman Khan. As per the terms of the agreement, some of the erstwhile Afghan territory became part of the British Indian Empire. The British recognized Abdur Khan as the undisputed king of Afghanistan and accorded him a stipend of Rs 18.5 million a year along with weapons to mitigate the frequent Russian incursions into the region and secured an agreement to maintain a nominal British military presence in Afghanistan. If Russia ran over Afghanistan, it could potentially threaten the British Empire in India. The one-upmanship between the Russians and the British to hold sway over Afghanistan came to be known as The Great Game. The 1,610 mile border dividing Afghanistan and British India came to be known as the Durand Line after the then foreign secretary of the British Indian Government, Sir Mortimer Durand. This Durand Line cut across Kafiristan, resulting in part of it falling on the British side of the border.

The first chief nodded his head in agreement. 'This is the best possible option under the circumstances.'

Consensus was finally reached—the book would be placed in the part of Kafiristan under British rule and the locals would have no choice but to embrace Islam and give up their way of life. The circulation of the book between the three chiefs too would come to an end to allay the risk of it falling into the wrong hands.

December 9, 1940: Chitral, North-West Frontier Province, British India

Oblivious to the fascination or even to the presence of the man they had been calling 'the foreigner' for the past week in their local Kalash language, the residents continued their festivities.

Initially, the women were dressed in traditional black robes decorated with cowrie shells of various sizes and hues. The men wore traditional white robes and stood separate from the womenfolk and were divided into two groups—the pure ones and the impure ones. On cue from the Shaman, the pure men burst into melodic songs about chastity and honour and praise of the God Indra.

Once they were done singing, the impure men too burst into a song, except theirs was raunchy, wild, passionate and downright obscene, representing Indra's younger and trouble-making brother Balimain. This further weakened the God Indra, who was already weak after aiding the people in the harvest season. Meanwhile, a group of young boys formed a chain, the *anvārambhana* and snaked through the village. They were ritualistically offered bread by the men and women alike and their feet were touched in an act of worship— they were impersonating the ancestors of yore. The impure men then exchanged their clothes with the women and now danced, dressed as women. The trouble-making Balimain was exercising his boon from Brahma to change his form at will. The Shaman then blew a conch toward the small hillock and the lucky teenage boy who was to be the cynosure of all eyes at this festival emerged from the hut atop the hillock and climbed down with the fifteen goats given to him. He had been living alone with the goats for a fortnight and was supposed to get fat and strong by living exclusively on goat milk.

For his efforts he was now given a golden opportunity—a 24-hour window in which he could have sexual intercourse and lose his virginity with any woman he wanted, married or unmarried, related or unrelated. A child born of this 24-hour rampage was considered to be blessed by both Indra and Balimain. He would be born in a special section of the community building known as the *bashaleni*—the building where all Kalash women gave birth or were sent to when menstruating. As the young boy shyly looked at the women, they made cooing calls, urging the boy to select her over any other.

He finally chose a girl slightly older than him and the Shaman blew his conch once again. The impure men, still dressed as women, stopped dancing and lined up and the Shaman proceeded to wave juniper brands over their heads. They were finally men once more and again exchanged their clothes with the women, reverting to their original attire. What followed was the last ritual of the evening, *ghona dastur*, the great tradition. Some of the women handed over letters to men containing the price the men had paid to the girl's family to marry her. Now, she wanted to marry a new man and sought him out through the letter. If he was able to pay the current husband double of what the original had paid, he could have her!

The foreigner immediately thought of the verse he had heard from the Russian lady the first time:

Wife-elopement here is a custom
So tell me dear Rustom
Do you want to pay double
For a wife who causes so much trouble?

He would have to head to the garrison at Peshawar right away and send a telegram.

January 12, 1941: The Rathore Residence, Malabar Hill, Bombay, British India

As Prithvi entered his home with dark circles under his eyes, an unkempt beard and what now seemed like a perpetual pain in his back and shoulders, he expected a friendly greeting. Babu, chewing tobacco as usual, opened the door and sized Prithvi up from head to toe and muttered, 'Oh young master is back! You look like shit and smell like cow dung.'

Prithvi said, 'I couldn't have asked for better reception considering I haven't been home in over a year.'

'Okay, okay. Go have a shower and rest tonight.'

'I can't—is Pandey here? I have to speak to him.'

Babu winced and grumbled, 'Yes, for the past two weeks he has been staying here as if he is the Master of the house. And he likes his tea with extra sugar. I am not a sugar baron. When is he leaving?'

Prithvi sighed and said, 'I don't know, Babu. Just send him to my room. And get me a drink, a nice whisky on the rocks.'

As Prithvi sipped the Jack Daniels, he heard a soft knock on the door. 'Come right in.'

Pandey was shocked at how Prithvi looked; he had always seen him impeccably dressed. 'Oh my God—what happned? You look like shit…'

Prithvi completed the sentence for him '… and smell like cow dung. I know. Just grab a chair if you actually find one that is dusted. Would you like a drink as well?'

Pandey asked, 'No thank you. Just where have you been?'

Prithvi replied, 'Well, after a month of cooling my heels in London, they finally issued me a fresh passport. The verse that the Kalmyk lady gave me, I could only relate one word to anything I knew, "Rustom". You may have read the Persian poem *Rustom and Sohrab*. So I assumed the clue was referring to the area around the Indian and Iranian border. I have been to more places than I remember—Islamic, Zoroastrian, Buddhist and Hindu. I was even beaten up at a Zoroastrian fire temple once for entering their religious premises. I just came up against dead ends everywhere. I gave up my quest on numerous occasions when I was hungry or thirsty or both. But every morning I woke up and tried harder, till I finally received the message from you. I made it a point to go once every week to a telephone booth and make a call to Bombay and check for messages. Of course, telephone connectivity too was a problem. Babu told me that you had left a message for me—"the fifth wicket is down"—if I remember correctly. So I assume Youdale found the fifth book?'

Taking a moment to collect his thoughts Pandey replied, 'First, the Oxford and Cambridge scholars were at a loss to decipher the verse. A call was then taken to release you by giving you your passport back; after all, they couldn't keep you stranded in London forever. The British too associated "Rustom" to the India-Iran border. Seven teams of three people each were sent to the region and without divulging much detail each was told to look for any community which had a wife-elopement tradition. Initially, they were amused but after a while three of the teams returned empty handed. Then, quite by chance there was a breakthrough. One of the team members was smoking opium with a soldier of the Gorkha Regiment and asked the Gorkha if he knew of any wife-elopement tradition. It so happened that the Gorkha had earlier been posted at Kafiristan in Afghanistan and had heard about such a tradition there but never seen it practised. This news was then conveyed to London which dispatched Youdale to the region. After looking for such a custom in Kafiristan, he ended up on the British side of the Durand Line in the town of Chitral where he found the Kalash people practising such a tradition. Only about 3,000 of them currently live there and their religious beliefs are an eclectic mix of Vedic and Buddhist traditions. Convinced that he had hit the jackpot, Youdale proceeded to Peshawar and sent me a telegram to meet him there immediately. Youdale believed that the Kalash would be reluctant to hand over the book to a British officer, so he needed someone he could trust implicitly to approach the Kalash for the book. That someone turned out to be me. I only realized what I had been called for once I reached Peshawar and could not risk sending a telegram from there to Bombay informing you, even in code, about my whereabouts or the task assigned to me.'

Prithvi asked, 'So did you acquire the book?'

Pandey said, 'It was far easier than I thought. The people there are very simple-minded and trusting. All it took was a gift of forty goats to the village and some pen and paper for the girls to write their elopement letters with. They did not realize the value or importance of what they were parting with. Apparently, the village chiefs down the years have been told that a dark-skinned man will one day ask for a book and recite a verse in Sanskrit and they should hand him the book.'

Prithvi queried, 'They speak Sanskrit?'

'No, they speak Kalash, but some of them also speak Pashto. We had a translator with us. But that particular verse, almost all of them knew in Sanskrit. I did not have much of a choice—I had to hand the book over to Youdale, who took it with him to London.'

Prithvi said, 'This is Book Five we are talking about—it teaches how to build a weapon of mass destruction by splitting the tiniest of particles. It can cause the deaths of millions with just a single blow. And now this book is in London!'

Pandey said, 'Not quite. Much has changed in the past year when you were on a wild goose chase at the Indian-Iran border and was getting beaten up for entering fire temples. The British and the Germans are locked in fierce battle—the Phony War is over.'

The nine-month period between the invasion and occupation of Poland by Germany in September 1939 to May 1940 was known as the Phony War or the Bore War (a play on the actual Boer War) because, although a lot of countries in Europe and indeed in the world had declared war on each other, no troops were mobilized and no major battles actually took place. Hitler still hoped to secure peace with UK and France and back channel diplomacy between the great powers of Europe was trying to avoid all out war. But the chasm was too wide to bridge. Hitler invaded and conquered Norway and Denmark without facing any resistance whatsoever. Sick of Chamberlain's appeasement policy, the reins of the British Government were now firmly in the hands of Winston Churchill. On the day Churchill was sworn in, the status quo ended and Hitler invaded Belgium, Netherlands and Luxembourg and more importantly, France, in May 1940. The French long believed that their nation would be secured through the unbreakable Maginot Line. The rest of the borders were believed to be too tough a terrain to mount an offensive from. Hitler's Panzer tanks circumvented the Maginot Line and entered through the

Ardennes forest. By June 10, 1940, Paris was in Nazi hands. To avenge the humiliation meted out to the German nation in Versailles at the end of World War I, Hitler had a train carriage removed from a museum and placed on the railway track in the Compiegne forest. It was the same carriage placed at the same spot where Germany had been made to sign the Treaty of Surrender at the end of World War I in 1918. He then made the humiliated French sign the Treaty of Surrender on June 22, 1940. Now it was only the English Channel which separated German forces from the UK. It was like two alpha males staring down at each other, waiting for the other to blink.

Pandey continued, 'In such a scenario, the British did not wish to take any chances in case Great Britain too falls to the Nazis. Given the sensitivity of the material in the book and the fact that it will takes a few years to translate and build the said weapon, the book has been transferred to the British Embassy in Washington DC, in the USA.'

Prithvi asked, 'So are the British going to give the book to the Americans?'

Pandey replied, 'I am not privy to that decision and I don't think Youdale is either.'

'Damn it! The book was acquired a while back. Chances are that Youdale is close to the sixth one that is if he has not acquired it already.'

Pandey said, 'Not quite. He knows exactly where it is, but he can't get there.'

'Where is it?'

Pandey smiled and said, 'It is in Druk Yul—the Land of the Thunder Dragon.'

Prithvi let out a short laugh, more out of relief than anything else, 'What a lucky break!'

Jan 13, 1941: British High Commission, Washington DC, USA

The young man had been on the verge of refusing to come to Washington DC from Berkeley, California. He hated the East Coast in general and in the East Coast he hated Washington DC in particular. The people were too formal, dressed in stiff suits, the weather was dreary and the red tape was legendary. The jacket and neck-tie made him uncomfortable but he had a feeling the Brits were sticklers for appearance so he went through with the charade; curiosity having gotten the better of him. He decided to make the long trip from California.

The British Ambassador had already introduced him to the American four-star General. He now pointed to a stooped man whose hassled looks clearly indicated that he needed some sleep. 'And this is Baron Butler, the Under-Secretary of State for India in the British Government.'

'India?' asked the man.

Butler cut off the Ambassador and decided to take control of the meeting. 'Indeed, young man. You must be curious to know why we sent for you from Berkeley to meet a rather diverse group, is it not?'

The man said, 'Yes, I am very curious.'

Butler continued, 'Well you have a rather interesting background. For starters you are a Jew of German heritage. At this moment in history, I couldn't have asked for a better soldier to help us fight Hitler and his Nazi Reich. You have degrees in physics and chemistry from Oxford and Harvard.'

Butler shuffled through some papers before continuing, 'And you have a PhD in physics from the University of Göttingen in Germany.'

The young man was getting restless now. 'I know my educational and anthropological background, sir. I sincerely hope you did not get me from California to tell me something I already know. Can we please just get to the point?'

Completing ignoring him, Butler continued, 'Apparently the professor administering the oral exam for your PhD remarked, "I am glad that it is over. He was on the point of questioning me!" Ha! That is quite impressive. But what is most impressive about you is that you speak, read and write Sanskrit fluently.'

The young man felt something he usually did not— confusion. 'You want me to help you in the war effort with my Sanskrit skills? It is a dead language, sir.'

'Not that dead. It is not just the Sanskrit skills either. It's all of it. It goes without saying that what is said in this room never leaves it. Are you willing to help?'

The young man responded, 'Will my life be in danger?'

Butler replied, 'No, you will stay in America and if you trust yourself around laboratory equipment, there is no imminent or foreseeable danger to your life.'

The young man said, 'Well, then I would certainly like to do everything to help win the war against the Nazis.'

Butler continued, 'I thought as much. We are in possession of a book; it is in Sanskrit. It details out the process of building a weapon of mass destruction by splitting the tiniest of particles. Given the proximity of the UK to Germany, we can't risk building it there, just in case the UK falls.'

The young man said, 'A weapon of mass destruction—in a Sanskrit book? You know, the Hindu holy text the Bhagvad

Gita, speaks of such a weapon. It is written, "If the radiance of a thousand suns were to burst at once into the sky, that would be like the splendour of the mighty one!" And you have an ancient book which details how to build it?'

Butler said, 'Yes, we do. And you will be heading the team which will build this weapon. You won't be going back to California for a while. The weapon will be built in New Mexico; at least, that is what your General tells me. So are you up to the task?'

'Of course, I am!' the young man exclaimed.

'You must remember that this entire project is being bankrolled by the British Government. So updates should come to British High Commission here in Washington DC on a fortnightly basis. From time to time, you may have to appear in person at the office and meet the Ambassador or any other British official. Are you fine with that?'

Oppenheimer nodded his approval.

Butler nodded at the General indicating that he should speak now. The General removed a folder from his briefcase and handed over a sheaf of papers to the excited scientist and stated, 'Read it all carefully and sign it. You will be reporting to the army and your designation will be Scientific Director.'

Butler extended a handshake and said, 'Well, Dr J. Robert Oppenheimer, welcome to 'the Manhattan Project.'

January 21, 1941: Jaigaon, West Bengal, British India

As Youdale walked toward the ornate border gate separating the two nations for the fourth time in three weeks, he was confident of gaining entry this time around. The first three attempts had revolved around requesting, cajoling and bribing, all in vain. But this time he was armed with a letter signed by His Excellency the Viceroy himself. It had taken him over a week to acquire that letter through the good offices of 'Rab' Butler.

Youdale handed over the letter to the old soldier heading the border guard in his tiny cabin. He was not an inch over 4' 10", was armed with a wooden stick and had a frown on his weather-beaten face.

'It is you again!' the guard sounded exasperated.

'Please read the letter!' implored Youdale.

The soldier stood up from his chair, raised his arm as high as he could and waved the letter angrily under Youdale's nose and shouted, 'Who is it from?'

Youdale stated, 'His Excellency, the Viceroy of India.'

The guard said, 'Oho, you must be well connected. I must read the letter.' He tore open the envelope and held the letter two inches away from his eyes as he squinted to read.

To whom it may concern,

This is a request to let Major Richard Youdale unrestricted access across the border from India into

Druk Yul to carry out his duties in the service of His
Majesty.

Thank you.

(Signed)

Victor Alexander John Hope, 2nd Marquess of
Linlithgow, Governor-General and Viceroy of India

The soldier sized Youdale up as if this letter did indeed
warrant a thorough physical check of the bearer. 'The letter
does look genuine.'

Youdale smiled, 'So, can I now enter then?'

The soldier smiled back. 'No.'

'You are refusing to entertain the order of the Viceroy of
India?' asked a perplexed Youdale.

The guard was getting irritated. 'Read it for yourself. It is
a request and not an order. And requests can be turned down.
Besides, I am not a subject of the British monarch to follow
orders from any Viceroy.'

Youdale pleaded, 'Surely you must at the very least consider
his request and show it to someone who is your superior.'

The guard said, 'My superior is over 100 miles away. You
reckon I should now borrow a bicycle and go to fetch him?
Who do you think will be in-charge of this post then—my
incompetent subordinates?'

Youdale continued to plead, 'Please—it is extremely urgent
that I cross the border.'

The old man sighed. 'As per the Treaty of Phunaka
signed between our two great nations, only ten white people
are allowed in every month, be they on official or personal
business. The quota for this month has been met. I will accept
the Viceroy's request on February 1.'

Youdale said, 'You can't possibly be serious.'

The old guard said, 'There should a copy of the Treaty in your capital in Calcutta. Please go ahead and read it and you will be back in time to enter in February.'

Youdale said, 'The capital is now in New Delhi.'

'Really? When did that happen?' the soldier frowned.

'Some thirty years ago!' snapped Youdale, now annoyed.

Their conversation was interrupted by a knock on the cabin. Another wooden stick-wielding guard entered the cabin and said, 'Sir, there is a new traveller who wishes to enter the country! He has been waiting outside the cabin for the last ten minutes.'

'Who is it this time? The Viceroy himself? What is this, an invasion?' the soldier barked.

Smirk firmly in place indicating that he had overheard the entire conversation, Prithvi entered the little cabin and watched the blood drain from Youdale's face. He greeted Youdale with a polite nod and a wink. 'Oh! It is an Indian. Do you have your passport?'

Not bothering to actually check the passport, the old man simply turned to the last page and stamped it. He handed it back to Prithvi with a warm smile and stated, 'Welcome to Bhutan—Druk Yul, The Land of the Thunder Dragon!'

January 22, 1941: Punakha, Bhutan

Unlike other states and kingdoms in the region, Bhutan enjoyed the unique distinction of never being governed, occupied or conquered by any outside power. The tiny land-locked state nestled between India, Nepal and China guarded its sovereignty with the kind of ferocity one wouldn't associate with a Buddhist nation. Tibetan, Chinese, Indian, Nepali and British invasions had all been thwarted, often by allying itself to one of its former aggressors.

Prithvi had the distinct feeling of having stepped into some kind of time warp as he looked outside his hotel window. He had been assured at the border town of Phuntsholing that the ancient capital of Punakha was the most modern city in Bhutan. Prithvi realized the relativity of that statement through the minor fact that it lacked electricity, telephone facility and running water. The hotel itself had only six rooms. The only nod to the 20th century was the seven automobiles in the town, five of which were owned by the king. But these were minor travails as he savoured the sheer majesty of the place. The capital Punakha was situated in a valley at the foothills of the snow-capped Himalayas at the confluence of the two main rivers of Bhutan, Po Chu and the Mo Chu at 1,200 metres above sea-level. Even the names made Prithvi smile at the utter simplicity of the place. Most of the people were employed in rice farming whilst the others spent their days in tiny, picturesque monasteries which dotted the city. It was as if postcards had been invented for places like these. Every person he had met had been helpful and had smiled, trying their best to communicate to him in broken Hindi or English. If they couldn't get their point across they would lead him to a friend whose language skills were marginally better. This was as close to Shangri La that he would ever be. Since there had been no wars for a while now, the Bhutanese had altered the name of their country to Deki Druk Yul, Land of the Peaceful Thunder Dragon.

After having a bath with water which nearly gave him hypothermia, Prithvi met his tour guide assigned to him by the hotel. The chubby boy was not a day over 14 but claimed to speak both Hindi and English fluently.

'What's your name, little fellow?' asked Prithvi.

The boy said, 'I am not a little fellow and my name is Jigme Ugyen.'

'And which ones of these is your last name? Both are fairly unusual.'

Jigme snorted and parroted, 'Except in the case of royal births, Bhutanese names do not include a last name. Instead, two time-honoured auspicious names are chosen at birth by the village lama or by the parents or grandparents or great-grandparents of the child. My parents chose my name. You can call me Jigme.' He was clearly used to the question.

Prithvi said, 'Thank you. And how long shall it take us to reach Paro Taktsang?'

Jigme replied, 'We should get to Paro village in eight hours by the hotel car. If you wish to trek, it will take three to four days.'

Prithvi laughed and said, 'Not a chance! We are definitely taking the car.'

'Come this way then.' Jigme led Prithvi to a barebones shed outside the hotel, the roof of which was made of hay. As he entered, Prithvi whistled. He had just spotted a Rolls Royce Phantom II in pristine condition. As if reading his mind Jigme chirped, 'It is the king's old car. He gave it to the hotel to ferry guests around.'

'That is very generous of him.'

'Our king is very generous and kind. Plus, he also owns the hotel.'

'I would never have guessed.'

'Enough petrol to fuel the cars is brought in once a month from India.'

'That's fantastic. Where is our chauffeur?' asked Prithvi.

Jigme looked hurt. 'I am the chauffeur.'

The journey was bumpy to say the least. Obviously roads were not as much of a priority for the king as the latest Rolls Royce cars were. Jigme was definitely an enthusiastic tour guide. 'The Paro Taktsang monastery where we are headed is one of the oldest Tibetan monasteries in the world. It was founded by the great Guru Rinpoche. In English it means "tiger's lair" because legend has it that Guru Rinpoche flew there on the back of a tiger. Everyone in Bhutan is Buddhist but there are a few Nepalese who are Hindu. On holy days, the people don't work and spend their entire day listening to the sermons of the lama. The holy days fall on the 8th, 10th, 15th, 25th, 28th and 30th day of each month. The last sermon the lama gave was about chastity. What's the use of a sermon when I am to get married this summer to Yangki? So then I asked the lama ...'

Prithvi interrupted him, 'Jigme, you have been talking non-stop for the past four hours. I would like to catch some sleep now, if you don't mind.'

'May I sing you a nice Bhutanese song to help you sleep?'

'No thank you, that will not be necessary.'

'It is a very soothing song.'

'No!'

Jigme was not about to cede ground. 'But I am a tour guide—I am paid to talk.'

'How much is the hotel paying you?'

Jigme said, 'They pay me 10 Ngultrum for each day, so 20 Ngultrum for this trip.'

Prithvi said, 'I will give you 50 Ngultrum if you get me there without behaving like a radio.'

'You will give me 50 Ngultrum? And what is a radio?'

'Never mind! I will give you 100 Ngultrum—just please keep quiet!'

The eight-hour journey took a tad longer and it was almost 11 hours before a still sleepy Prithvi was told, 'We are in Paro village, sir.' He had been catching short naps every few hours in between enjoying the spectacular if monotonous scenery. Rubbing his eyes as he stepped out of the Rolls Royce he looked around the small town which, he was told by Jigme, was a miniature version of the capital. At the edge of the street he could see a fairly large and tall monastery. Pointing at it he asked, 'Is that the Taktsang monastery?'

Jigme laughed. 'No, no. That is the Rinpung Dzong. It is the tallest structure in Bhutan. In the old days, because of its heights it served as a watch tower to guard against Tibetan invasions. Today it houses sacred masks and costumes. The costumes themselves have been …'

Prithvi quickly cut him short, 'Then where is the Paro Taktsang Jigme?'

Jigme protested, 'You never let me finish …

Prithvi smiled and said, 'That is because you never seem to finish Jigme. Where is the Taktsang?'

Jigme replied, 'It is further away but cars can't go there. We will have to walk eight kilometres and …'

Prithvi said, 'Walk eight kilometres? We can't possibly do that today. We will have to leave early tomorrow morning.'

Jigme said, 'You should have let me complete. Not only do we have to walk eight kilometres but we have to climb 700 metres.' He rummaged in the Rolls, handed Prithvi a pair of ancient binoculars and pointed toward the mountains. Focusing the binoculars, Prithvi finally saw the monastery surrounded by a swirl of clouds and mist.

While he was still looking at the monastery Jigme helpfully added, 'The Taktsang is at 3,100 metres and we are in Paro which is 2,400 metres above sea-level. So we only have 700 metres to climb.'

Prithvi gaped at the sheer steepness of the cliff. 'Who do you think I am—George Mallory?'

Jigme asked, 'Who is that?'

Ignoring the question Prithvi continued, 'The sport I chose in university was cricket, not mountaineering. Do you have any equipment for mountain climbing?'

Jigme mocked, 'What equipment could you possibly need to climb a mountain? Everyone climbs it. I first climbed it when I was 11.'

'I assume that was only last year then.' It was Jigme's turn to ignore him this time.

By noon the next day, the duo reached the base of the hill atop which the imposing monastery stood. Much to Prithvi's relief, he would not require the skills of George Mallory after all. Eons ago, the architects of the monastery had built steps on one side of the hill's slope. Nonetheless, it wasn't exactly easy. The stone steps were wet and slippery and covered with moss. The mist and fog affected visibility and did not make the task any easier. Given the thinness of the air, Prithvi was often left panting, much to Jigme's amusement.

'You must really like Buddha to put yourself through so much trouble to reach the monastery!' said Jigme.

'Far from it,' replied Prithvi, 'the Buddha and Ashoka have become the bane of my existence.'

On reaching the top, Prithvi finally sat down on the top step, half collapsing from lack of breath and thirst. He laid flat on his back and shut his eyes. He heard some laughter and felt water being sprinkled on his face. He opened his eyes to see Jigme holding a jug of water and a bald, weather-beaten Buddhist monk smiling. The Buddhist monk said in broken English, 'You have taken so long to arrive. Your friends have been waiting for you for quite some time.' Not bothering to get up, Prithvi turned his head to the general direction in which the monk was pointing. The blood drained from his face as he saw Josef Heidler and Max Kahn dressed in saffron Buddhist robes and smiling at him. Much to the monk's consternation, the first words that came out of Prithvi's mouth at the doorstep of the holiest Buddhist monastery in the country were, 'Oh fuck!'

January 24, 1941: Paro Taktsang Monastery, Bhutan

Prithvi was in saffron robes as was customary to wear inside the monastery. He sat across the table from Heidler and Kahn, who were sipping tea from chipped mugs. Prithvi left his mug untouched.

Heidler said, 'Go ahead, drink it. It's rather delicious.'

Prithvi said, 'No thanks.'

'It's not poisoned,' Heidler laughed. 'It's just butter tea. The locals call it *cha suma*, churned tea. It is made of tea leaves, salt and yak butter. Go on, try it.'

Prithvi reluctantly took a sip. 'So how in the name of the devil did you two get here?'

Heidler said, 'Unless you have forgotten, Bhutan also shares a border with China.'

'But how did you know about this place? The clue was …' retorted Prithvi.

'… with the Kalash people near the Afghan border.' Heidler's reply stunned Prithvi.

Kahn cut in, 'We found the Kalash people first. I stayed there for a while and they knew me only as "the foreigner". Unfortunately, they refused to hand us the book because it would have to be given only to a dark skinned-man. Of course, there was no restriction to look at the book—we copied it. There was no restriction in giving the next clue either.'

Prithvi was stunned once again, 'You copied the entire book outlining how to make a weapon of mass destruction?'

Kahn continued, 'Unfortunately not. Youdale and his cronies arrived three days after we started copying the book. We only managed to get half of it. To make sure it wasn't easy for the British, I had torn out three extremely important pages from that book. The locals did not notice but the British are going to have a hard time filling the gap. Before Youdale arrived, they sent some troops to seal the area. We escaped at that time. But we did get a sizable head start on Youdale since he was waiting for some Indian to come collect the book. The restriction of ten Europeans entering Bhutan is only from the Indian side of the border. No such restriction exists on the Chinese side. So we got in quite easily.'

Prithvi incredulously asked, 'And you were waiting for me to come?'

It was Heidler who spoke this time. 'We did not have a choice. At the border, we were disarmed—we were not allowed to bring weapons into Bhutan. That should be a relief to you. Once we got to this monastery, the lama refused to give us the book or the next clue. Without weapons, the two of us were not about to take on the forty Buddhists monks who stay here. We convinced them of our interest in Buddhism—which in Max's case is genuine. Apparently instructions accorded to the lama are to give the book and clue to an Indian. So even if Youdale got here before you, we would have to wait for you or for Youdale to get some Indian.'

Prithvi asked, 'And why are you telling me all this?'

Heidler said, 'You probably think I want to kill you, and with good reason. Max here probably does want to kill you given that you killed a man whom he thought of more as a son than a mere protégé. I am a soldier, not a barbarian. I am carrying out my duty in the service of the Fatherland just as you are carrying out yours and Youdale is carrying out his. Who understands the futility of war better than a soldier?'

Prithvi said, 'Fancy that—such words being spouted by a war-mongering Nazi. Just look at how you have treated the minorities in your land.'

Heidler took a moment to respond. 'First of all, I have never formally been an active member of the Nazi Socialist Party. I am an avowed Roman Catholic and joined it merely because I had to. And how have the British treated you Indians? How have the Americans treated the ancient tribes of America? How have the Belgians treated the natives of the Congo in Africa? How have the French treated the Algerians? We do it for three years and we are animals; the British do it for 300 years and do they become benevolent? All Europeans are made of the same cloth. Through the ages, the European colonizer, whether German or English or French, has viewed the Asiatic and the African with jaundiced eyes—associating them with duplicity, cunning, hypocrisy and treachery. Lest we forget, your faiths and beliefs have long been viewed with repulsion and Jesuits have tried to convert the colonized peoples, sometimes through sermons and sometimes by force. So tell me are you proud to sing "God Save the King" when you hear all this? Or have you never thought about it at all?'

Prithvi retorted, 'Spare me the lecture! What makes you insinuate that I am in any form or manner aiding the British?'

'Inadvertently you are helping them—whether you are reconciled to this fact or not. If the British win this war you will continue to be a part of the second-class citizenry of the British Empire. If Germany wins, it has no interest in keeping India as a colony—the Asiatic people will be free. The Germans want to establish their Reich only in Europe. The Japanese wish to liberate the Asiatic people. We have no territorial ambitions in Asia or Africa. Help us acquire the books and win the war. Do it for your country. Do it for India.'

Prithvi decided to cut the conversation short. 'You know, I had promised Jigme a 100 Ngultrum. I think I better go pay.'

Heidler said, 'You need time to think about it. You have a few hours. I do not want to kill you in order to acquire that book. There are two of us and one of you and you are not even a trained soldier. Celibate Buddhist monks are not going to help you even if they wanted to. Either way, we will acquire the book.'

Prithvi paused for a minute. He then replied, 'I will hold on to the book while I decide my course of action.'

'That is acceptable.' Heidler extended his hand across the table which Prithvi shook after an instant's delay.

At the appointed hour, a young Buddhist monk escorted them to the chamber of the lama. The old man gave them a wide smile as they entered. He seemed delighted at having something to do which broke the monotonous cycle of his monastic existence. He placed his monocle firmly in place to check the faces of his visitors and smiled even wider.

'I have been waiting for this moment for last 50 years since I became lama. My predecessor and his predecessor too waited in vain all these years for this moment—probably a few lamas before that as well.' He laughed. 'The last time an Indian came visiting was in 1799. According to our history, a learned monk from a faraway part of India came and replaced the old article with a new one. I don't know why.' The old man walked toward the bookshelf and slowly moved the books one by one, causing Max to grow increasingly inpatient. Finally, the lama directed Prithvi to help him remove a thin 44-inch long box made of wood. Sliding it open, he asked Prithvi to remove the velvet cloth which hid the item. Prithvi lifted the cloth and held out its contents for the two mesmerized Germans.

The 40-inch sword curved gently to ease beheadings; its scabbard was encrusted with jewels and made of gold. The hilt too was made of gold with mounted grenade and wire wrapped leather grip from which the gold peeped out in places. As Prithvi slid the sword out of its scabbard, the gleaming blade shone in the dingy room. It was a French sword whose design had been inspired by the Egyptian campaign of its original owner. Prithvi brought the blade closer to see the inscribed French words, *Pour le tigre de Mysore. Votre ami, Napoleon Bonaparte.* Beneath the cloth in the box was a tiny envelope which contained just a small slip of paper. Unfolding it, Prithvi read the English line to himself, 'Blood is thicker than water'. Not bothering to show it to the Germans, Prithvi quickly tore it into little pieces much to their chagrin. The last thing Prithvi removed from the box was the leather bound sixth book on alchemy. Max moved forward to grab it from Prithvi's hands but Heidler motioned to him to stop. There was no need to create a scene in front of the lama, he reasoned. Prithvi gave the two Germans a wry smile and flung the book outside the window. Much to their mortification, a fiery arrow appeared from nowhere and pierced the centre of the book while it was still in mid-air resulting in the book instantly bursting into flames. Acting on impulse, Kahn grabbed Prithvi by the throat and pushed him into a corner trying to strangle him as Prithvi struggled to get Kahn's strong grip off his throat. Another arrow hit the throat of Kahn as he collapsed onto the floor of the confounded lama's room. Jigme was standing on the ledge and his next arrow was pointed straight at Heidler's head.

Prithvi was glad he had told Jigme to come to his aid if he saw anything untoward happen. He knew the little bugger would come in handy.

'Heidler, you introduced me to the local drink. Let me introduce you to the local sport. Archery is their national pastime and Jigme finished second in the archery contest in his village.' He looked at Kahn choking on the floor, almost dead. 'I am sorry about your friend.'

Jigme interrupted, 'I have three other arrows which are poison-laden too. Even a minor scratch and you will be dead almost instantly.'

Irritated at the interruption, Prithvi continued, 'Did you really expect me to sign a blank cheque for the Nazi regime? Unlimited supply of gold during a war—Hitler would have found his El Dorado for sure. Now I suggest you stay put here while we leave the monastery. I abhor violence; I want to avoid it as far as possible.'

Heidler was surprisingly composed and asked, 'But how did you get weapons into the monastery?'

Jigme replied, 'We did not get anything in. Given its height, the monastery was also used as a watch tower to keep an eye out for invaders and some weapons have always been stored here.' Jigme turned to Prithvi, 'He has given you a lot of trouble, isn't it? Should I just kill him?' Jigme reached for his poison tipped arrow.

Prithvi noticed Heidler flinching for an instant before regaining his composed and calm demeanour. Both men stared at each other without blinking for a full minute as Prithvi considered Jigme's offer. Not turning his gaze away from Heidler, Prithvi thought about their earlier conversation and replied, 'No—just use the other arrow and render him unconscious.' Heidler finally blinked and nodded his head ever so slightly, acknowledging Prithvi's decision. He then felt a surge of pain as a shot from Jigme's arrow pierced his thigh and everything went dark.

January 29, 1941: Bombay, British India

The Indian orderly snapped to attention as he entered Youdale's unorganized cabin. The number of loose papers on his desk prevented Youdale from switching on the fan and instead, he was periodically wiping the sweat off his brow. Youdale said in a brusque manner, 'At ease soldier. What is it?'

The orderly crisply replied, 'We have received word from the North-East Frontier Agency. As per your instructions, all Indian citizens of the Crown entering back into India from Bhutan were detained for an hour before being allowed to re-enter India to verify their credentials. One of the persons matched the description you had given in your Red Alert Notice. Your instructions were carried out to the letter. His belongings and his person were given a thorough check; no books were found in his possession at all.'

'Of course, no books were found on him. He wouldn't carry them so openly, he's not stupid!'

The orderly continued, 'He was followed and not arrested. He sent a telegram to Calcutta from the closest post office at the border from Jaigaon. He waited for a day and then sent another telegram. Here are the contents of both the telegrams.'

Youdale tore open the two envelopes and carelessly flung both of the envelopes on his already littered desk much to the amusement of the orderly who struggled to keep a straight face; that fan would never be operated at this rate!

The contents of the first telegram were:

WICKET 6 DOWN BOWLED. STOP. INDIA WON STOP. AUS LOST. STOP.

'So the resourceful bastard did acquire the sixth book after all. No surprise there.'

The second telegram was longer:

WICKET 7 IN TIGER'S LAIR. STOP. BLOOD THICKER THAN WATER. STOP.

Youdale frowned; this message was a lot less obvious than the previous one. He looked up at the orderly who had also begun sweating now. 'Do we have any other information?'

'Well, he did ask the post master at the post office if he could tell him the fastest way to get to Mysore.'

'Thank you. You can go now.' Youdale replied.

He said to himself, the Tiger of Mysore! Not so smart after all, Mr Rathore.

February 1, 1941: Shantiniketan, West Bengal, British India

Prithvi's grandfather opened his monogrammed leather bag and passed around eight glasses while he placed one firmly in front of himself. He then removed a peculiarly shaped bottle from his bag and filled his glass nearly to the brim. 'It is time for a mini celebration, my comrades.'

'Comrades? Are you a communist now? Just what is in that bottle? And what is the occasion?' asked one.

The old man said, 'It is called *chuak*, it is a traditional Tripuri rice beer, very potent. The occasion is that the sixth book on alchemy has been destroyed by my grandson. Apparently the Nazis were there too, so we should be happy that the possibility of them having an unlimited supply of gold during the war has been eliminated.'

One person out of the nine present over there asked, 'I read the telegram. How did you gather that the Nazis were there and the book destroyed?'

The old man chuckled, 'We use a cricketing analogy. If he writes "caught" it means the book has been acquired; if he writes "bowled" it means the book has been destroyed. "India won" means of course that we have acquired or destroyed the book and so on.'

'But Germany doesn't play cricket,' cut in another.

He said, 'That is the reason why he uses Australia in place of Germany.'

'What about the next book? What is the status on that?'

The old man picked up his glass and took a sip of the *chuak*. 'He is on his way to Mysore to acquire it. I don't think that we should be afraid of the Nazis getting their hands on that one.'

February 3, 1941: Derry/Londonderry, Northern Ireland, United Kingdom

Derry/Londonderry was the only settlement on the planet which had still not resolved the name with which it should be addressed. The nationalists favouring integration with Ireland called it Derry whilst the unionists who favoured continued integration with the UK insisted on calling it Londonderry. It also enjoyed the distinction of being the last European city which was completely walled; its defenses had never been breached. Oppenheimer had been told that this was selected as the meeting point because of its closeness to the Irish border, Ireland being neutral in the War. Besides, as it was the westernmost port in Europe in control of the Allied Forces, British, American and Canadian ships were often docked here and it served as an American military base. It was probably the safest town in Allied control in Europe.

Oppenheimer's host did not bother to get up, but nevertheless greeted him with a gruff, 'Welcome to Londonderry, Dr Oppenheimer.'

Not that his unionist credentials were ever in doubt! thought Oppenheimer. 'Thank you err … Mr Prime Minister.'

Winston Churchill looked exactly in person as he did in the numerous press photos, thought Oppenheimer. He was dressed in a three-piece suit with polka dotted bow-tie firmly in place. Oppenheimer wondered whether it was the weight of the heavy suit which made him sit in a slouched position. In his right hand was a Cuban cigar and in his left it was a glass of scotch on the rocks. The puffed red cheeks of the Prime Minister clearly illustrated that the scotch was not an occasional indulgence. Perfect! So the victory of the Allied Forces depends on a chain smoker who drinks regularly during the day, thought Oppenheimer.

The Prime Minister opened his drawer and placed a British Alfred Dunhill humidor in front of Oppenheimer and offered him the Cubans cigars, 'Romeo y Julieta?' Oppenheimer shook his head. Churchill then removed another humidor; this one was a slightly older Swiss Zino Davidoff humidor and asked, 'Perhaps you prefer La Aroma de Cuba?'

Exasperated at the pomp Oppenheimer shook his head with more vigour and said, 'I don't smoke, sir. Can we just get on …?' Oppenheimer rolled his right hand in a circular motion, trying his best not to sound rude to the Prime Minister.

Churchill said, 'Of course, of course my good man! I take it that your time is very valuable and you are extremely important to the war effort. Pray let me underline that my time is far more valuable and that I am more important to the war effort. That is precisely why it was you who had to hop across the Atlantic Ocean and not I. So pray let us get on with the conversation.'

'Pardon me. Do you use "pray" a lot in your conversations sir?' asked an irritated Oppenheimer.

Churchill said, 'Yes I do, my good man. In fact on the little notes on which I scribble instructions to my staff I use it so often that at Ten Downing Street they refer to them as "Churchill's prayers"!' he guffawed as he put down his glass and slapped his palm on his thigh.

'So what is the agenda of this meeting, Mr Prime Minister?' posed Oppenheimer as he struggled with a forced smile.

'Well, you do realize that the weapon of mass destruction that you are building across the pond under the name of the Manhattan Project is completely funded by the might of the British pound. Unfortunately, it is difficult to spare much of it when the Krauts are banging on the doors of the British Isles. So the agenda of the meeting is to ascertain that British investment is in safe hands. Besides, I want to size you up as a man, see if you are capable of delivering what you purport to deliver. While the rest of your credentials are laudable, why choose Sanskrit as a language over something superior like Greek or Latin? It's akin to a brilliant engineer choosing to repair sewing machines rather than build an aircraft, isn't it so?' posed Churchill.

Oppenheimer retorted, 'With all due respect Prime Minister, Sanskrit is a great language, older than Greek or Latin. That is precisely why I am currently using a Sanskrit text to build a weapon like no other—nothing in Greek or Latin comes close.'

'First, I refuse to believe for one minute that something so spectacular could emerge from an Asiatic civilization, least of all from India. As a young lieutenant, I served in the Fourth Hussars in India. I led my Sikh soldiers against the Afghan hordes. The Sikh soldiers taught me two words, *maro* (kill) and *chalo* (let's go). I introduced them to an English word as well, "Tally ho!"' Churchill guffawed once more. Then he stated, 'Ah! You didn't get the joke. "Tally ho" is a British expression used by a hunter to alert his hounds during a foxhunt.'

Oppenheimer struggled to remain polite. 'I still don't see the humour.'

Churchill said, 'Of course you don't. You are one of those who are enamoured by all things Indian. Personally, I have never seen a more beastly people or a more beastly religion. We are the ones who built that nation; else India is a geographical reality as is the Equator. We introduced them to the concept of western justice and education and I find it repulsive when a fellow Harrovian like Nehru dons a nationalist mantle or when a Middle Temple lawyer like Gandhi dresses half-nakedly in the garb of an Indian peasant and demands independence from the King Emperor as if he is His equal.'

Oppenheimer stated, 'But surely the Indians have a right to demand independence.?

'I do not agree that a dog in a manger has the final right to the manger even if he has lain in it for a rather long time. A country where the population multiplies like rabbits does not deserve the kind of respect you accord it. We built the railways there, generated employment and gave direction to a bunch of barbaric fanatics. Why should a stronger race, a more worldly-wise race give up India to be run by a slew of inferior people who will exploit the even inferior people they govern?'

Oppenheimer frowned, '… And what is the point of telling me all this when you clearly know that I will never agree to any of the points you made?'

'The point my good Dr Oppenheimer, is that I am not willing to waste a single penny of the British taxpayer or the British Crown on developing a weapon based on a book which emerges from that land of uncouth imbeciles when the sheer existence of Great Britain is under threat.' Churchill replied.

Oppenheimer opined, 'But we need that weapon to stop Hitler. How can you just …'

Churchill interjected, 'I am the Prime Minister of the greatest empire to have ever straddled this planet. I can do what I please. That will be all. Have a pleasant journey back.'

Oppenheimer considered for an instant if he should say what he was thinking. Well, what had he to lose? 'Mr Prime Minister I have come across some arrogant imperialists from Great Britain in my time. They seem to have found the most bull-headed amongst themselves and elected him Prime Minister. You have a pleasant journey back to London, too.' Oppenheimer caught a glimpse of the red-faced furious Prime Minister stubbing his cigar into the ashtray before he turned around and stormed out of the room.

MAY 3, 1799: MYSORE KINGDOM, BRITISH INDIA

Although I never supposed that Napoleon possessed, allowing for some difference of education, the liberality of conduct and political views which were sometimes exhibited by old Haidar Ally, yet I did think Napoleon might have shown the same resolved and dogged spirit of resolution which induced Tippoo Saib to die manfully upon the breach of his capital city with his sabre clenched in his hand.'

—Sir Walter Scott

Tipu was short, tawny and had the habit of twirling the moustache above his clean shaven chin when he was pleased. His dark grey eyes zeroed in on whomever he was engaging with, shutting out the people in the background. The focus of his attention today was his Chief Minister, Purniya Pandit. Ignoring the pleas of the Muslim clergy and his Muslim courtiers he had appointed a Hindu as his Chief Minister. It was a decision he did not regret for a single minute of his reign. But the Pandit was asking for the unthinkable today.

Tipu said, 'Pandit, you of all people should know that I will never surrender. I have defeated the British before; I will defeat them again today.'

The Chief Minister retorted, 'There is a time for bravado and there is a time for prudence. If you surrender, you can fight to live another day. The eyes of Mysore are on you; the eyes of India are on you.'

'That is precisely my point. All the eyes of India are on me.' He pointed to a document that adorned the wall on the back of his throne. 'Do you know what that document is, Pandit?'

The Chief Minister replied, 'Of course I do. Everyone in the kingdom knows the Treaty of Mangalore.'

Tipu proudly said, 'It is more than just a treaty, Pandit. It is a testament to the defeat of Colonel William Baille at Pollilur; it is a testament to General Hector Munro dumping his cannons in the sea and fleeing to Madras; it is a testament to the capture of the fortress at Arcot; it is a testament to the defeat of Colonel Braithwaite at Tanjore; it is a testament to the capture of Chittur from British hands; it is a testament to an Indian kingdom dictating the terms of surrender to a European power.' He paused, as if considering his words. 'The eyes of all India are on me. By what right do I command my men to die for my cause if I should be afraid to lay down my own life? When a calamity befalls a land, must a king be insulated from the suffering and sacrifice of his people by virtue of his rank? Tell me Pandit, many years from now when the Europeans are long gone from our shores, how would you have the people of this vast land remember me: as a tiger who went down fighting or as a jackal who took the easier way out?'

The king walked toward his favourite contraption and turned the lever. The mechanical life-sized tiger roared as he attacked the British soldier who flailed his left arm in vain. The button keys on the tiger's carcass could be used to make music using all thirty-six brass pipes and leather bellows. The king was particularly proud of his toy. But his obsession with the tiger was not limited to merely this contraption.

On his personal firearms tigers prowled along the barrel, often wrestling their prey. Tigers adorned the blades of his swords and cannons and of course his regal throne. The Chief Minister knew that any talk of surrender was going to fall on deaf years. 'Just as it is my duty as your Chief Minister to give you the best advice I can conjure, it is also my obligation to respect your wishes. I will stay here with you till the end.'

Tipu Sultan did not expect anything else from his most loyal courtier but he was not about to sacrifice his Chief Minister's life given that he had some important tasks outlined for him. 'Do not be foolish, Purniya. All women, children and ten selected men to accompany them have been offered a safe passage by the British. I can't think of anyone else I could trust more than my Chief Minister to ensure their safety.'

The Chief Minister interrupted him, 'But what kind of Chief Minister leaves his king in the hour of his utmost need? I do not think …'

Tipu retorted, 'That is not all. During the last war with the British I was given a book by a mystic. You need to make sure it is kept out of reach of the British and in the safe hands of my family.'

His Chief Minister looked at him quizzically. 'I am sure there are more important things to protect than a book; we should get as much gold out of here as possible for the future of your family.'

Tipu said, 'Gold can be bought and stolen; knowledge must be earned and acquired. Give me your solemn word that you will protect the book at all costs.'

The Chief Minister looked at his king with a touch of melancholy knowing that this was in all probability their last conversation. 'You have my word. I will ensure that the book does not fall in British hands.'

February 12, 1941: Mysore, British India

Mysore was not an Indian village or a hamlet as Prithvi had thought it to be. Neither did it have the hustle of Bombay or Calcutta, nor the self-important air of Delhi; it was a sleepy little town where things moved at their own pace. The town was rife with temples and palaces, all of them bearing the hallmark of Tipu's reign. There were a number of buildings built by the British in typical Victorian architectural style as well. Mysore seemed like a sponge which had soaked in the architectural waters of all its rulers and was emerging relatively dry from the ordeal.

'Patience, Prithvi! What do we know of the involvement of Tipu Sultan with the Nine Unknowns?' Pandey asked.

Prithvi considered whether it was safe to tell Pandey what his grandfather had told him about the Nine Unknowns helping Tipu Sultan fight the British and decided that he would have to trust Pandey for now. 'Well, for starters he was helped by the Nine Unknowns during the Anglo-Mysore wars. Secondly, he had more advanced weaponry than the British did, especially rockets. The Royal Artillery Museum houses two rockets recovered from the arsenal of Tipu Sultan when the kingdom of Mysore finally fell. They were the most advanced pieces of military hardware ever seen.'

Pandey retorted, 'The problem of course is that the trail gets cold here. He fought the British and he lost. He was found dead defending his fort with a sword clutched tightly in his hands. Everything that was valuable in his palaces was shipped to London.'

Prithvi exclaimed, 'So are you suggesting that the book is in London?'

'It is a possibility. What are your thoughts?' asked Pandey.

Prithvi replied, 'I am fairly sure it is not there. Tipu Sultan went into the battle knowing quite well that the odds were stacked against him. He would have either smuggled it out or kept it hidden or, in the worst case scenario, destroyed it.'

Pandey considered the three possibilities. 'If the book was destroyed, then the trail goes cold and we don't have to worry about the rest of the books either. If it is hidden in Mysore the next clue would have been slightly more specific. It must have been smuggled out. Put yourself in his shoes—whom would you trust with your most valued possession if you knew you were going to die in battle?'

'If I were to put myself in his jewel encrusted shoes I would turn to my immediate family or my most trusted aide. Were any civilians given safe passage during the siege?' asked Prithvi

Pandey replied, 'There is only one place where we can find that out—the Oriental Library.'

Commissioned by the House of Wodeyar in 1891, the Oriental Library housed some of the rarest manuscripts in India including over 30,000 ancient palm leaf manuscripts. As more and more ancient books and manuscripts in India were found, they were often sent to this library to prevent decay and destruction by silverfish. The library regularly applied lemon grass oil on the manuscripts which acted as a virtual pesticide to mitigate the risks posed by the silverfish.

In the library, as both of them browsed the numerous titles preserved in the Tipu Sultan section, Pandey came across a log book. He flipped the pages and on seeing an entry he beamed at Prithvi. The journal maintained by the British quartermaster involved in the siege had an entry on which Pandey placed his index finger. Prithvi squinted to read the horrendous handwriting:

Prince Muhammad Yasin Sultan Sahib; son of Tipu Sultan: born 1784, age 15, Belongings: Blunted ornamental sword and ancient Sanskrit book.

Pandey smiled at Prithvi and asked, 'Now why would a Muslim prince carry a Sanskrit book as his sole possession on being given safe passage? It has to be the book. Now we have to trace his lineage.'

'We will have to travel a fair bit for that.' replied Prithvi.

'What do you mean?' posed Pandey.

'Why do you think it was a sword given by Napoleon, which was mentioned in the clue? His family migrated to France—the book is in France!' said Prithvi.

Pandey nonchalantly replied, 'So then we better get going to France as soon as possible.'

'Are you serious? Have you forgotten? You do realize France is under German control. How do you expect us to enter Nazi territory?'

Pandey paused for dramatic effect, raised his chin and declared, 'Legion Freies Indien!'

February 5, 1941: Office of Under-Secretary for India Rab Butler, London

The Baron Butler always made it a point to keep his voice and cynicism down in the presence of a lady. This lady was of blue blood, so he had to be extra careful to keep his manners in check. He sized her up. She was tiny—not more than 5' 3", he gathered. She also looked a lot younger than the 27 she was supposed to be. Her hair was cropped extremely short and even though she wore an Army cap, it was obvious that the length had been shortened to keep the curls in place. She was quite light skinned and her brown eyes shone with defiance. She did not fidget and maintained an aristocratic air, as if she was used to being in the company of barons and lords.

Butler asked, 'Would you care for some tea, miss?'

'If it is Darjeeling, I shall have a cup. Thank you.'

'Of course it is Darjeeling.' He poured her a cup from his kettle. 'You do realize that the average life span of a British operative working for the Resistance in occupied France is six weeks.' She was uncertain if he paused for effect or for her to react with shock. He repeated, 'Six weeks! Princess, if you go in there, the probability of you getting out alive is next to zilch. Why don't you just tell us where the book is hidden and you can enjoy a luxurious life here in London. If you wish to help us against the Nazis, you can do so from England.'

She replied, 'Please stop calling me Princess. I no longer use my old name. My new British name is Nora Baker.'

'To everyone else you might be Miss Nora Baker, the radio operator. To those of us who know you, you will be Princess Noor Inayat Khan, the descendant of Tipu Sultan and one of the two people who know the location of that book.'

'I told you, I'd rather go there myself.'

'Your training officers say that while you speak French fluently you are completely and utterly incapable of operating in occupied France.'

She retorted, 'Well, if I can't retrieve the book myself than you can forget about it.'

'And what if you die on your noble quest, Princess?' he delicately asked.

'Well, I can't do much if I am dead now, can I?'

Butler said, 'The least you could do is to give us the clue for the next book so we can get working on acquiring it. Your brother claims that he does not know what the next clue is! The trail will simply go cold.'

She continued, 'I have already told you that I do not know the next clue off-hand either. It is safely tucked away in a note in a locker in Geneva in neutral Switzerland. My banker has been told that I am currently residing in England. On the day I leave England, I shall be informing him that if he does not hear from me for 15 days at a stretch, he must provide the package containing the clue to the British High Commissioner in Berne. Of course the 15-day period only starts once I am in France. So either way, you will have your clue—whether I am successful in acquiring the book or not.'

Butler posed, 'Why should I trust you?'

She countered with, 'What choice do you really have?'

'And what makes you sure you will be able to get through to Switzerland on schedule from occupied France?'

'I am training as a radio operator to help the British and the Resistance cause, for crying out loud! Of course, I shall have a radio and will be able to make contact.'

Butler said, 'Your training is still not over. While it is on, I urge you to reconsider your stance. Please.'

She nodded politely and stated, 'I shall definitely give it a thought, Baron Butler.'

He formally said, 'Thank you. I appreciate you coming over.'

No sooner had she left that Butler pressed a buzzer below his table. A false door in the corner of the room slid open to reveal a perspiring Youdale. 'You definitely need some ventilation in there,' he said.

Not bothering to acknowledge the remark Baron Butler said, 'She is one tough nut to crack. I did read the dossier, but she is far worse than I expected. At least your trip to Mysore brought us back on the trail.'

'Yes, we followed Prithvi Rathore to Mysore.' Youdale thought about mentioning Pandey's presence with Prithvi but decided against it. He continued, 'We figured that the book was in France with Tipu Sultan's descendant by tailing them. Once the Nazis invaded France the obvious place where Tipu's descendants sought refuge was across the English Channel. Finding an Indian seeking refuge from occupied France wasn't exactly very difficult; we found Princess Noor Inayat Khan and assumed that she had carried the book with her. Unfortunately she did not do so and has kept the book hidden in France itself. Furthermore after some coaxing and some threats we thought she would reveal the location of the book to us and that we could try and retrieve it from occupied France ourselves. She did not budge; the girl is made of stern stuff. When we told her about the Nazis being on the lookout for the books as well, she was genuinely taken aback and offered to retrieve the books from France. She would rather the books be in British hands than fall into Nazi hands.'

Butler asked, 'Well and what was your impression of Princess Noor?'

'She seems very sure of herself. I am not so sure if she would be able to maintain that swagger in occupied France. Most of the agents we send are caught in a few weeks. But all she has to do is get the book and we bring her here. Her brother is with us; he is the collateral.'

'Where is her brother?'

Youdale answered, 'He has been assigned a desk job in the Royal Air Force and he is not allowed to leave the Air Force premises.'

'Excellent. Well, you already know what you have to do.'

Youdale sheepishly said, 'There is one thing, though. We've lost track of Prithvi and Pandey.'

'Damn it! I told you we could not trust Pandey! Are they operating in tandem?' Butler fumed.

Youdale tactfully avoided a direct answer to the question. 'They were last seen in Nepal where we tailed them in the hope of getting more information. Now they've disappeared from the face of the planet.'

'Do you think they will actually try to enter Nazi-occupied France?' asked Butler.

Youdale said, 'That would require some nerve and Mr Rathore certainly doesn't lack nerve. But for all the money at his disposal, it would be completely impossible for an Indian to enter a territory ruled by Nazi Germany. He is a cricketer, not a soldier. Talk about putting your head in the lion's mouth—in his own den no less!'

July 20, 1941: Berlin, Nazi Germany

'I, Major Azad, swear by God this holy oath that I will obey the leader of the German race and state, Adolf Hitler, as the commander of the German armed forces in the fight for India, whose leader is Subhash Chandra Bose.'

With these words the cricket loving Prithvi Rathore of Bombay became Major Azad in the Legion Freies Indien at Berlin in Nazi Germany. The Legion Freies Indien (also known as the Tiger Legion) was an older replica of the Indian National Army formed by Subhash Chandra Bose with the support of Nazi Germany. It had the optimistic aim of invading British India from the west—from Persia through Baluchistan while the INA would invade British India from the east. Initially started by Indian students and residents in Nazi Germany, its ranks swelled when Indian POWs, captured by Germany were indoctrinated to pick arms against the British Empire for the cause of Indian freedom. Besides the POWs, a number of Indians in Europe voluntarily joined the Legion as well.

From Bombay, Prithvi and Pandey had made their way to Kathmandu, the capital of Nepal, another neutral country in the war. Despite pressure from the British Government, the monarch of Nepal had not cut off ties with Germany or any other Axis powers, mostly because of his fondness for Mercedes cars which the German Government was glad to gift! In Kathmandu, Prithvi and Pandey had tried vainly to get an audience with the German Ambassador and offer their services to the Axis cause. Giving up on Germany, they tried their hand at the Italian Embassy where they were finally able to express their desire to join the Axis cause after acquiring an audience with the Italian Ambassador. After a few months of doing the rounds convincing the Italians about the sincerity of their cause, the Italians finally issued them permits to move to Italy. While the Italians wished to have a thorough background check of any such Indian applicants, the fog of war prevented any clarity. Thankfully, for the two of them, the main problem of the Legion was a lack of officer cadre; hundreds of foot soldiers had defected or volunteered into the Legion but the number of soldiers in the officer cadre to manage the troops was marginal—this was the clincher for Prithvi and Pandey.

After another month cooling their heels in Rome, Nazi Germany finally gave them the permits to enter Germany where they were kept in barracks along with other Indian soldiers, most of them being POWs. Every single day, they were bombarded with fliers and information about British atrocities against Indians. Some didn't fall for the bait, but many did. As soon as they agreed to support the Nazi cause, they were given better beds, better food but still kept captive in the barracks. The routine became mundane and monotonous and Prithvi and Pandey often discussed if they had taken the right decision.

Then one fine morning, all those who had signed up to support the Nazis were given new uniforms and they were told to assemble at 8 am in the gymnasium. As is usually the case in such situations, rumours abounded about their fate. The general consensus was that they were being shipped to the frontlines. In the gymnasium, the officer cadre stood in the first line with rows of soldiers behind them. Thus, both Prithvi and Pandey got a clear glimpse of the balding, rotund man with horn-rimmed glasses as he walked into the quickly put up stage to address the crowd. He did not need an introduction—all of India knew him as Netaji Subhash Chandra Bose.

'It is my privilege, honour and pleasure to address you fine men of the Tiger Legion. Some of you might still have doubts about taking up arms against the British. After all, some of you have served for the British all your lives—some of your fathers may also have served the British all their lives. And that is the problem I have; I do not wish to serve anyone. If I fight a war alongside anybody, it should be my choice and not my pre-determined destiny. The British arrested me eleven times and the last time they finally thought they had put me away for good. The radio waves in India are agog with news of my death. Some say I died in custody, some say I was shot as I escaped from Calcutta and some say I was killed in the mountains of Afghanistan as I escaped. These rumours about my death are greatly exaggerated.

'So why do I choose to fight for freedom rather than subscribe to the Gandhian ideals of non-violence and peaceful non-cooperation? I love and admire Gandhiji like a father and as in any father-son relationship we are in disagreement about India's freedom movement. History has witnessed many revolutions; the ones successful have always been bloody.

'It may well be that we will eventually acquire our freedom through non-violence, but what kind of freedom will that be? Will it be a mere transfer of power from the hands of a few Englishmen to the hands of a few upper crust Indians? Will that change anything for the Indian farmer in Punjab or the fisherman in Bengal? Will it heal communal wounds and fissures of many centuries? Look at the American War of Independence, look at the French War of Independence—every home lost a man, every aspiring free citizen sacrificed something for his country.' There was a ripple of visible discomfiture in the Nazi ranks as Bose gave the example of the French to be emulated.

Completely unfazed, he continued, 'I want every Indian to sacrifice so that he may learn the value of his independence and understand the responsibilities that come with independence. The glue that will bind us together will be our own blood. Hindus, Muslims, Sikhs and Christians; Brahmins and the Untouchables; Pathan and Tamil; Gujarati and Bengali; rich and poor, we will all be bound to our nation, to our independent nation by our blood. Give me blood and I will give you freedom!' There was wild cheering in the ranks which brought a smile to the Nazi ranks. Bose was charismatic and no one in India doubted his patriotism. Coming from a fairly rich family in Calcutta and having been educated at Cambridge University, Bose could easily have taken the easier route and joined the civil service, served the British Raj and enjoyed a very comfortable life. Yet here he was, in Nazi Germany having escaped from British clutches despite a shoot at sight order, willing to give up his life for a cause he so dearly believed in. He was neither a military tactician nor a student of war; he was just one really, really angry Indian. Prithvi's thoughts were interrupted by a Nazi soldier announcing, 'Herr Bose will see each commissioned officer personally in his office now.'

Prithvi hesitated before he knocked on Bose's door. Through his grandfather, he had met a few prominent Congress leaders, but not someone as notable as Bose; he felt a touch uneasy. Calm down, calm down, he repeated to himself. He just wants to ensure that you are not a British spy and wants to gauge your patriotism. It will be over in five minutes. Prithvi finally knocked once faintly. Unsure if it was loud enough he knocked a second time with more force as if to show purpose.

'Come in!' said the welcoming voice. 'Sit down, officer.' Bose measured him from head to toe with what seemed like mild amusement to Prithvi. Bose continued, 'You seem to have strong arms officer. Do you play a lot of sport? Hockey, is it?'

As Prithvi hesitated Bose cut him off, 'I bet it is not hockey. It is cricket, right? And what should I call you—Major Azad or just Prithvi?'

Prithvi tried to display outward calm and he diplomatically said, 'Look at the file sir. My name is Azad.' But even Prithvi realized that his voice had a quiver.

Bose looked at the file and said, 'I know what the file says Major Azad. Don't worry; your secret is safe with me. The question that bothers you is …'

'… how could you know? There is only one explanation.'

'Which is …'

'That you are one of the Nine Unknowns,' Prithvi replied with his left eyebrow arched, half asking, half stating.

'Close but no cigar. Let's just say you and I have something in common—a relative amongst the Unknowns.'

'So you have been sent here to help me?'

Bose let out a short, infectious laugh. 'Quite the pompous brat you are, isn't it? No I have really come here to raise an army to drive away the British from India. Both of us are serving the motherland to the best of our abilities. I will go out of my way to help you if I must.'

'Do you really believe the Nazis are the right kind of allies?'

Bose looked hard at Prithvi before asking, 'Have you read the *Mahabharata*?'

'Of course, I have read it. Which Indian hasn't?' asked Prithvi rhetorically.

'For a book filled with such fascinating characters, it is always hard to pick a favourite. Generally, people pick Arjuna who faced the moral dilemma of fighting his cousins. But there is another who is my favourite—Karna, his older brother. Karna faced the moral dilemma of fighting against his heroic biological brothers or not standing by his evil best friend who had given him everything he did not get from his family—fame, fortune and recognition. And whom did Karna choose?'

Prithvi's reply was a poem in Hindi—

> *Hey Krishna, zara yeh bhi suniye*
> *Sach hai ki jhoot man mein guniye*
> *Dhoolon mein tha main padha hua*
> *Kiska sneh pa badha hua?*
> *Kisne mujhko sanman diya, nripta de mahimavaan kiya?*
> *Tan, man, dhan Duryodhan ka hai*
> *Yeh jeevan Duryodhan ka hai*
> *Surpur se bhi mukh modunga*
> *Keshav, mein usay na chodoonga*
> *Jis nar ki ba rahi maine, Jis taru ki chav rahi maine*
> *Us par ne vaar chalne doonga, kaise kuthar chalne doonga?*
> *Mitrta badha anmol rattan, kab taul sakta hai ise dhan?*
> *Dharti ki toh hai kya visaat*
> *Aajaye agar venkuth haat*
> *Usay bhi nyauchavar kar doon*
> *Kurupati ki charnon mein dhar doon!*

Hey Krishna, hear me out and
Correct me if I you think I have chosen the wrong side

I lay in the dust

Who helped me out and helped me grow?

Who gave me self respect and self belief?

My body, soul and wealth belongs to Duryodhana

This life belongs to Him

I'd rather turn away from all the riches than leave him

The man who lent me his shoulder

The tree which gave me shade

I will not let the man receive a blow, how can I let the tree be axed?

Friendship is a precious jewel

Can one set a value to such a jewel?

Let alone the whole Earth

Even if I become the Lord of the Heavens above

I would gladly give it all up for my friend!

Bose smiled and said, 'I haven't heard that one before. Who is it by?'

'I honestly don't remember. I did read it as a kid in some book and memorized it because I liked it so much.'

'What a beautiful ode to friendship. Yes, he chose his friend over his biological brothers. In this war, India is Karna. Either choice it makes, whether to support the British or the Nazis could be construed as right or wrong depending on the prism from which one views the decision. The Nazis may have wronged others but the British have definitely wronged India. Compulsions make strange bedfellows, Prithvi. The enemy of my enemy is my friend. We *will* achieve independence, young man.

'If the British win this war, perhaps we will achieve it through Gandhiji's way. If the Germans win, we will achieve it through mine. Either way, the end of the war will result in the re-birth of a nation, a civilization.' He suddenly seemed a lot more animated than he initially was. He seemed to realize this and checked his enthusiasm. 'So now tell me Major, how can I help you?'

'Where do you intend to deploy the Legion? I need to remain in France.'

'The Legion is too small to be deployed militarily as a fighting force. Besides, the Germans are not convinced about the loyalty of the Indian troops. So till we win their trust and our ranks swell, I have been asked to station the troops in non-combat duties at the Atlantic Wall or in Occupied Netherlands. In France, which has the most hostile population of the lot—we intend to have a small propaganda unit. Would you like to be part of that?'

'Propaganda unit? Who else do the Germans want to convince now?'

'Ha! The Indian troops fighting against the Nazis. You plant a seed of doubt in a soldier's mind and he begins to question the cause he is fighting for. The British too are using propaganda to convince Indian troops to fight the Nazis. Have a look at this.' Bose unfolded a pamphlet which he removed from his pocket.

Nazi propaganda pamphlet. Courtesy SGM Herbert A. Friedman (Retd.), US Army.

'Here you have the Indian tiger striking down the Nazis and the Japanese under the Allied flags. We are doing exactly the opposite in France, that is dropping pamphlets to implore the Indians to break rank with the Allies and join us.' Bose now showed him a Nazi propaganda pamphlet. It depicted an elephant with a mouse controlling it. The mouse's tail was flying the Union Jack.

Prithvi flipped the pamphlet over and the same paragraph was repeated in three languages—English, Hindi and Urdu.

Once upon a time, an elephant was sleeping so soundly that a mouse came up to him and tied him to a chain. Ever since, the elephant has remained a slave of the mouse. One day a cat came by and wanted to eat the mouse. The mouse ran to the elephant and asked for help. He promised the elephant that if he helped the mouse would set him free. The innocent elephant helped the

Nazi propaganda pamphlet. Courtesy SGM Herbert A. Friedman (Retd.) of the US Army.

193

mouse against the cat and then asked him to release the chains. The mouse laughed at the elephant and replied, 'You don't deserve to be set free; you are not fit for it.' After a few days the same cat came again and attacked the mouse. The mouse once again went to the elephant for help. The elephant replied, 'You are dishonest; a traitor and deceiver! I won't help you. I'll try to break my chains by myself. It is good for the cat to eat you.' And that is exactly what happened, the cat ate the mouse and the elephant applied a bit of strength to break his own chains and was free.

Prithvi asked, 'So what will be my role in France?'

'You will have to approve the designs and figure out which pamphlets are dropped to Indian troops based on their ethnicity and language. Bengali for Bengali troops, Punjabi for Punjabi troops, Urdu for Muslim troops and so on. I assume your crony too would have to be stationed there?'

'Yes, sir. That would be very helpful.'

Bose pointed a finger at him. 'You mustn't arouse any suspicion whatsoever. Even if you do not believe in the Nazi cause, make sure you carry out your duties diligently and to the best of your ability in France. Remember—this conversation never happened.'

'Thank you, sir. I wish you luck in your endeavour. I do hope with all sincerity that you succeed.' Prithvi saluted Bose.

Bose returned the salute, held out his hand and said, 'May you succeed as well, young man. Jai Hind!'

For the first time in his life, Prithvi said the slogan that would have appalled most of the members at the Cricket Club of India. 'Jai Hind!'

August 11, 1941: British High Commission, Washington DC, USA

The Ambassador wasted no time with the niceties—no greetings and certainly no tea. The American military attaché too was biding his time to intervene.

Pointing his index finger at a bemused Oppenheimer he said, 'Oppenheimer, it has been six months since we gave you that book and your progress reports are utterly hopeless.'

'Seven months.' Oppenheimer corrected him. 'And your Prime Minister has already made it amply clear that he is pulling the plug on any funding for the Manhattan Project.'

The Ambassador continued, 'That's right. Seven months. And we have been spending money like one of your Hollywood producers. Where is the damn movie?'

Oppenheimer retorted, 'Let me correct you there. First of all, it is not one book. It is a series of books encapsulated in one book. And yes, along with being a physicist, I am very well versed in Sanskrit. But I did not study physics or chemistry in Sanskrit. I studied religious texts and not scientific manuals in Sanskrit. It's akin to asking the Pope well-versed in the St James Bible to understand and explain the Theory of Relativity to you simply because both happen to be in English.'

The military attaché intervened, 'The Pope wouldn't happen to know it since it would be part of the Anglican Church and it is the King James Bible, not the St James Bible.'

A visibly irritated Oppenheimer snapped, 'Well, I am fucking Jewish but am sure that you get my fucking point.'

'All right, I get your point. But where do we stand so far? Have you learnt anything of note?' asked the attaché.

Oppenheimer became less agitated and continued, 'Well. For starters we have been reinventing the wheel for quite a while now. As I said, it is a series of books. To add to the complications, they are written in poetic form. Ancient Indian scientists placed as much emphasis on their prose as they did on their scientific knowledge—it was the pursuit of perfection, I assume. Think of it as Einstein meets Shakespeare. One of the first books was the *Samara*, dealing with every possible aspect of avionics. I had to translate and understand 250 stanzas in that book. It deals with everything—engineering of an aircraft, take-off, landings, normal and forced, cruising at high altitudes in tough weather conditions and believe it or not, possible collisions with birds.'

The Ambassador said, 'You expect us to believe that the ancient Indians knew how to build aircraft. Come on! Surely, you are joking.'

'Oh it gets much better! Like you, I too was not thoroughly unconvinced. I thought of it as the Jules Verne syndrome. Jules Verne, the great French author wrote *20000 Leagues Under The Sea* describing submarines decades before we acquired the technology to build one. Perhaps by coincidence, the captain of the ship was an Indian prince named Nemo. Anyway, I had to be sure. So I did some further research. Here is a picture of an artifact from the Harappa ruins in India and now kept in the Imperial Museum in London. It is marked as "Bird—Toy in ancient India".' He opened his briefcase and put forth a picture for the two men to consider.

Looking at the picture, the Ambassador exclaimed, 'It is a toy bird. What is your point?'

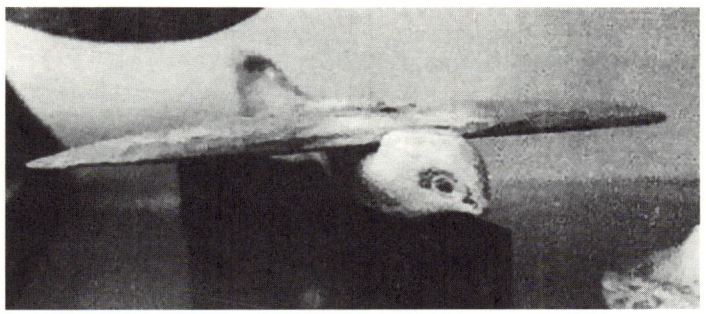

Toy bird, Egyptian Antiquities Museum, Cairo, Egypt.

'My point Ambassador, is that I would really like you to explain to me which bird has a tailfin?'

Looking more closely he said, 'Oh my God! That's not a bird, is it?'

'It is not a bird—it is a plane. Not only did the ancient Indians know how to do it, they did build it after all. Why else would a child have a model to play with otherwise? I suggest you move this artifact away from London and associate it to another ancient civilization if you wish to keep things quiet about this little discovery. Perhaps, the Egyptian civilization?'

'Is there anything else?' asked the American military attaché.

Oppenheimer replied, 'Oh, it just keeps getting better. I looked in the ancient texts to see if there are other references to this weapon of mass destruction that you want me to build.'

The attaché said 'And what did you find?'

Oppenheimer closed his eyes and recited from memory, 'The *Mahabharata* states in one stanza:

Flying in his swift and powerful Vimana,
Hurled against the three cities of the Vrishnis and Andhakas,
A single projectile charged with all the power of the universe.
An incandescent column of smoke and fire,

As brilliant as ten thousand suns,

Rose in its entire splendour.

It was the unknown weapon—the iron thunderbolt,

A gigantic messenger of death,

Which reduced to ashes,

The entire race of the Vrishnis and Andhakas.

The corpses were so burnt beyond recognition.

Hair and nails fell out.

Pottery broke without apparent cause

The birds turned white and foodstuffs were poisoned.

To escape, the warriors threw themselves in streams

To wash themselves and their weapons!'

Oppenheimer hesitated for an instant, frowned as if trying to remember and then continued, 'Another stanza states:

Birds croaked frantically,

The very elements seemed troubled,

The Sun seemed to dither in the Heavens above

The Earth shook,

Scorched by the appalling violent heat of this weapon,

Animals and humans burst into flame,

Running to and fro in a frenzy

Finally crumpling into the ground and dying.

From all points of the compass

The arrows of flame rained incessantly.'

Oppenheimer finally opened his eyes and looked directly at the Ambassador, 'Now, do you wish me to build such a weapon? I can build it in a couple years if I can get the translation and technology in place. I am convinced this book contains the know-how to build such a destructive weapon. However, your government has refused to fund me anymore.'

The Ambassador had called the meeting at Churchill's insistence to make the Americans look foolish and probably get a few more dollars out of them. Oppenheimer had completely turned the tables. Unsure of the next course of action, the Ambassador feebly replied, 'I don't know. The Prime Minister says that British funding must stop with immediate effect.'

The military attaché, playing second fiddle to the Ambassador, felt emboldened enough to take control of the meeting. Ignoring the Ambassador he turned toward Oppenheimer and said, 'Yes, we do want you to build it. Out of sheer curiosity how old do you reckon this book is?'

Oppenheimer said, 'The *Mahabharata* and the *Ramayana* are supposed to have been written in 4000 BC.'

The Ambassador exclaimed, 'So that makes it about 6,000 years old! Well before the time of Ashoka—he must have acquired them from somewhere!'

Oppenheimer said, 'No. According to Hindu belief, the books which describe these wars were written 6,000 years ago; wars which took place in the last Kalyug—the age of darkness and destruction—we are living toward the end of the next Kalyug. In between there was the Tretayug—the age of decline and the Krishiyug—the golden age. Each of these eras is supposed to last 6,000 years—which means that the knowledge contained in the book you gave me is at least 18,000 years old!'

The military attaché stroked his chin in confusion and retorted, '18,000 years! How is it even possible? Human history doesn't stretch that far back.'

Oppenheimer emphatically stated, 'Correction—recorded human history doesn't stretch that far back. In the last 100 years or so, humanity has made unprecedented progress; we moved from horse driven carriages to railways to planes. The recorded history of our civilization is about 5,000 years old. Yet it is a scientific fact that the modern human has been around for at least 100,000 years. It would actually defy logic if there had been absolutely no progress in any field in the preceding 95,000 years. It goes against the grain of human nature.'

Oppenheimer glanced back and forth at the two men and saw that they were still not convinced. 'Let us imagine that both the British and the Germans had the knowledge to build these weapons of mass destruction and decided to use them on each others' territory. Whom would they target? The main targets would be cities which house the best libraries, factories, shipyards, research laboratories and are home to the doctors, engineers, scientists and lawyers. All these would be destroyed and killed and we would be hurled back to the Stone Age with very few survivors in a largely inhospitable planet. What would happen to a world without London, Manchester, New York, Berlin, Tokyo, Calcutta, Rome or Moscow? It would take thousands of years to make this planet habitable and then the cycle of human development would start again. We would have to start from scratch—we would literally have to reinvent the wheel.'

Noticing the look of sheer disbelief on the faces of his hosts, Oppenheimer continued, 'All ancient civilizations that we know of perished—the Romans, the Egyptians and the Greeks. These are the civilizations that we know of. However, there is no major evidence of a civilization perishing in India; the Indic civilization has simply continued to flourish. Or perhaps, there was an ancient civilization there which did perish? This book certainly seems to indicate this very feasible possibility. This weapon can kill millions of innocents. There is a reason why this book has been kept hidden for so long. Are you certain you wish me to build such a weapon?'

'We need to stop Hitler and perhaps at a later date, even the Communists. However, it seems to me that you are not very sure if you want to build it. Remember what Hitler has done to the Jews and Gypsies and the homosexuals and anyone whom he considers inferior,' said the attaché.

Oppenheimer replied, 'You don't need to remind me. I will build it but I will need unrestricted access to funds and other resources as I deem fit. Are we in agreement?'

'Let me assure you that the US Government has every intention of seeing the successful completion of Project Manhattan. If the British do not wish to invest in this venture, that is completely their prerogative. America is the land of possibility. This is the land of Washington, Lincoln and John Adams. It is the land of Ford and Rockefeller. We know how to win wars and we sure as hell know how to raise funds.'

August 14, 1941: Signing of the Atlantic Charter, Ship Harbour, Newfoundland, Canada

On board the HMS Prince of Wales, a Class Five battleship, Prime Minister Churchill thought that it was not too often that he met someone whom he considered his intellectual equal. It was even rarer for him to ask a world leader for help; the US had offered its support to the British war effort against the Nazis but had not formally entered the war. Churchill knew that American force could provide the decisive thrust that the Allies needed against the Nazis. It was under these circumstances that Churchill met President Roosevelt who was due to arrive in the USS Augusta cruiser. The agenda was to seal an agreement to shape the post-war world. Prime Minister Churchill had enjoyed the secretive voyage playing backgammon, watching movies and reading while the crew along with the escort ships tensely avoided German U-boats. Although the agreement could not be implemented till the Nazis were defeated, it would send the correct message to the Fascists—the US was firmly behind the British.

The Prime Minister was used to getting his way in any negotiation with a world leader and dominating the conversation. But President Roosevelt was aware of the sticky situation the British were in and he was pulling no punches. The new world would be shaped according to American values and not by antiquated European values. Churchill tried to remain as civil as possible but the bloody American was annoying him with his intransigence.

Roosevelt said, 'We are against trade agreements in the future—no countries should be favoured over others. All markets should be open; that will ensure healthy competition.'

Churchill said, 'Mr President, the British Empire trade agreements define …'

Roosevelt cut in, 'Prime Minister, it is precisely because of agreements such as those rather antiquated ones that the people of India are poor and backward.'

'Please keep India out of it. It is not in the realm of American business. Mr President, England does not intend for a moment to lose its favoured position among the British dominions. The trade that has made Britain great shall continue under conditions prescribed by Britain's ministers.'

Roosevelt said, 'It is here, Winston, that you and I disagree. The American people and nation are against any policy which takes wealth in raw materials out of a colonial country, but returns nothing to the people of that country in consideration. How can the United States fight a war against fascist slavery, while at the same time not work to free people all over the world from a backward colonial policy. I will have to stand my ground as far as India is concerned.'

Churchill's cheeks reddened as he tried to maintain his composure. He had just called Roosevelt 'Mr President' and the Yankee upstart had called him 'Winston' instead of 'Mr Prime Minister'. 'We will not allow the Empire's economic agreements to be tampered with. They are the very foundation of our greatness.'

Roosevelt refused to blink. 'Then the Empire's greatness is artificial. If you want American support, the post-war world cannot under any circumstance include any continued despotism. The structure of the peace demands and will get equality of peoples. Equality of people involves the total freedom of all nations. I had a word with Oppenheimer yesterday—India is the country whose ancient knowledge will help us win this war. India should be made a Commonwealth at once. After a certain number of years—five perhaps, or ten—she should be able to choose whether she wants to remain in the Empire or have complete independence. As a Commonwealth, she would be entitled to a modern form of government, an adequate health and educational standard. But how can she have these things, when Britain is taking all the wealth of her national resources away from her, every year? Every year the Indian people have one thing to look forward to, like death and taxes. Sure as shooting, they have a famine. The season of the famine, they call it! Surely, as great a nation and civilization as India has a right to chart its own course. The American Declaration of Independence espouses that every man has the right to pursue happiness. This is applicable to all people, not just Americans. And the American nation does not see the Indian man being able to pursue happiness till he remains under the sway of the Union Jack.'

It was at this defining moment that Churchill saw the baton of world leadership which the British had held for centuries slip into American hands. Churchill considered his response and finally said in a resigned voice, 'You want to do away with the Empire in the post-war world, is it not? History has chosen me to preside over the demise of the greatest Empire the world has borne witness to. Am I to be the Nero of the British Empire? Bloody hell!'

The final outcome of the meeting was a joint statement termed the Atlantic Charter. The Americans and the British agreed upon eight points to shape the post World War II years:

no territorial gains were to be sought by the United States or the UK; territorial adjustments would have to be in accord with the wishes of the people concerned; peoples right to self-determination was to be recognized; the lowering of trade barriers; the global economic cooperation and advancement of social welfare; the promise to work towards freedom from want and fear; freedom of the seas; and the disarmament of aggressor nations and common disarmament post-war.

August 25, 1941: Office of Under-Secretary for India Rab Butler, London

Butler and Youdale sat across the desk from each other. The frequency of their meetings had led to an air of informality in their conversations and a begrudging respect for the other's professionalism.

'So when do we get her out of France? I don't want her falling in Nazi hands,' said Butler.

Youdale replied, 'Air-dropping her via parachute into occupied France was the easiest part of the operation. She has a radio set and in all probability will acquire the book in a day or two. Getting her out of there is a logistical nightmare. We will have to find a safe airstrip to land on in the dead of night. We haven't done anything like that so far and as most military rescue operations go, this one is fraught with risk.'

Butler responded, 'Can't we get her out by sea?'

'Through the German U-boat infested waters of the English Channel? It would take a miracle for us to get to the coast of France. And it would take an even bigger miracle to get back to the British Isles.'

Butler said, 'And can you at least give me a realistic time-frame of when we can expect her back?'

Youdale replied, 'I am working with the Royal Air Force to coordinate the rescue operation. They tell me it will take about a month to do the reconnaissance and then shortlist and finalize a worthy air strip. Of course, it has to be in proximity to a location where Princess Noor can access that airstrip—in a way, I would say that limits the geographical extent of the reconnaissance project.'

Butler exclaimed, 'I sure as hell hope that the Royal Air Force is as good at landing as it has so far been in shooting down the bloody Krauts over the English Channel. Goddamn Indian royals! And this one in particular. Can you believe it, her forefather Tipu Sultan fought us tooth and nail and here we are, relying on that damn woman. We are just too damn liberal! We should be able to order these Indians around.'

Youdale fumed but tried to be as delicate as possible. 'With all due respect sir, she is putting her life at risk for the Empire. Wouldn't we alienate the Indians if we ordered them around?'

'Stop being such an Indian lover. Being born an Englishman, it has been your right by divine intervention to lord over those Indians. What would you have us do—give them independence? They'll run back to us; they are just incapable of governance. India is meant to be British, old boy.'

Youdale mumbled, half to himself, half to his superior, 'Is it, really?'

October 17, 1941: Paris, Nazi-occupied France

Lieutenant Colonel Rohrbreck would have preferred to be on the battlefield but his gifts lay elsewhere. They had been recognized, tuned and polished to serve the Third Reich to the best of his abilities. While usually stringent about outside personnel—official or unofficial—entering the premises, the prison guards now knew the Lieutenant Colonel well enough to relax their identification routine for him. He gestured to the guard to slide open the door to the cell. He wiped the imaginary creases off his immaculate uniform, adjusted the pistol on his leather holster and walked right in as the prisoner twirled around to see who the visitor was.

'Princess Noor,' he said, 'I hope things are to Her Majesty's likeness in this little cell.' He paused for a reply. Since none was forthcoming, he continued, 'I am Lieutenant Colonel Rudolf Rohrbreck from the Waffen SS.' The name Waffen SS had the desired effect as he satisfactorily noticed Noor flinch ever so slightly. 'You seem to recognize the name. What have you heard about the Waffen SS? Good things I hope.'

Turning her back at him Princess Noor replied, 'Hitler's thugs. The Waffen SS is officially responsible for internal security in the Nazi Reich. And you use the sweeping powers to torture and murder political opponents, dissidents, spies or whoever catches your whim and fancy.'

The officer smirked. 'Is that your personal opinion or was this "information" drilled into you by the British propaganda machine?' Once again he waited for an answer. 'I tend to forget you are royalty. You will only answer questions which you feel like, isn't it? Well, let's start with what we know so far, shall we?' Once again there wasn't a response.

He continued, 'Your last transmission to London by radio was "Item acquired". You are part of the British Women's Auxiliary Air Force, the WAAF, and three of you were air-dropped into France. We acquired this information from another captured WAAF operative. On arresting you in Paris, we found radio equipment and seized all your possessions. Of course, arresting you wasn't easy; one of my soldiers now wears an eye patch since you used a paper cutter to stab him in the eye. As you can imagine, you are not exactly very popular in this prison. It gets more intriguing now. We initially thought you had acquired an item related to troop movements or positions and all your items were sent to Berlin for inspection. But the item which you had acquired was entirely different; it was not even Nazi. It was a book in Sanskrit which caught the eye of the Indian desk at Berlin. Now a Major Heidler informs me you that you are supposed to tell me the location of what he calls "the next book". I can't begin to imagine why an Indian book in Sanskrit would be of such importance in Berlin—but that is not my job. My job is to find out the location of the next one. So why don't you just give it to me?'

This time she spoke, 'You can kill me if you like, but you won't get anything from me.'

'Hmm. Have the guards here beaten you?' He stroked her cheek. She slapped his hand away. Turning her around forcefully; the Nazi removed a pair of handcuffs and cuffed her hands behind her. He then forced her to sit on the chair and bound her feet together with a rope. 'They did beat you I think? What a bunch of cave dwellers! A princess like you has to be treated right.' He unbuttoned the top of her shirt and said, 'I have never seen a princess naked before.' As she spat on his face, he gagged her mouth with his handkerchief. 'This can stop any time you like. Just answer the question—where is the next book? When you are ready to answer, just nod your head and I will take off the handkerchief.' He then proceeded to unbutton the shirt completely and yanked off her bra. He grabbed her breast and pinched a nipple as he heard a muffled cry through her gagged mouth. Tears were streaming down her face. 'Now I need to get off these pants.' As he unbuttoned and unzipped her trousers, there was a knock on the door before it was pushed open. The visitor announced, 'Lieutenant Colonel Rohrbreck, I am Major Pandey from the Legion Freies Indien. According to the rules and protocols in place, when any member of the Indian race is arrested, he or she will first try to be recruited into the Indian Legion by us. I shall have to ask you to release the prisoner to me for now.'

His eyes ablaze in rage, Lieutenant Colonel Rohrbreck responded, 'You do realize Major, that I outrank you and that she has information that is needed by Berlin right away! Get out of here.'

Pandey said, 'You do outrank me sir. I have had a word with Major Heidler in Berlin. You incidentally outrank him as well and he is in agreement that the protocol be followed. Would you like a word with him?'

Despite outranking Heidler, the Lieutenant Colonel knew that Heidler had the ear of some of the most senior men in the Reich. Rumour had it that he directly reported to the Fuhrer. Rohrbreck knew better than to cross his path but he did have to be completely sure, 'Yes, I shall have to check with him.'

'Please feel free to do so. In the meanwhile, do you think you can circumvent the protocol? If not, I shall have to ask you to release the prisoner to me.' Pandey stood his ground.

No words were exchanged for the next minute as the two men stood glaring at each other, neither of them blinking. Finally Rohrbreck announced, 'Very well. You have 72 hours to recruit her into the Indian Legion and get the information from her. If you are unsuccessful, she will be my prisoner again.' He turned to Princess Noor who still had tears in her eyes and raised his officer's hat while bending down. He then moved his hand on her breast once again and whispered into her ear, as if he were her lover, 'So long princess. I hope we can complete what we started.'

Pandey immediately untied the Princess and passed her clothes back to her. As she buttoned up, Pandey said, 'I am sorry for all that has happened, Princess Noor. We really need to get out of here right away.'

'I am not going to fall for any ploy of yours either. You can kill me if you like.'

Pandey said, 'So much for gratitude! We have come specifically from India to acquire that book. Where is it?'

'What book?' she retorted.

A clearly exasperated Pandey said, 'I think it is best you speak to my colleague, Prith… err… Major Azad.'

October 17, 1941: Office of Under-Secretary for India Rab Butler, London

Baron Butler leaned back on his armchair and tilted his head away from Youdale toward the heavens. 'It can't possibly get any worse. When did the Princess get captured?'

'It has been a week by our estimates.'

'A week! Why is it that I have been informed of such a serious development so late?' asked Butler.

Youdale replied, 'The Nazis were using her radio and log book to send updates. The password was wrong but this was not paid attention to. We assumed that she had forgotten the password or perhaps it just slipped under the radar.'

'Well, if she has been captured by the Nazis it means that we need to collect the next clue from Switzerland before she spills the beans to them. I know she is strong but everyone has a breaking point. I hope she hasn't wilted under the pressure yet. If the Nazis get the next clue then the trail goes cold and we can bid goodbye to the last book as well.'

October 19, 1941: Paris, Nazi-occupied France

Princess Noor knew that her time was running out. She seemed to have two choices—believe what the erudite and polite Prithvi Rathore had told her about his quest or be returned into the hands of that German pig. Prithvi had claimed he was known here as Major Azad and insisted that is how he should be addressed in public but he responded quite naturally when Pandey addressed him as Prithvi. Unlike many other Indian soldiers serving the Reich, Prithvi seemed far too knowledgeable and intelligent to be swayed by Nazi rhetoric against the British. But what if all of it was a Nazi ploy to garner the information that they sought from her? They were master manipulators after all. How could she be sure?

As they sat in Prithvi's tiny office in Paris in a Nazi military garrison, she shuddered at the thought of Lieutenant Colonel Rohrbreck barging in at any moment and whisking her away. She did feel relatively comfortable in Prithvi's presence. She leaned over to look at the leaflet that lay on Prithvi's desk. In it, a caricature of Churchill was about to chop off the fingers of an Indian worker in a textile shop. Other fingers littered the floor and the background showed the British having set the shop ablaze. The leaflet was written in Hindi and Bengali.

'What does it say?' she asked. 'I am afraid I am not very good at reading Indian scripts.'

'It says: To save Manchester, the British rulers shed the blood of Indians and in return gave them hunger and poverty.'

Nazi propaganda pamphlet. Courtesy SGM Herbert A. Friedman (Retd.), US Army.

'And there are more like these?'

'Yes, we do have many more. Here, take a look. The former is aimed at Bengali troops. This one is meant for Punjabi troops. It asks the Indians to vanquish the brutal British.'

She looked at him and asked, 'Do you expect me to believe this really happens in India?'

He answered, 'You can believe whatever you want to, Princess. But it does happen. In the British neighbourhoods of India, Indians are not allowed to walk on the sidewalks—they must use the gutter. In Punjab, the Indians have to crawl off the road if a British person passes by. That is the law.'

The expression on her face changed from wry to incredulous. 'I did not know this. That is just terrible.'

Prithvi shook his head and said, 'That makes two of us. I did not know either; the likes of us have been living in a some kind of a bubble.'

Nazi propaganda pamphlet.
Courtesy SGM Herbert
A. Friedman (Retd.), US Army.

She asked him, 'I would like to ask you some questions in private. Is that okay?'

Prithvi turned to the Indian orderly assigned to him and gestured to him to get out of the room and leave them alone. As the orderly left he said to her, 'Fire away, Princess Noor. However, you need to realize that time is short. I can't hold back Rohrbreck forever. What's more, if it is Major Heidler who comes to Paris then I am in deep trouble. I had him incapacitated in Bhutan with a poisonous arrow. I am now in a territory controlled by the Nazis; he will certainly want his pound of flesh.'

She allowed herself a little smile and said, 'It looks like you have been having quite an adventure.'

He smiled back and said, 'It was not too long ago that my greatest adventure was walking down the pitch to an Aussie fast bowler and hitting him for a six. It does feel like a different life now. I would honestly rather be sipping a single malt in the bar at CCI in Bombay after a nice game of cricket rather than try convincing a pretty princess of my intentions in Nazi-occupied France. But life is about the choices we make. I could have chosen to ignore my grandfather's instructions and continued my relaxed existence in Bombay and you could have just as easily given the British what they sought. But we both chose otherwise and now here we are—for better or for worse.'

She asked, 'Till death do us part? So what exactly are you doing for the Nazis here in Paris?'

'I am helping the Nazis by aiding them in their effort to lure Indian soldiers away from the British and into the Nazi ranks. That is what my department does.'

She asked, 'What made you choose the quest?'

Prithvi scratched his chin as if considering his answer. 'I can't point my finger to a particular trigger. I guess I lacked direction and a sense of purpose in life. I have been the eternal fence-sitter. Some of my friends chose the Indian nationalist movement to channelize their energy; others chose to support the British Raj in India. Some joined their fathers' business and others got into the arts. I was happy playing cricket and drinking. At that point, I neither supported nor was against the British.'

She asked, 'So what coaxed out the patriot in you?'

Prithvi let out a small laugh. 'Unfortunately, in India we don't seem to differentiate between patriotism and jingoism. For me, it has been a realization that it is not India as a geographical entity that I need to feel patriotic toward; rather it is India as a civilization that I need to embrace.'

She retorted, 'All civilizations rise and fall.'

He replied with a line from Iqbal:

yūnān-o-miṣr-o-rumā sab miṭ gaye jahāñ se ab tak magar hai bāqī nām-o-
nishāñ hamārā kuchh bāt hai kih hastī miṭṭī nahīñ hamārī
sadiyoñ rahā hai dushman daur-e ẓamāñ hamārā.

She frowned and queried, 'What does that mean? My Hindi isn't very good I am afraid.'

He replied, 'It isn't Hindi. It is Urdu. It is Iqbal's take on India as a civilization. It means:

In a world in which ancient civilizations of Greece, Egypt, and Rome have all vanished without trace, our own name and sign live on to this date. There is something about us which prevents our existence from meeting its end. Even though, for centuries, the cycle of time has been our enemy.

'So it has survived unlike other ancient civilizations. What's the secret?'

'I honestly believe that is the ability to assimilate. Other civilizations have always been resistant to change, be it social or religious. India simply embraces all religions and peoples and keeps on adding to its diversity. As a civilization it is on a perpetual evolutionary path—that is what keeps it alive and kicking,' Prithvi replied.

She nodded her head slowly in agreement and said, 'To get back to our topic, let's assume I take you to Geneva—what next for me?'

He replied, 'Well once I have the clue I follow it to wherever it leads me. You can of course choose to stay on in Switzerland; it is neutral. The money needed for the Nazi cause is often routed through Switzerland so I don't think it is in any danger of being invaded. Of course, you can also go to the UK. If you wish, I can even arrange for you to be sent to Bombay or any other city you choose in India. If you have any financial needs, those will be taken care of.'

She thought of Rohrbreck, his hands on her, and felt an instant revulsion. 'I don't want to fall into Nazi hands again. The trip to Switzerland is fraught with danger.'

Prithvi felt a tightening in his chest. He had grown very fond of the Princess. He looked her straight in the eye and promised, 'I shall not let you fall into Nazi hands again. You have my word.'

She leaned across and planted a kiss on his cheek.

October 21, 1941: Paris, Nazi-occupied France

It is not too often that a serving Lieutenant Colonel gets a dressing down from a Major. Rohrbreck avoided eye contact as Major Heidler went completely ballistic on him; he knew that he was in the wrong this time.

Heidler said, 'I wonder what I should be more furious at—your sheer incompetence or your sheer stupidity. Let me get this right, you were given instructions from Berlin to gather information about the next clue. You reacted by first trying to literally rape the Indian princess and then you released her to a Major Pandey from the Legion Freies Indien for recruitment to fight for the Nazis? You honestly believe that a girl who was almost raped by a Nazi would be willing to join the Nazi cause? Are you completely daft?'

Rohrbreck managed to mutter, 'Well, I was trying to garner information from her to the best of my abilities.'

Heidler barked, 'There are other ways of gathering information! Whatever happened to threats of electric shocks or hammering nails? Imbecile! At the first chance, you start pulling down your trousers! And under whose authority did you release her to this Major Pandey?'

Rohrbreck replied, 'He said it was under your orders. He even asked me to contact you and double check.'

'And did you see any such written orders? And did you even bother to contact me and double check as he so generously asked you to do?' Heidler asked angrily.

Rohrbreck said, 'Yes, I tried to get in touch with you but you were on your way here.'

Heidler fumed, 'That was not very smart now, was it? This Major Pandey—take me to him at once. I need to speak to this girl as soon as possible.'

Still not moving his gaze toward Heidler, Rohrbreck fumbled, 'Well—he is no longer in Paris. As soon as I heard you were coming I sent for them earlier this morning. Neither Major Pandey nor Princess Noor are in Paris.'

Heidler threw up his hands in despair, 'This just keeps getting better and better Lieutenant Colonel Rohrbreck. Where the fuck are they, then?'

Finally looking up at Heidler, Rohrbreck stated, 'Three of them—Major Pandey, a certain Major Azad, both attached to the Legion Freies Indien and the Princess—have made arrangements to travel to Ferney-Voltaire. These are the files of Major Pandey and Major Azad.' From under his arm Rohrbreck handed two files to Major Heidler.

Heidler quickly flipped through the file of Major Pandey as he asked, 'Where exactly is Ferney-Voltaire?'

As Rohrbreck replied timidly, 'Near the Swiss border.' He was not expecting Major Heidler to look completely ashen and shell-shocked.

Heidler turned the file around pointed to the picture and queried, 'This man is Major Azad?'

A confused Rohrbreck looked at a picture of Prithvi Rathore in Nazi regalia and replied, 'Apparently, it seems so.'

Heidler whistled softly and said, 'This man is in Nazi territory! The sheer nerve! Lieutenant Colonel Rohrbreck, you need to escort me to Ferney-Voltaire in a plane right now. We must not let them get into neutral Switzerland!'

October 23, 1941: Ferney-Voltaire, Border of Nazi-occupied France and Switzerland

The Nazis had wired the border with fences and the outposts themselves were manned by armed guards and ferocious dogs to prevent any Jews or Gypsies from escaping to neutral Switzerland. Since Prithvi had the necessary documents, he did not foresee any roadblocks on his path towards getting into Switzerland. However, Pandey cautioned him as they were about one kilometre from the outpost. Pandey removed the Nazi standard issue Carl Zeiss Wehrmacht Dienstglas, military service binoculars, from the leather pouch and handed them to Prithvi. Prithvi was surprised at how light they were, given their size.

Pandey said, 'You are not a military man—let me handle this. I go in first while you observe from this vantage point. If something is amiss, just take a decision on what has to be done. Do you know how to operate these?' He turned the binoculars in the direction of the border post and focused the lenses. All he saw was a bullet from the outpost whizzing from the barrel of a shotgun magnified by the lenses. He had just enough time to shout 'Duck now!' and moved his head away from the binoculars; he himself did not have time to duck. The bullet pierced the right lens of binoculars and went past the spot where his head had been an instant earlier. Then they heard another shot.

'Damn it Pandey! Are you okay?' shouted a crouched Prithvi. 'We are sitting ducks and all we have are Walther P38s.

We're fucked!' As he heard another firing shot, all three altered the positions once again and Pandey shouted, 'Behind that boulder! Now!'

'Why aren't they firing more rounds?' Princess Noor asked, ducking as quickly as she could.

Prithvi shrugged as he looked at Pandey for an answer who said, 'They only have one long range telescopic sight on a rifle. They must have seen me scanning the check post and decided to fire at us—perhaps they panicked. Given that we are in Nazi uniforms, they were clearly expecting us, else they would not have shot. It is safe to assume that it is Heidler. We have about four minutes before the dogs get here and about six before the troops which will follow the dogs. Thank God for the hilly terrain or else they would be here in three minutes.'

Princes Noor suddenly looked ashen. 'Oh God, I think I've been hit!'

Still crouching, Prithvi asked, 'How badly?' Noor pointed to her stomach as it bled profusely. Prithvi winced and asked Pandey, 'What do you know about gunshot wounds?'

Unlike the panicked Prithvi, Pandey maintained his composure. 'The way it is bleeding, it has hit one of the vital organs. With the necessary medical equipment there would have been a chance...' his voice trailed off.

Prithvi asked, 'What can we do then? There has to be a way to save her.'

Pandey replied, 'A war is a fluid situation. You take stock of your current situation, cut your losses and try to survive so that you may live to fight another day.'

A visibly shaken Prithvi asked, 'How can you be so cold and calculated? I promised her that I would protect her. We can't just let her die.'

Between gasps Princess Noor intervened. 'No Prithvi, you said you would not let me fall into Nazi hands. The books are more important than my life. Give me a pen—fast!' Prithvi stood still as Pandey handed her a pen. She grabbed Prithvi's arm and wrote a number on his palm. 'This is the password for my bank account at Tagand, Pivot, Rosset et Cie in Geneva. Just go and get the books.'

Prithvi was adamant. 'I can't bring myself to do that. You are coming with us.'

Pandey gently said, 'She is right you know. We can jump over the fence. We can't hold off the soldiers with two pistols for a very long time. We do as she says.'

Prithvi said, 'Jump over the fence? The Swiss guards will turn us over to the Nazis. They must have already informed the Swiss to do so. And what if the fence is electrified?'

Pandey said, 'Damn it! You have to argue about everything! The Swiss are neutral and the Germans need them—who do think is bankrolling the German war effort? By law, the Swiss are required to return German subjects; we happen to be British subjects. Once they determine this fact, the worst they can do is hand us to the British High Commission. The Germans are not about to waste precious coal electrifying a fence with a country which is actually not their enemy. Nor are the British about to invade Germany through Switzerland.'

Unwilling to expend more of her quickly draining energy, Noor looked at Prithvi and nodded. The barks were getting closer but Prithvi was still reluctant to leave her. She grabbed him by the collar, brought his ear close to her mouth and mumbled softly, 'Maybe in a different time, in a different place this could have ended differently. Now go get the books; even Tipu Sultan died protecting one of them.'

For one instant, their lips met as Prithvi steeled himself not to shed a tear. Pandey and Prithvi then proceeded to jump over the fence.

She then looked at Pandey and nodded ever so slightly in resignation. From across the fence Pandey said, 'I am sorry for this, Princess.' He shot her with his P38 at practically point blank range.

Pandey put his arm around Prithvi whose eyes were teary as he struggled to keep his emotions in check. 'I am sorry, Prithvi. I had no choice.'

October 24, 1941: Berlin, Nazi Germany

Doctor von Buren did not like Herman Goring. But as the head of the Luftwaffe, Goring was his boss, and he did not have a choice but to accept his meeting invite. As soon as he walked into the room he noticed that Goring barely managed to fit into his already generous chair. The man seemed to get fatter every time the Doctor encountered him.

Herman Goring was very cordial to the Doctor. Most people realized that he was one of the smartest men in Germany, perhaps even the world. Rumour had it that he was constantly in touch with the Allied Powers and if the Nazi war machine tumbled, he had secured his future in America. No one had been able to substantiate the rumours so far. Goring said, 'Dr von Buren, I thank you for joining me at a short notice. From what I understand, our rocket development program has been stalled—are you having problems?'

Dr von Buren knew that like most important military and political leaders, Goring would not be interested in technical details, so he decided to keep it as simple as possible. 'We are facing problems with the liquid fuel engines and the gyroscopic guidance mechanism.'

Herman Goring waved his hand in dismay, 'As if I actually understand that.' He then produced a document with a flourish. 'This is the first translation draft of a book we acquired about a week ago from occupied France. The book was in Sanskrit; the Fuhrer asked me to hand it to you. You must take it as a serious scientific document. The Fuhrer himself has used some of these Sanskrit books.'

With a frown Dr von Buren accepted the book. He flipped through the book and was astonished to see one of the pictures in it detailing liquid-fuel rocket engines, rudders in jet control, gyroscopic guidance mechanisms and supersonic aerodynamics. 'How old is this Sanskrit book?'

Goring replied, 'I don't know for sure, but it is at least a few thousand years old. How long do you think you will take to build the one we seek? Does this book help?'

The Doctor replied, 'A lot less than a few thousand years. I need to look at this book in detail but it seems to have answers to many of our development problems.'

Goring asked, 'So how long will it take?'

The Doctor said, 'I can assure you and the Fuhrer that the V-2 rocket will be ready by the spring of 1943. We will rain Apollo's fire on London.'

October 25, 1941: Tagand, Pivot, Rosset et Cie, Geneva, Switzerland

Prithvi and Pandey had barely exchanged words since Pandey had pumped a bullet into Princess Noor. Whilst he understood the logic behind Pandey's actions, he was still grappling with the loss of a woman for whom he had developed a strong affection.

Pandey had decided that it would take a couple of days for Prithvi to come around and decided to give him his space. He liked Switzerland; he was used to bitter cold during his postings in the Himalayas, but this was different—the cold here did not bite. He found it fascinating that there could be so much snow but the climes could be so pleasant in Switzerland.

The signboard was silver plated with a big 'T' in black. Below the 'T' the sign in black said, Tagand, Pivot, Rosset et Cie, Banquiers depuis 1869.

Pandey helpfully translated, 'Bankers since 1869.' Prithvi gave a slight nod; this was the first interaction between the two men in the last four hours.

Located on the Rue du Stand 60-62, Tagand, Pivot, Rosset et Cie was an establishment which serviced only a handful of clientele who appreciated it for being low key and discreet.

The doorman raised his T-monogrammed black hat as he opened the door for the two Indians. Upon introducing themselves, the receptionist asked them to wait. After about five minutes she announced, 'Monsieur Pierre Pivot will see you now.'

The room itself was tastefully done, clearly decorated to make the customer feel at home. It seemed more like a place where one entertained guests rather than a client. Pierre Pivot was unexpectedly young, probably not a day over 40, guessed Pandey. His jet black hair was suitably combed with an elaborate side parting and he was dressed in a fashionably cut wool suit. He firmly shook their hands before saying, 'I apologize for keeping you waiting. We are in the process of dropping the "Tagand" from our corporate name—soon we will be called "MM. Pivot, Rosset et Cie" only. This has been keeping me busy. Would you like some coffee?'

'No thank you,' replied Prithvi.

Pivot asked, 'Perhaps I might interest you gentlemen in a drink of whisky?'

Prithvi kept a poker face and did not reply. Slightly embarrassed Pivot continued, 'Very well, very well. We better get to business then.'

This time Prithvi said, 'Thank you. Here is the account number for the locker.' He gave Pivot the number along with the password.

Pivot raised his right eyebrow and said, 'Interesting. How very interesting. Please excuse me for a few minutes. I shall be right back.'

Prithvi's jaw dropped as he saw Pivot entering the room with Major Richard Youdale. He managed to say, 'Wonders will never cease!'

Pivot himself was slightly amused; as a Swiss banker he was used to invariably seeing unconventional phenomena during the course of business but even he did not expect to see both the Allied and the Axis uniforms at the same time in his cabin.

Youdale held out his hand which Prithvi reluctantly shook as Youdale said, 'How nice to see you again, Prithvi.' He then proceeded to shake hands with Pandey who seemed to take Youdale's materialization in his stride without appearing either flustered or fazed. Apparently nothing shocked him at all, thought Prithvi.

Pivot exclaimed, 'So you know each other. How wonderful. We have an issue—perhaps a minor one really. Major Youdale from the British armed forces has a letter of authorization from Princess Noor's lawyer allowing him access to her locker. Unfortunately for him, he does not have the password. He has been imploring the bank to give him access to the locker—a request which we have been considering.' He then turned toward Youdale and said, 'Monsieur Azad on the other hand does have the password for the locker but he does not have an authorization letter either from Princess Noor or from her lawyer.'

Pivot then scanned the room for any change of expression on the faces of his visitors. Prithvi was the only one scratching his brow while the two military men remained completely impassive. 'Given this deadlock and our endeavour to be fair to both the involved parties, a decision on who can access the locker will have to be taken by our board. However, if the two said parties can come to an agreement, this issue can be resolved promptly. The next quarterly board meeting will take place on the 8th of December. Do you think you can share access to the locker right away? If you are in agreement, it would save both the parties a considerable amount of time.'

Before Youdale could say anything, Prithvi replied in a curt tone, 'No, not at all. We have the password—we should get access to that locker.'

Pivot calmly replied, 'That is a decision that has to be taken by the board. I suggest we reconvene here on the 8th of December.'

Youdale turned toward Pivot and said, 'Yes, Monsieur Pivot, that would be much appreciated.'

November 25, 1941: Office of Under-Secretary for India Rab Butler, London

The war had begun to take a toll on everyone in the official circles of London and Baron Butler was no exception. Everyone was burning the midnight oil to keep the war juggernaut rolling and Butler's bloodshot eyes clearly indicated his lack of sleep. This did not do wonders for his mood which Youdale could only describe as snappy, even by Butler's own standards. 'The sheer nerve of these bloody Krauts!'

'What happened, sir?'

Butler replied, 'This morning I received a circular. Two Luftwaffe officers made an audacious attempt to escape from the POW camp in Penrith, Northumbria.' He shuffled the paper on his desk and read out, 'Lieutenant Heinz Schnabel and Harry Wappler forged papers that identified them as Dutch officers serving in the Royal Air Force and made their way to the RAF airfield at Kingston near Carlisle. They sneaked into a Miles Magister aircraft and took off for Nazi-occupied Holland! The bloody nerve!'

A surprised Youdale asked, 'They managed to escape from right under our noses?'

'Not quite. They realized the aircraft did not have enough fuel to fly them to Holland and they were forced to land in a field five miles north of Great Yarmouth. Their cover was blown; they have been thankfully recaptured and sent back to the POW camp in Penrith. The bastards have also deservedly been sentenced to four weeks of solitary confinement. The circular has asked us to be vigilant about forged documents. So Major Youdale, besides enjoying cheese, milk and chocolates in Switzerland, you have pretty much returned empty-handed from Geneva. We have the approval of Princess Noor's lawyer but we still can't access her locker?'

'It is all there in the report I sent you last month. I have been trying to talk some sense into Prithvi Rathore; he simply refuses to budge from his stubborn stance. He styled himself a military man named Major Azad in Nazi territory.' He cleared his throat as he considered his words now. 'Even Pandey has been trying to stuff some sense into him there.'

Lines of confusion creased Baron Butler's face. 'What in the name of the devil is Pandey doing there—is he in cahoots with Mr Rathore?'

Once again Youdale hesitated before continuing. 'You are not going to like this. After you decided to keep Pandey out of this mission, I had a word with him. I convinced him to win Prithvi's trust and keep me informed about his whereabouts. Pandey successfully implemented that part of the mission.'

The confused face of Butler was turning a few shades redder now. 'You ignored my direct orders?' He lowered his voice, 'So Pandey is still providing us information, I hope?'

Youdale reluctantly replied, 'My intention was to keep the book out of Nazi hands at all costs. I would rather have the books fall in Indian hands than the Nazis. In direct answer to your question, Pandey stopped providing me information a while ago; he has switched sides now. He is very loyal to Prithvi and doesn't see much reason to support us.'

Butler said, 'You must be joking! I have enough trouble on my plate than to worry about a double agent. Does Mr Rathore know that Pandey was working for His Majesty?'

Youdale replied, 'Yes. When both Pandey and I were trying to convince him to share access to the locker, Pandey told him. It would be an understatement to say that Prithvi was livid. Equanimity is just not his style. He almost punched Pandey in the face and held him responsible for Princess Noor's death.'

'What is 'almost' punched?' asked Butler

Youdale said, 'Well, Pandey ducked and avoided the blow. There is now a bit of a fissure between them but Pandey has proved his stripes to Prithvi. While their relationship is not what it was, Prithvi needs Pandey's military insight and Pandey well and truly believes in the Indian cause.'

'And what in the name of God is this Indian cause? India is British, you fool, and India is part of the Allied war effort.'

'I meant to say the cause of The Nine Unknowns sir. India, of course, is British.'

'Youdale, sometimes I wonder whose side you are on.'

Sometimes I wonder too, Youdale thought to himself.

Butler knocked his desk thrice with fisted knuckles and queried impatiently, 'So what is our next course of action to gain access to that locker?'

'We don't have many options. We wait for December 8th and see what the board of the Swiss bank decides.'

Timeline of World War II

November 25, 1941—
In the midst of monitoring the assault on Moscow, Hitler meets Haj Amin al-Husseini, the Grand Mufti of Jerusalem in Berlin. While Hitler abstains from giving a formal Nazi sanction to Arab nationalist aims in the Middle East for fear of upsetting Vichy France, both of them agree on the need for the 'destruction' of the 'Jewish element'.

November 27, 1941—
Japan rejects USA's demand for withdrawal of their forces from China.

December 1, 1941—
State of Emergency is declared in British territory of Malaya (former name of Malaysia) and British colony of Hong Kong is put on 'stand by'.

December 2, 1941—
Churchill introduces a new National Service Bill, including compulsory service for women mainly in fire brigades and women's auxiliary units.
Germans patrols are just five miles from the Kremlin in Moscow, Soviet Union.
Soviet troops evacuate their territory of Karelia, ceding it to Finland, which is now a Nazi ally.

December 5, 1941—

Britain declares war on Finland, Hungary and Romania.

December 6, 1941—

Roosevelt makes a personal appeal to the Japanese Emperor Hirohito for peace.

December 8, 1941: Tagand, Pivot, Rosset et Cie, Geneva, Switzerland

'Good morning Mr Rathore; good morning Mr Pandey!' greeted the impeccably dressed doorman as he doffed his T-monogrammed hat to the two Indians and swung the heavy oak door open. Prithvi was amazed that he could remember their names even though they had been there only once and left in rather unpleasant circumstances. Swiss professionalism, he concluded.

Youdale was already present in Pivot's office when Prithvi and Pandey were led there. He had shunned his uniform for a suit this time. The suit was not ill-fitting but looked rather plebeian relative to the finely cut one donned by Pivot.

After a round of handshakes, which while being firm could hardly be described as warm, Pivot announced, 'Gentlemen, thank you for coming in. As you are aware our board met as scheduled earlier today. We had a series of issues to discuss—including your rather, for a lack of a better word, peculiar problem. After much discussion we have come to the conclusion that it is not for the bank to prefer one party over the other so the status quo stands till you resolve your differences amongst yourselves or get an order from a court of law either in Switzerland or in the UK or even from India. We do not wish to take a decision which might be ruled illegal or illegitimate by a court of law—under Swiss law it would be a criminal offence. Perhaps you would like some time in private to consider your options?'

Before Prithvi could respond Youdale cut in, 'Thank you, Monsieur Pivot. That would be very useful. We appreciate it.'

'Very well then, gentlemen. You are free to use my cabin for any discussions. If you need anything there is a buzzer below my desk. I shall now leave you to hold your discussions.' Pivot straightened his tie before leaving the room.

Pandey spoke first. 'Do you think this room has some kind of equipment which might record our conversation?'

Youdale replied, 'Absolutely not! The Swiss value their clientele and their privacy laws are air tight. Both of you can rest assured that the room is secure and our conversation is not being recorded. Anyway Prithvi, I would once again like to say how sorry I am about Princess Noor.'

Pandey looked at Prithvi who seemed to twitch on reflex and said, 'She is dead Major. We encountered Heidler on our way to Switzerland at the French-Swiss border but the British are equally responsible for her death.'

Youdale's eyes softened a bit. 'She was a brave girl—a bit foolhardy but very brave indeed. Did the Nazis get any information from her?'

Pandey replied, 'No, but God knows they tried but she did stand her ground. In fact one of the Nazis …'

Prithvi cut him short by saying, 'Clearly this is not an interrogation session and we are not obliged to give you any any kind of information.'

Pandey put an arm on Prithvi's shoulder as Youdale said, 'You need to relax. I am just as sorry about losing her as you are, believe me.'

Prithvi retorted, 'Is that why you sent her behind Nazi lines when you could easily have sent anyone else to acquire the damn book?'

Youdale was growing impatient. 'I don't owe you an explanation either. But if you must know, it was her own bloody decision. We tried to dissuade her. It would have been far easier for us to escort her straight to Switzerland and send someone else to acquire the book left behind in France. That way we could have chased two books at the same time and saved ourselves a lot of grief. She was adamant. Are we clear?'

Pandey said, 'Calm down gentlemen. Let's remember one thing quite clearly—Switzerland is a neutral country which still has excellent diplomatic relations with the Nazi regime. We must expect that Heidler and his cronies are here in Geneva as well looking for us. Can we just agree to get the next clue and go our own ways?'

Youdale asked, 'What if it is an artifact which needs further probing? You have the tendency to run into the bloody Nazis; I could safely take it back to England.'

Prithvi said, 'Absolutely not. I don't differentiate between the bloody Nazis and the bloody British at all. They are two sides of the same coin. I shall take the artifact if indeed there is one in the locker.'

Youdale got up to speak but Pandey interjected once again. 'Once again, calm down. Let's take stock of the situation. Neither of you is going to budge from your respective positions. We just open the locker, look at what is inside and if there indeed is an artifact, we just put it back. Neither of us gets to take it—is that fair?'

Youdale was the first to reply, 'That is acceptable to me.'

Not getting a response from Prithvi, Pandey asked him pointedly, 'Are you okay with the arrangement Prithvi?'

Prithvi reluctantly nodded his head ever so slightly prompting Youdale to ask, 'Is that a yes?'

This time Prithvi spoke forcefully, 'Well, yes, considering I don't have much of a choice, Youdale.'

Unwilling to wait for any more fireworks between the two, Pandey proceeded toward Pivot's desk and pressed the buzzer. After about three minutes Pandey was about to press the buzzer once more but just that instant Pivot appeared in to the room and queried, 'So Monsieur Rathore or is it Major Azad and Major Youdale—do we have an agreement?'

Prithvi replied, 'The name is Rathore.'

On receiving confirmation from the two parties, he led the three men to a deposit section underground. A mechanical ladder was used by Pivot to get the box from a section too high for an average person to reach. He placed the box under his arm and directed the three men to follow him to a secluded, private room. He then produced a key from his waistcoat pocket and unlocked the deposit box. He opened the box while appearing completely disinterested in its contents and simply said, 'You are free to take the contents of the box or place them back in it. The box has been paid for till 2050 so it will remain under the name of the royal family of Mysore irrespective of the contents in the box. Once you are done, there is an electric bell under the table. I shall be here within five minutes of you ringing it and will take the box back to the deposit section. You are also free to ring the bell if you need any other assistance. Thank you.'

Realizing that Prithvi would be adamant about opening the box himself, Youdale did not bother to move and gestured to him to go ahead and open it. Let the baby suck on the teat! he thought to himself. The box itself was rather plain looking, made of copper, a lot like boxes found in Indian towns and villages.

Prithvi unhinged the box to find something wrapped in plain brown paper. On unwrapping the plain brown paper he saw a slew of articles: a small statue of Buddha, a miniature sailboat, a miniature anchor carved of stone and a green-brown swastika. As creases of confusion appeared on his forehead he passed the articles to Youdale who appeared just as confused and said, 'Why is there a swastika? Have the Nazis already been here?' Pandey who had not yet handled the articles exclaimed, 'Is it just me, or does this Buddha have breasts?'

Prithvi rudely snatched the statue from Youdale's hand and said, 'It is not a Nazi swastika; it is a Buddhist swastika, you illiterate buffoon. You are right Pandey, it seems to be a Buddha in feminine form. I have never seen this before.' He rotated the statue to see if something was written on it. On not finding anything, he flipped it over. Inscribed on the statute were the words in Hindi, 'May the merciful goddess help protect the seamen and bring them heavenly happiness.'

It was Pandey who spoke. 'Does either of you know what this means? Where do we begin looking?'

The reply was an utter silence from the duo. What followed was a gentle knock on the door. Pandey opened the door to let Pivot in who stated, 'Gentlemen, we usually do not disturb our customers. But we live in unconventional times. Considering you are military men, I thought you would like to know the news that is currently doing the wires. Yesterday the Empire of Japan declared war on the US and attacked their naval base at Pearl Harbour. The entire US Eastern fleet has been destroyed. And the UK has declared war on Japan a few hours ago.'

Once again, what followed was only stunned silence.

February 1, 1942: Makeshift Office of Under-Secretary for India Rab Butler, Edinburgh, Scotland

Due to the incessant German bombing of London, as a precaution some of the offices of mid-ranking to high British officials had been moved to Scotland. Butler wasn't very happy about this. 'I want to be in the thick of things,' was his refrain.

On the brighter side Youdale thought that he looked a lot less tired and irritable than he did in London in the midst of the Luftwaffe bombings. Youdale asked, 'So what is the news? I hope you called me in because you have some good news from Oxford!'

'As you are aware Youdale, our scholars have been trying to discern the meaning of the clues you came across in Geneva. It has taken close to two months of extensive research and they finally seemed to have actually made a breakthrough!' said Butler, visibly excited.

'About bloody time! I was beginning to think we have hit a dead end. Where is the book?'

'It's in Singapore,' said Butler.

'Singapore, eh?' asked Youdale.

Butler nodded his head and queried, 'Do you reckon Mr Rathore has been able to figure that out?'

'I wager that both those bastards are already in Singapore. It is a shame we did not have enough men on the ground in Switzerland to keep an eye on them!' said Youdale emphatically, shaking his head.

February 5, 1942: Raffles Hotel, British Singapore

On Prithvi's request and to keep himself and the remaining Unknowns abreast of the situation, Prithvi's grandfather had flown down to Singapore. They sat at the table in one of the restaurants in the grand Victorian themed Raffles Hotel.

Prithvi's grandfather said, 'Both you lads must have the Singapore Sling cocktail—this is where it was invented.'

Pandey said, 'I don't drink, sir. Thank you.'

After ordering two Singapore Slings for himself and his grandson, the old man said, 'It has been a long time, son. Irrespective of what happens now, you have made me very proud. You would have made your mother proud, too. '

'Thank you. If given the choice, I wonder if I would do it all over again. Believe me, it has taken its toll. I even have a few grey hairs now.'

The old man smiled, 'We all get them. I am still to figure out if Pandey was using you to help the British or were you using Pandey to thwart the Nazis?'

Prithvi smiled wryly, pointed at Pandey and said, 'That makes two of us, probably three since I bet even Pandey is trying to figure that one out.'

Prithvi's grandfather asked, 'Singapore, eh? Who would have ever thought?'

Prithvi replied, 'It did take some time to make the connection. First, we weren't aware of where the book could be—it could have been anywhere on the planet. Who could have possibly guessed a Russian connection to Buddhism? I concentrated my energies on predominantly Buddhist regions in Asia—that significantly reduced the geographical extent that I needed to explore. The inscription on the base of the female Buddha said, "May the merciful Goddess help protect the seamen and bring them heavenly happiness", but in reality it wasn't a feminine form of the Buddha at all—there is no such thing. It was a statue of Kuan Yin, the Bodhisattva of mercy, hence the line "may the merciful goddess" …'

His grandfather cut in, 'Okay, but how did you still figure it was Singapore and how did you figure which temple it was?'

'The goddess of the sea and protector of all seamen is Matsu, a goddess in Taoist mythology. There is only one temple in the world which is dedicated to both Taoism and Buddhism and it is in Singapore. It is called the Thian Hock Keng Temple.' Prithvi allowed himself a smile before asking, 'Do you know what that translates to?'

His grandfather replied, 'No, I don't, but I have a feeling you just can't wait to tell me.'

Prithvi replied with a mild laugh, 'It translates to "Temple of Heavenly Happiness!"'

His grandfather whistled softly and said, 'Wow! "May the merciful goddess help protect the seamen and bring them heavenly happiness"—it all fits! Get yourself another round of Singapore Slings.'

The old man then got up and shook Pandey's hand before proceeding to peck Prithvi on his forehead. 'I must leave today itself. The remaining Unknowns are awaiting my update.'

Pandey watched as the upright old man gulp down the cocktail and reach for another. Now I know where Prithvi gets his love of alcohol from, he thought.

February 7, 1942: British Singapore

The gates had bright tiles portraying roses, peacocks and bigger versions of the Buddhist swastikas that they had found in Geneva. Pandey winked at Prithvi as he pointed to one of the swastikas. Guarding the doors were the traditional sentinels of Taoist places of worship—tigers and lions. Prithvi said, 'It is a pretty big temple—we better get to work.'

Just then a voice boomed, 'Search away as much as you like. Perhaps it will keep you engaged. I have been here for a week. I knew that you would get here sooner or later.'

Both Prithvi and Pandey turned around to see a smiling Youdale propped up against a wall with his arms folded across his chest.

'Major Youdale—you have become the bane of my existence!' Prithvi exclaimed.

Pandey said, 'He may have found the book, but we can still look for the clue.'

Youdale was about to say something when a series of loud explosions filled the air. He said to no one in particular, 'What in the devil's name is that, an earthquake?'

An orderly came rushing into the temple, 'Sir! We must get out of here as soon as possible! The Japanese have invaded!'

Youdale snapped right back, 'You must be out of your fucking mind. Singapore is the Gibraltar of the East; we have one of the best naval defense systems on the planet here. How can they be so stupid as to try an invasion?'

The clearly shaken orderly replied, 'Sir—it was not a sea invasion. They came through Malaya.'

Youdale shouted, 'Are you suggesting that the Japanese actually came in through the impenetrable jungles of Malaya? It has only been one week since they even mounted an attack on Malaya. Are you saying that they have overrun all of Malaya in one week?'

He replied, 'It does look that way, sir.'

Prithvi intervened, 'Well Youdale, do you have the fucking book? If your Gibraltar of the East falls, how long before they decide to invade India through what the British think of as "impenetrable" jungles?'

Youdale said, 'I have the book, don't worry it is safe.'

Prithvi queried, 'And what about the next clue?'

Youdale retorted, 'I most certainly can't give it to you. That would be dereliction of duty. However, as both of you are civilians and citizens of the British Empire, in my capacity as a British officer, I can evacuate both of you to India or the UK as soon as possible.'

Pandey cut in, 'Thanks but no thanks. I am hardly a civilian. We will take our chances.'

After two days of extensive combing amidst the increasing frequency of random gunfire Pandey finally found what seemed like the next clue. He was not quite sure if this indeed was the clue and asked Prithvi to look at it. 'Do you think this is it?'

There was no inscription on the obverse side of the tablet. The only thing there was a circle—Ashoka's Dharmachakra, or Wheel of Righteousness with one minor variation. A conventional Dharmachakra had spokes representing the eight Noble Paths a human being must follow to attain nirvana, or the state of being free from suffering and the cycle of rebirth. Each spoke represented righteous view and righteous intention which comprised *Pragna* (Wisdom); righteous speech, righteous action and righteous livelihood which comprised *Sheela* (Ethical Conduct); and righteous effort, righteous mindfulness and righteous concentration which comprised *Samadhi* (Concentration). A conventional Dharmachakra had eight spokes; this one had nine.

Once again Pandey asked, 'Is this it? Is this the clue? Do you know where the next book is?'

Prithvi tried to erase the sound of the gunfire from his mind and looked around at the beautiful temple. Being righteous— that was what life was all about, wasn't it? He smiled sincerely at Pandey for the first time since the death of Princess Noor and said, 'How very appropriate. Yes, this is the clue. I know where the last book is.'

On February 15, 1941 the British surrendered Singapore to the Imperial Army of Japan.

April 5, 1942: Makeshift Office of Under-Secretary for India Rab Butler, Edinburgh, Scotland

Observing the more prominent stoop of the Baron, Youdale decided that he looked older than ever as he addressed the Major in a voice which had clearly lost its boom. 'You did a remarkable job in acquiring the eighth book. The Prime Minister does not think that Great Britain can spare the resources to work on the book; he doesn't think it amounts to much. He never did think very highly of India or Indians.'

Youdale asked, 'So is the book useless? Where is it?'

Baron Butler replied, 'You and I both know that the book is not useless. I had a word with the American ambassador and the Americans are very keen to have it. After a word with the Prime Minister, we handed it over to them. They claim to have made remarkable progress with the earlier book. In fact it was Oppenheimer who really wanted it.'

Youdale was aghast. 'That book tells of the possibility to travel to the moon. When the war is over, doesn't the Prime Minister want the first man on the moon to be a Briton?'

Butler replied, 'Apparently not. Coming back to the clue of the ninth book, the men at Oxford and Cambridge are at their wits' end. Not only India but the whole continent of Asia is replete with your Buddhist circles.'

Youdale corrected him, 'Not circles sir—Wheels of Righteousness—Dharmachakras.'

Butler said, 'Well, then I stand corrected. Wheels of Righteousness, if you insist. We don't even know where to begin looking. Every monastery in India and across world has many such wheels. The scholars' opinion is that you seem to have the wrong clue. Since Singapore is under the Japanese now, it's not as if I can send you there in the next ship. What's the news on Mr Rathore—did he find the next clue?'

Youdale replied, 'I am not sure if he did, we have no idea of what has happened to him or to Pandey. I offered him the opportunity to be evacuated but to be honest, I did not press him. I was sure that we would be able to defend Singapore.'

Butler said softly, 'All of us were sure. The Prime Minister termed the surrender of Lieutenant General Percival as the worst disaster and largest capitulation in British history—and the Pacific War was only ten weeks old! What a disaster!'

Youdale asked, 'So what are my orders?'

'You are to return to active duty in India immediately. There is a fear the Japanese might invade Bengal. We will need every fine officer there. You will be stationed in Calcutta. Hopefully, it will not go the Singapore way. If there is any word on the location of the next book, you will either be summoned here or receive your orders in India itself. But I sincerely doubt the scholars will make much headway. Godspeed, Major.'

April 17, 1942: Japanese-occupied Singapore

The two of them sat bound and gagged on chairs next to each other, still recovering from their bruises. But they were glad for it; there was a lot more space in this interrogation room than they had enjoyed in the overflowing barracks, now converted into a prison. Having acquired the next clue, Prithvi and Pandey had tried to flee Singapore. But by then the Japanese were in complete control of the city and citizens of the British crown were unable to leave Singapore.

For the third day in a row, Major Josef Heidler arrived in the room at precisely 10 am. He removed the gags from their mouths but still kept their hands bound behind their backs and said, 'You must be hungry, Herr Rathore. It has been three days and my patience is not infinite. All you have to do is tell me about the eighth book and the last clue and I will see to it that you are sent back to India. It's the word of a soldier.'

Pandey sighed and said, 'We have already told you. Major Youdale has the eighth book and we don't know the next clue. You can look for it all you like.'

'But you can at least point me in the right direction, Pandey. Where do I begin looking?' asked Heidler.

Pandey's jaw still hurt from the blows of the previous day as he struggled to spit at Heidler. Disgusted, Heidler threw some water on Prithvi's face to force him to open his weak eyes. 'I want you to look at this Mr Rathore.' Prithvi looked up to see Heidler cock his gun and hold it to Pandey's head who was merely smiling at the German. An infuriated Heidler continued, 'I will count till five. All I need you to do is point me in the right direction, else I blow his brains. One ...'

Pandey said, 'Prithvi, I am ...'

'Two!'

'... sorry I couldn't be of more help. I did ...'

'Three!'

'... help the British initially but I switched my loyalties to you and to India. I am sorry about Princess Noor too ...'

'Four! I will shoot him Mr Rathore.'

Prithvi said, 'I have already forgiven you, my friend.'

'Five! Last chance Mr Rathore!'

Pandey's mind went back to the Great War and to the General quoting Kipling. Aloud Pandey said, '"Tho' I've belted you and flayed you/By the livin' Gawd that made you/You're a better man than I am, Gunga Din!" I am no Gunga Din—I die for India, not England.'

Heidler once again looked quizzically at Prithvi who remained unmoved. On getting no reply from Prithvi, Major Heidler pressed the trigger. Blood from Pandey's head sprayed all over Prithvi. Heidler said, 'You really won't budge, will you?'

A Japanese officer assisting Heidler cocked his pistol at Prithvi's head and asked Heidler enthusiastically, 'We need room for more interrogation. Can I kill this one too?'

Heidler moved the gun away from Prithvi's head and pulled him closer by yanking his collar. He turned to the Japanese soldier and said, 'No. He once had a chance to kill me but he did not. Send him to the camp! Let us see if he is resourceful enough to survive that!' He then turned to Prithvi, 'You spared my life once in Bhutan—now consider us even!'

April 20, 1942: Shantiniketan, West Bengal, British India

The meeting of the Nine Unknowns lacked the usual chatter; the atmosphere was sombre. Prithvi's grandfather was grave when he spoke. 'As you are well aware, we have not heard from Prithvi since the Japanese captured Singapore. Our last interaction was in February in Singapore. We must resign ourselves to the fact that, maybe ...' his voice trailed off.

One of the Unknowns said, 'Don't give up hope. Your grandson has proved to be very resourceful. Whatever happens, all of us are hugely indebted to the young man.'

The old man continued, 'I should not let emotions get in the way but I can't help it. I suggest we disperse to our hometowns and meet only if and when required.'

Another said, 'It is only natural to feel a glut of emotions. He was your grandson. While we sat discussing the events, he was right there trying to accomplish a job which we should have been doing. He was indeed "The Tenth Unknown."'

Timeline

April 29, 1942 -
'The fruits of victory are tumbling into our mouths too quickly.'—Emperor Hirohito of Japan to his Generals on the occasion his birthday.

May 5, 1942 -
'Japan is operating in the Pacific in the hope of extending her hold over New Guinea ... from such a position she could carry out raids on Australia whilst awaiting our final defeat by Germany.'—British General Alan Brooke.

May 5, 1942 -
British forces retreating from Burma reach the Indian frontier – the Japanese overrun Burma and plan attack across the border on India through Bengal.

June 3, 1942 -
'Our citizens can now rejoice that a momentous victory is in the making. Perhaps we will be forgiven if we claim we are about midway to our objective.'—US Admiral Chester Nimitz.

July 14, 1942 -
Annoyed at having forced India into a war, the Indian National Congress passes a resolution demanding complete

independence from Great Britain failing which a massive civil disobedience movement will be launched.

August 8, 1942 –
The commander of US ground forces General Eisenhower establishes a HQs in the UK.

The Indian National Congress passes the Quit India Resolution at Gowalia Tank, Bombay. Mahatma Gandhi asks Indians to follow non-violent civil disobedience; he asks the masses to act as an independent nation. The British respond with mass arrests of over 100,000 Indians, levy mass fines and when the jails begin to overflow, resort to public flogging of peaceful demonstrators.

September 1942 –
German forces enter Stalingrad and are met with stiff resistance. Stalingrad railway station changes hands several times.

October 29, 1942 –
The first major offensive by the Allied Forces against the Empire of Japan launched. American naval forces compel the Japanese fleet to retreat in the Solomon Islands after shooting down over 100 aircraft, two carriers, three cruisers and a battleship.

November 1942 –
Fierce fighting continues in Stalingrad between German and Soviet forces. Stalin tells American journalists in an interview that American military aid has been of little help. The Soviets launch a counter offensive against the Germans.

December 20, 1942: Calcutta, British India

Youdale resided at the top floor of an apartment block in Mission Row, close to Dalhousie Square. He had been offered a bungalow as an officer of the Armed forces but he loved the view from up here and had declined government accommodation. The building itself was very cosmopolitan; besides a few wealthy Indian families, there was a Portuguese family which had recently moved there from Goa and a wealthy Chinese merchant couple who had fled with all their belongings and a lot of gold from Rangoon after the Japanese invasion.

The Indian children in the building loved to play with Major Youdale whom they affectionately called 'Major Uncle' or 'Military Uncle', and he entertained them by giving them British military standard issue steel whistles. Early in the morning Youdale stood with his tea cup in the verandah admiring the view. Through the leaves of the trees he could see the steeple and weather cock of St Andrews Church and in the background was the magnificent Howrah Bridge—the lifeline of Calcutta—connecting the two sides of the great city of the Empire, separated by the mighty Hooghly River. The children on various other rooftops were flying kites; some of them had coated the strings of their kites with crushed glass to engage in a game of trying to snap the strings of the other kites as they fluttered in the breeze.

Calcutta was rife with military personnel as the UK looked towards attacking and re-capturing Rangoon. He was thinking

about the festivities on New Year's Eve in Calcutta that year—
would they be muted or as boisterous as ever? His choice of
living in a cosmopolitan area rather than the British locality
had raised a few eyebrows. The incessant if muted insinuations
questioning his loyalty to the British right had never irked
him. He had himself never doubted his British credentials.
But recently, he had begun to question his own beliefs. What
business did he have here in a far corner of the world flying
the Union Jack? The Nazis were irrefutably evil, but how much
better were the British? Worse, he wondered whether the Nazis
had merely taken British views on treating certain people as
sub-human and merely amplified them.

It was the opposing circular dovecot that his Scottish
neighbour McArthur insisted on calling 'doocot' that
interrupted Youdale's thoughts. The pigeons in it started
flapping their wings and one after the other, flew off. Then he
heard the unmistakable sound of airplane engines flying far too
low for comfort. He turned his gaze toward the Hooghly and
saw them through his binoculars. The white and red sun flag
was unmistakable; the Japanese planes were approaching the
Howrah Bridge. The second biggest city in the British Empire
after London was under attack!

Timeline

January 28, 1943—
The whole of the German workforce is mobilized for 'complete war'.

January 31, 1943—
Large parts of the German 6th Army surrender to Soviet forces in Stalingrad. Friedrich Paulus, the German Field Marshal in Stalingrad becomes the highest ranking Nazi to surrender in the War.

February 2, 1943—
Battle of Stalingrad comes to a complete end with official surrender of Nazi 6th Army.

March 16, 1943—
Stalin implores his allies for the ninth time to open a second front against the Nazis.

May 3, 1943—
British and Indian forces recapture Rangoon from the Japanese.

July 23 and July 24, 1943—
Heaviest bombardment of German city as British Royal Air Force bombs Kiel.

September 3, 1943—

The Allied Forces invade Italy and Germany begins evacuation of civilians from Berlin.

September 8, 1943—

Eisenhower publicly announces surrender of Italy to the Allied Forces.

October 13, 1943—

Italy switches sides; declares war on Nazi Germany.

November 28, 1943—

Roosevelt, Churchill and Stalin meet in Teheran, Iran, to discuss war strategy against Germany—Operation Overlord is planned.

December 6, 1943: Berlin, Nazi Germany

Dr Wernher von Buren tried to remain as calm as possible under the fire of the Fuhrer's barrage. 'Dr von Buren', said Hitler 'you had promised me the delivery of rockets that would rain Apollo's fire on London. The only rain seems to be British bombers bombing the daylights out of Germany. Every German man, woman and child is at risk. That Churchill is a mad man, hell bent on destroying Europe completely.'

Dr von Buren replied, 'We are facing issues at the Mittelbau Dora camp. We have already hanged 150 men for sabotage and many more have died assembling those rockets—it is a dangerous activity.'

Hitler shouted back, 'This is war! The German nation's ideals and its very existence are at risk. I don't want to hear lame excuses. I want the rockets ready for launch!'

'I am working on it sir. We need more trained engineers.'

Hitler said, 'We have a lot of French and Jewish engineers in some camps—I will arrange to get them transferred to Mittelbau Dora. Now leave!'

Timeline

June 6, 1944—
Operation Overlord commences as the Allied Expeditionary forces of the USA, UK, Canada, Poland and free France invade Nazi-occupied France.

September 8, 1944—
Dr Wernher von Buren delivers his promise and Nazi Germany fires V-2 rockets at London leaving it in a state of ruin— 20,000 inmates die at Mittelbau Dora constructing the 3000+ V-2 rockets.

April 30, 1945—
Hitler commits suicide.

May 8 (May 9 in USSR)—
Germany formally surrenders—the Western War is over.

June 12, 1945: Calcutta, British India

The General sized up Youdale and said, 'Congratulations on your promotion Lieutenant Colonel Youdale.'

Youdale politely said, 'Thank, you sir.'

The General acknowledged Youdale's thanks with a nod and continued, 'As you are probably aware, this is not a courtesy call. I understand that the war is just over and troops like you have earned their rest. It seems we have on our hands a Nazi prisoner of war in Berlin who claims that he is in possession of documents which could be of great service to His Majesty. However, he insists that he will only talk to a certain Major Youdale from the British Indian Army. So my dear man, prepare for a trip to Berlin. However, we can't send you for the next couple of months. The Americans are going to extract as much information from him as they can before they let us see him.'

Youdale asked, 'What's his name?'

The General rubbed his forefinger and thumb on his forehead as he said, 'Colonel Josef Heidler.'

July 16, 1945: White Sands Proving Ground, Alamogordo, New Mexico, USA

Oppenheimer tapped his desk absent mindedly as he waited for the news. The underground bunker was insulated and self sufficient. If something went wrong, he and his colleagues could survive underground for the next five years, maybe seven with rationing. His senior colleague Kenneth Bainbridge, a physicist from Harvard asked him, 'So Robert, why did you choose the name Trinity?'

Without ceasing the tapping Oppenheimer responded, 'It is 5.35 am already. Where is the news of the test? In answer to your query, Trinity is a tribute to the Holy Trinity.'

A confused Bainbridge asked, 'The Father, the Son and the Holy Ghost? What is the connection to the test?'

Finally stopping the tapping Oppenheimer smiled despite the tension and said, 'No Ken, not that one. It was a reference to the Hindu holy trinity—Brahma, Vishnu and Mahesh—the Creator, the Preserver and the Destroyer.'

Bainbridge said, 'Then it is a very apt name you have chosen indeed. We would have not been able to make much headway without that book.'

Before Oppenheimer could respond, a soldier barged into the room unannounced and read excitedly from the paper in his hand, 'At 05.29 hours, Mountain Time, the device exploded with an energy equivalent to 20 kilotons. It left a crater 10 feet deep and 1,100 feet wide. The mushroom cloud reached 7.5 miles in height. Trinity is a success!'

'No, we are all sons of bitches,' Bainbridge stated to the rest of the scientists.

Oppenheimer stood up and raised his arms toward the assembled scientists and quoted from the Bhagvad Gita, 'Now I am become Death; the destroyer of worlds.'

Timeline

August 6, 1945—
The atomic bomb *Little Boy,* is dropped on Hiroshima.

August 9, 1945—
The atomic bomb *Fat Man,* is dropped on Nagasaki.

August 15, 1945—
Japan announces its surrender to the Allied Powers. World War II is over.

September 4, 1945: Charlottenberg, British Sector, Berlin, Germany

Till all four of the Allied powers came to a mutually satisfactory agreement they had decided to carve up Berlin into four sectors with each of them—the Americans, the British, the French and the Soviets occupying one sector each. It was like carving up a heap of ruins; Hitler's Berlin lay in tatters. Berlin itself fell in a zone completely occupied by the Soviet Union and for the surrendering Nazis in the vicinity, the non-Soviet zones were like a gift from the heavens above. The Soviets had lost 25 million men against the Nazis, by far the most by any nation in the war. They vented their anger on the general German population, but reserved the worst treatment for the Nazi soldiers.

Youdale had been waiting patiently in the cell of what was formerly a Nazi prison in the British sector of Berlin; he wondered if he should go out and check if all was well. It was distinctly eerie to be sitting in a major city in Europe without the sound of sirens, bombs or aircraft—it made Youdale edgy.

The doors to the cell finally swung open and an American soldier led Colonel Josef Heidler into the room. Youdale observed that his German foe looked a little gaunt but still remarkably-well fed for a prisoner of war. Youdale was about to offer his handshake to Heidler, but checked himself once he realized that Heidler's hands were handcuffed.

He recollected crisscrossing the globe—each of the men trying to outdo and out-think the other. It had finally boiled down to a cell in Berlin in the British occupation zone. Youdale was the one who spoke first, 'I see that you have become a Colonel now. I could merely become a Lieutenant Colonel.'

Heidler replied, 'Yes, there were a flurry of promotions by Hitler toward the end of the war, apparently to boost morale. It didn't quite help to be honest. Congratulations on your promotion, Lieutenant Colonel Youdale.'

'Thank you. Now that you have had me flown all the way from India, what exactly is this about?'

Heidler glanced at the American soldier who still stood behind him. Youdale said, 'The Americans are very careful. It seems most of you Germans prefer to surrender to the British or the Americans than to the Russians. So the Russian spies try to wean away as many Nazis as they can; almost all high-ranking Nazis are in British or American hands.'

Heidler replied, 'That is because the Americans and British treat us better. The Soviets treat us worse than dogs.'

Youdale said, 'But still not quite as badly as you treated the Jews and the Gypsies.' Heidler winced as Youdale continued, 'What do you expect from the Russians? They lost 25 million men fighting you off. That's more than the rest of the Allies put together.' Youdale then gestured to the American to leave them alone who didn't seem too happy about the directive. He left the room reluctantly.

Youdale asked, 'So what is it, Colonel Heidler?'

'I want you to get me and my family out of here in exchange for the books that were found by us,' Heidler said.

Youdale said, 'I am not Eisenhower or Montgomery—you are barking up the wrong tree. But do continue, I am all ears.'

Heidler said, 'There is no food in Berlin. My children are malnourished—the queues for bread are getting longer than ever. Just the other day a Russian soldier offered my wife an extra loaf of bread if she let him feel her up. The worst part is, she agreed. What is next in store for her—rape? I haven't felt so impotent in my life. I followed orders and served my country as any soldier should. Even if you can't get me out, please send my family to the UK in exchange for the books. If they try me for war crimes, I know I will be hanged, but I need to secure the future of my family before that.'

Youdale said, 'I can certainly arrange for your family to find safe refuge in England in exchange for the books. I can even spare you a public hanging. But there is one more thing.'

Heidler eagerly said, 'Anything! Ask for anything!'

Youdale asked, 'Where are Pandey and Prithvi?'

Heidler replied, 'Ah, you want to secure all the books. I had to shoot Pandey during an interrogation in Singapore.'

A slightly shaken Youdale queried, 'And what about Prithvi?'

Heidler said, 'That boy is something else. He refused to divulge any information. In normal circumstances, I would have killed him in the course of an interrogation. But he had the chance to kill me in Bhutan and yet he spared my life. As a soldier, I too spared his life. He was taken to a Japanese Prisoner of War camp in New Guinea.'

'So where are the books?' asked Youdale.

'My wife has them. She will hand them to you once my family is safe in England.'

Youdale said, 'We have a deal then. She and your family will be in England before the end of the week.' He slid a small metal box of Altoids into the front pocket of Heidler's shirt who replied by saying, 'Thank you.'

One week later upon hearing that his family had been given safe haven in the UK, Colonel Josef Heidler was found dead in his cell in the American sector of Tempelhof in Berlin. He had committed suicide by consuming cyanide; no one knew how he acquired it.

December 7, 1945: Territory of Papua New Guinea, Australia

The Australian Colonel was hefty with an impressive moustache and spoke with the thick accent which Youdale guessed must be from Queensland. 'The name is Dudley Gibson. We have tried to rehabilitate the men both physically and mentally to the utmost extent in the time available and boost their morale. These Indians, they are a fine bunch of soldiers, a great race, great in adversity. They were weak and wearing tattered clothing. It was inspiring to see their sergeant pull them aside before they mounted the truck and make them tidy their clothing to the best of their ability so that they arrive at HQ looking as presentable as possible under the circumstances. Such a display of soldierly pride after so much hardship can only be called ennobling.'

'So what exactly happened to Prithvi?' queried Youdale.

Colonel Gibson held up a file and opened it as he said, 'Here is his testimony, Youdale. After the surrender of Allied troops in Singapore, the Indian troops were immediately separated from the European ones. They were constantly fed propaganda against the Allies; their alleged atrocities and their lack of moral authority to rule over Asia. Asia for Asians, an Asian economic sphere of co-operation, that was the message. The 40,000 Indian troops captured were all offered amnesty if they agreed to join the Indian National Army, the INA led by Subhash Chandra Bose in Burma. 35,000 of them did agree and were immediately dispatched to fight the Allies. About

5,000 of them did not and decided to remain loyal to the Allied cause. After a few more months of trying to cajole them, the Japanese transported them to New Guinea in their infamous Jigoku sen.'

Youdale interrupted Gibson by asking, 'What are those?'

Gibson looked up from the file and looked at Youdale as if he could not believe that he hadn't heard of them. 'Hell ships, my dear boy. Due to lack of transportation POWs were crammed into cargo holds of ships with little air, food or water on journeys which would last for weeks. Many man became delirious and unresponsive to the environment and died from dysentery, starvation, thirst or asphyxia. As these hell ships were unmarked and non combat units, they were often bombed by our own Allied aircrafts. Stories abound about hell ships being so bad that the soldiers inside tried to kill each other to drink the blood of their comrades. Often the only movement possible in such ships was over the heads and bodies of other soldiers, lying in their own filth and urine.'

'So Prithvi was in one of those?' asked Youdale.

Colonel Gibson returned to his file and said, 'Yes, he was. He finally made his way with about 3,000 other men to Wewak in New Guinea. They were put up in a swamp close to Wewak Point and forced to build their own huts using nothing but mud and grass. Their huts often got flooded and they had to sleep in the water. Lacking medical equipment and sanitary facilities, the fatalities were quite high. The men were forced to work at the harbor unloading ships. The lack of food led to a lot of the men suffering from beriberi.'

Youdale recoiled on hearing that. Once again Gibson looked up and asked, 'Do you want me to continue?' On seeing Youdale nod his head Gibson said, 'Very well.'

'It seems your man Prithvi Rathore was one of the few educated Indians held prisoner. Along with some other officers, he submitted a writ petition in English to Colonel Takano of the Imperial Japanese Army. They asked for better provisions, medication and access to doctors, scheduled working hours and a weekly day off to rest. They requested that they be treated according to the Geneva Convention of International Law and that their camp be marked so they were protected from any accidental attack by Allied aircraft. Takano dismissively described them as traitors of Asia and India. He said, "You have surrendered unconditionally and you must do the work you are ordered to do." Takano told his Japanese officers not to allow the POWs to make further petitions and to "see that they work hard".

'In August 1943, six Indians were killed and thirteen were wounded when Allied aircraft raided Wewak. Mr Rathore was not one of them. The wounded were carried to the beach, where they lay, some crying out in pain. Colonel Takano arrived and angrily threw handfuls of sand at them, shouting in broken English, "Why are you crying? This is not my fault. It is Roosevelt and Churchill." Mr Rathore arranged for the wounded to be bandaged but could not coax the Japanese to have them otherwise treated. All of them died of infected wounds in a few hours. After the Japanese officers refused to accept another writ petition, the enterprising Mr Rathore decided to take a leaf out of Gandhi's book and arranged a hunger strike. The Japanese commander of the party, Captain Itakura assembled the men and threatened to shoot them unless they ended their strike and ate. Quite clearly cut from a different cloth they refused saying they would rather die than be denied their rights. Finally Colonel Takano became involved and relented—he gave them better food but still refused to mark their complex as a POW camp saying it would be a "disgrace to the Japanese Army".'

Gibson paused and asked Youdale, 'Would you like some water?' Youdale shook his head and Gibson continued. 'The Japanese tried their best to coax the Indians to join the Japanese war effort. Knowing that Prithvi was one of their ring leaders, one fine morning they dragged him to a trench and placed the blade of a samurai sword on his bare neck as if to behead him. They then asked him to join the Japanese war effort. He refused. A gun was then pointed at his chest and the Japanese soldier pulled the trigger.'

Youdale interrupted, 'They killed him?'

Gibson continued, 'No, the gun was not loaded. He, along with his comrades, was liberated on September 11, 1945 from the camp by a joint force of American and Australian troops.'

Youdale asked, 'So where is he now?'

Colonel Gibson shut the file and smiled at Youdale. He twirled his finger and said, 'Turn around, Youdale.'

His hair had turned prematurely grey and he was as thin as a reed; the clothes he wore were ill-fitting, but there was no mistaking the focus in the eye—it was Prithvi Rathore.

'Hello, Major Youdale. You just can't get enough of me, can you?' asked Prithvi, giving a weak smile.

Youdale cleared his throat, surprised by the surge of emotion he felt. Giving Prithvi a smile, he said, 'It's actually Lieutenant Colonel Youdale now. You've had your share of the war, Prithvi. It's time to go home, old friend.'

December 19, 1945: Great Indian Peninsular Railway, Calcutta to Bombay, British India

There had been no mention of books so far. Perhaps he is waiting for us to get to Bombay before the questions start, thought Prithvi. Youdale had signed the papers authorizing Prithvi's release in New Guinea itself. However, it took a while for the Australians to process the documentation and arrange for Prithvi to be shipped to India. A steam ship had taken him to Bengal and it was there that he was greeted by Youdale. In the few hours that they had been together, Youdale had not mentioned the books at all. The journey by train to Bombay would last three days, so Youdale figured that the topic would come up for discussion sooner or later. So far the discussions had revolved around the negotiations taking place between Gandhi, Jinnah and Mountbatten regarding India's impending independence. Would Jinnah have his Pakistan? Would Sardar Patel be independent India's first Prime Minister, or would it be Nehru?

Youdale finally opened his suitcase and placed a bottle on the table in their carriage. Prithvi recognized the distinctive green bottle with the yellow label bearing the sail ship instantly. He picked up the bottle and read aloud, 'Cutty Sark! How nice of you.'

Youdale asked, 'This was your request to me in Scotland, wasn't it?'

Prithvi smiled and said, 'It has been a long, long time indeed. May I?' he asked and proceeded to uncork the bottle.

After a few rounds of drinks, Youdale excused himself to visit the men's room. On returning, he found the glass in Prithvi's hand had been replaced by Youdale's gun which was pointed straight at his chest.

'What are you doing, Prithvi?' asked Youdale.

Prithvi said, 'Well, now that we are done with the niceties, perhaps we can get on with business. You came looking for me in New Guinea because you wanted the remaining books, is'nt it?'

'Well ...' said Youdale.

Prithvi continued, 'Just tell me one thing. Was the book that you acquired responsible for the bombings in Nagasaki and Hiroshima?'

'Yes, it was,' said Youdale.

'Do you realize how many innocent people you have killed? The number of lives lost that you are directly responsible for?' fired Prithvi.

'Please listen to me Prithvi. If I had an inkling of what...' said Youdale.

Prithvi interjected, 'The time for inklings is over, Youdale. I have never killed a man intentionally but you don't deserve to live.' He emptied the magazine in Youdale's chest. Youdale's body slumped on the floor of the carriage. Using all his strength, Prithvi lifted the limp body and threw it over the next bridge the train crossed.

January 3-5, 1947: Nalanda, British India

The sun had set and it was raining. The only protection Prithvi had was an overcoat and even this seemed luxurious compared to what he had been through in New Guinea under Japanese occupation. For two days, he searched for the Dharmachakra with nine spokes. He finally found it near the erstwhile library of Nalanda, Dharma Gunj, Mountain of Truth. Once he found the Dharmachakra, he started digging. If he had regained his normal strength, it would have taken about ten minutes; but he was still weak from the time spent at the POW camp. He wondered if he would ever be as strong as he once was. Perhaps in due time, he would be able to hit the cricket pitch once again.

After about half an hour, the shovel finally hit something metallic and he bent down to pick out the box. On opening it, he found that there was no book, just a folder piece of paper. He curiously unfolded the paper and was shocked to see it addressed to him.

Dear Prithvi,

Your journey has been a long one. It has not been easy for me either. I served His Majesty to the best of my abilities, but there was always that question at the back of my mind—was I doing the right thing?

The catalyst which provided me the answer was my time in Bengal after the Japanese bombing of Calcutta began. Burma was in Japanese hands. Bengal still belonged to Great Britain. Fearing a Japanese invasion of Bengal, the British authorities decided to stockpile food grown in Bengal for British soldiers to prevent access to the Japanese in case of an invasion. A policy known as 'scorched earth' was implemented in Chittagong; all the rice grown in Bengal was either stockpiled or shipped to British troops in the Middle East and Burma. Officially, three million Bengalis died in 1943 alone. The real number is closer to 8 million. Some of us British soldiers who had not seen such death by starvation sent a request to Prime Minister Winston Churchill to let us release the food to the masses. He responded by asking that if food in India was so scarce, why hadn't Gandhi died yet? There was no shortage of food—we were simply starving the citizens of the Empire to death. The Indian National Army led by Subhash Chandra Bose sent three ships filled with rice to help the Indian people of Bengal. Churchill and Wavell refused to accept it.

Now that the war is over, the amount of hue and cry raised over the deaths of 6 million Jews, Gypsies and others affected by the third Reich has been made public. But what about the genocide of the Indians— doesn't that need to be told as well?

I was in Dacca helping in the distribution of the food that I could get. I was apologizing to an old Indian man who had lost his entire family, when he placed his hand over my head and stated, 'Life completes a full circle. Suffering is important so that you may savour the good times.' At that time it hit me like a truck—the last book was in Nalanda. Life comes a full circle—it ends where it began. I came here at the very spot you stand on and held it in my hands. But after what happened in Bengal, how could I possibly hand it to either the British or the Americans? I always believed that I had chosen the right side in the war. I wasn't so sure anymore. How can we possibly kill millions of our own citizens; what kind of British Empire is that?

Yes, I stopped you from acquiring those books. Yes, those books have been used to create mayhem around the planet. I did realize then what Ashoka wanted, why he wanted those books to be hidden forever. It is in the nature of man to be destructive, to use power for evil rather than good. You were always right Prithvi, you fought in a war which was not yours, to prevent death and destruction; I aided death and destruction.

Two of the books are with the Americans and there is nothing I can do about that. However, the ninth book and the books I acquired from Heidler are in my apartment in Calcutta hidden in a place which will be very obvious to you. Soon India will be free. I trust you will use these books to help build a nation which realizes the dream of Ashoka.

I hope to see you in your cricketing whites in Bombay very soon. And if you consider me your friend, we will perhaps celebrate a century of yours together. I don't know if you remember, but you owe me a drink you promised me all those years ago in Indo-China.

Yours truly,
Lt. Col. Richard Youdale

Prithvi then did something he had not done in a very long time—not when Princess Noor had died in front of him; not when the blood from Pandey's limp body had splattered across his face; not when he couldn't bear the stench or breathe in the hell ship suffocating with hundreds of other men, and not when the Japanese soldier aimed the blade of a sword at his neck in that filthy trench—he broke down and cried.

January 10, 1947: Bombay, British India

It was the last Sankrant in Bombay under British rule and the British residents wanted to mark this occasion with pomp. The local Indians too were enthused; their erstwhile masters were now mere guests. After so much bad blood between the rulers and the ruled, it was refreshing to see the children of both races with some adults in tow, flying colourful kites all over the city.

As the Plymouth cab pulled into the residence, Babu assumed it was another Englishman coming to greet the old Mr Rathore on the auspicious day. Initially he did not recognize the thin man who stepped out of the cab but his demeanour seemed very familiar. Babu then improvised his vision by placing his hands on his eyes to focus at the stranger. He could not believe his eyes—it was Prithvi!

Forgetting protocol, Babu did something he hadn't since Prithvi was a little boy—he gave him a hug and shrieked loudly, 'Prithvi is back! Prithvi Baba is back!'

Hearing the ruckus Prithvi's grandfather stepped out as well. He did not take as much time as Babu to recognize his own flesh and blood. He rushed to hug his grandson, his voice thick with emotion and said, 'All of us took you for dead, son. It has been so many years!'

After the initial excitement wore off and Prithvi had had a chance to rest and get cleaned up, he narrated his travails since they last met in Singapore. His eyes filled with tears when he revealed his rescue by Youdale and the incidents that followed. 'I killed a good man,' said Prithvi, his head in his hands.

'You did more than what anyone expected of you. You made a mistake in the end, but you did not do it maliciously. My fellow Unknowns refer to you fondly as "The Tenth Unknown", and with good reason,' said his grandfather.

Prithvi looked up and shook his head before saying, 'No. I know of someone else much more deserving of that title.'

EPILOGUE
AUGUST 15, 1947: NEW DELHI, INDIA

Mahatma Gandhi was in Bengal trying to stop the riots. In Punjab too, the Hindus, Sikhs and Muslims were at each others' throats killing men, women and children. Trains from either side of the border were arriving drenched in blood with limbs strewn across carriages. Prithvi considered going to Punjab or Bengal to help in any way he could. But he decided that he had seen enough bloodshed and he would rather see the spectacle unfolding in front of his eyes in Delhi.

The streets were packed and beyond the sea of people, he could see the magnificent Red Fort. The British soldiers who, less than a year ago, were raining blows against the Indians were perched on Indian shoulders and were being whisked around amidst cries of Jai Hind.

Every second person was trying to get near a radio to listen to Nehru's historic speech on the first day of India's independence.

Long years ago we made a tryst with destiny, and now the time comes when we shall redeem our pledge, not wholly or in full measure, but very substantially. At the stroke of the midnight hour, when the world sleeps, India will awake to life and freedom. A moment comes, which comes but rarely in history, when we step out from the old to the new, when an age ends, and when the soul of a nation, long suppressed, finds utterance. It

is fitting that at this solemn moment we take the pledge
of dedication to the service of India and her people and
to the still larger cause of humanity ....

Will this really be the India that Ashoka dreamed of? Taxila
is now in Pakistan; Pataliputra is in India—has the dream
soured? Prithvi asked himself.

At the dawn of history India started on her unending
quest, and trackless centuries are filled with her striving
and the grandeur of her success and her failures.
Through good and ill fortune alike, she has never lost
sight of that quest or forgotten the ideals which gave her
strength. We end today a period of ill fortune and India
discovers herself again. The achievement we celebrate
today is but a step, an opening of opportunity, to the
greater triumphs and achievements that await us. Are we
brave enough and wise enough to grasp this opportunity
and accept the challenge of the future? ....

Two hundred years is a long time, Prithvi thought. The
British have left their indelible imprint on the lives of all
Indians. Should we shake off that heritage, or accept it as our
own, just as we accepted the Parsis and the Mughuls in the
centuries of yore? What does Ashoka's vision encompass?

It is a fateful moment for us in India, for all Asia and
for the world. A new star rises, the star of freedom in
the East, a new hope comes into being, a vision long
cherished materializes. May the star never set and that
hope never be betrayed! .... The future beckons to us.

Whither do we go and what shall be our endeavour? To bring freedom and opportunity to the common man, to the peasants and workers of India; to fight and end poverty and ignorance and disease; to build up a prosperous, democratic and progressive nation, and to create social, economic and political institutions which will ensure justice and fullness of life to every man and woman ....

Frenzied crowds surged around the cars which led Lord Mountbatten and Nehru to the Red Fort. The recorded speech continued:

To the nations and peoples of the world we send greetings and pledge ourselves to cooperate with them in furthering peace, freedom and democracy. And to India, our much-loved motherland, the ancient, the eternal and the ever-new, we pay our reverent homage and we bind ourselves afresh to her service.

Prithvi was curious about the design of the flag. He knew that there had been a lot of discussion and debate about what it would look like. What had they decided?

Finally, it happened. The Union Jack was lowered by Lord Mountbatten and Nehru proceeded to unfurl the tricolour. Prithvi adjusted his binoculars as he focussed on the flag. Saffron on top stood for dedication, white in the middle for peace and truth and green at the base denoted the bond to the earth. And then, right at the centre, there it was—Ashoka's Dharmachakra. Prithvi finally allowed himself a smile.

Ashoka's vision would definitely live on.

Author's Note

Over many years I have lived in various parts of the world, but something drew me back to India. I can't point a finger to it. After six years in the US, when I first moved back to India, I realized that I had a smile on my lips walking through honking, filthy streets which I missed while I walked down Rodeo Drive. This book is my little way of giving back to a country which has given me everything, from my name to my identity. I wish to bring to readers a part of India which is all but forgotten.

While this book is a work of fiction, there have been rumours about the existence of the Nine Unknowns of Ashoka. I have tried to incorporate many real incidents and individuals related to Buddhism, India and to World War II. These include Butler, Churchill, Roosevelt, Hitler, Goring and Princess Noor among others.

Historical data and information about the city of Bombay was gathered and adapted from the article "The Expansion of Bombay" in the *Times* (UK), May 24, 1911. At times, I have used artistic license to alter certain historical facts. Although the character of Suryakant Pandey is a figment of my imagination, the choice of name is no accident. 'Pandey' was a synonym for 'mutineer' in the British Indian Army because of the sepoy Mangal Pandey who fired the first shot of what later came to be known as the First War of Indian Independence and the Sepoy Mutiny of 1857 in the UK. The revolutionary poems which the General Sahib shows Pandey have been adapted from the Ghadarite poems' cover page, a collection that was published in 1923. The original can be found at the Bancroft Library, University of California, Berkeley, USA. The excerpt of Sir Walter Scott has been taken from *The Tiger and the Thistle*, (http://www.tigerandthistle.net//tipu33.htm). The rockets recovered from the arsenal of Tipu Sultan can today be found at Firepower: The Royal Artillery Museum in Woolwich, London, UK.

Princess Noor was really a descendant of Tipu Sultan. She did seek refuge in England after the Nazis invaded France and returned as a radio operator to aid the Allied War effort. However, she was killed in a concentration camp in 1944 by the Nazis and not on the French-Swiss border as outlined in the book. The stanzas recited by Oppenheimer, a Sanskrit scholar and the father of the atom bomb, do seem to describe an ancient nuclear war in the epic *Mahabharata*. The nuclear test was indeed called Trinity.

A lot of information in the chapter set in Papua New Guinea has been fictionalized using the resources of the Australian War Memorial (http://www.awm.gov.au). Information about this period is patchy, and this is one of the few resources available which documented the plight of Indian soldiers who decided to remain loyal to the Allies and refused to side with the Japanese in the Pacific theatre of WWII. The history of World War II is easily one of the best chronicled and documented histories of our times. Perhaps so well chronicled and documented that the Legion Freies Indien became less than a footnote in that history. While this might be acceptable in the other nations and civilizations which participated in the war, its absence in the text books and collective memory of India is very surprising, given the pride and fondness with which Indians remember most armed uprisings against the British. Most Indians know about Subhash Chandra Bose and the Indian National Army (INA) which was aided and abetted by the Japanese to attack British India from Bengal, Burma and the North-East. While they met with limited success militarily, their contribution to India's freedom movement was much larger after the war, perhaps more significant than that of the Quit India Movement. While successive governments in India have attributed Indian Independence mostly to Gandhi's Quit India Movement, this movement was at best semi-successful and at worst, a complete failure. Indeed, the stories of the INA and the Legion were perceived to be so inflammatory that the British Government asked the BBC not to broadcast any information about them for fear of mass uprisings. When word did get out about the trial of INA officers at Red Fort, there were protests on the streets on such a scale that two bitter political opponents— Nehru, the first Prime Minister of independent India and Jinnah, the founder of Pakistan, offered their legal services to represent the officers.

Another major repercussion of this trial was the Bombay Mutiny. To protest against the prosecution of the officers of the INA, the Royal Indian Navy in Bombay refused to take orders from the British officers, and started offering them left-handed salutes and dubbed themselves the Indian National Navy. Much to the disbelief of the British administrators, this mutiny spread to every port in India, from Karachi to Calcutta and the British flag was lowered from the ships and flags of the Indian National Congress, the Muslim League and the Communist Party of India were tied together and hoisted from the naval ships. Elements of the Royal Indian Air Force and local police forces too joined the protests. This was the proverbial final straw which broke the camel's back—for close to 200 years British control of India was directly dependent on the loyalty of Indian troops in the British Indian Armed Forces, non-violent protests notwithstanding. As they revolted, much to Churchill's chagrin, the British had no choice but to leave India. My book is also a tribute to these brave men of the Tiger Legion.

APPENDIX OF IMAGES

Stamps issued by the Indian Legion in Germany for use in INA controlled Andaman & Nicobar Islands—these were printed by the Reichsdruckere (Government printing office) in Berlin.

A Nazi military officer inspecting Nazi Indian troops.

Indian soldier in the Indische Legion.

*Armband of Legion
Freies Indien.*

*Sikh Indian soldier in the Indian
Legion—observe the armband
and the Nazi eagle on the chest.*

Acknowledgements

I am indebted to a host of people without whose contribution this book would not have been possible. First of all, my parents, who bought me every book I wanted to buy and supported every decision of mine, including my decision to go to the US for my undergraduate degree. Bindi, my sister, introduced me to books through her own collection of Enid Blyton when I was a toddler; Ragesh Bhatia, my brother-in-law, was the first one to read the manuscript and give me encouragement; Neelay Bhatt, one of my closest friends since high school and his wife Baljeet, who scheduled calls across time zones to give me feedback. I must also thank Preeti 'Bunny' Maniar aka Bunzoo for her help. I am grateful to The Wallace Library at Rochester Institute of Technology, where as a Computer Lab Assistant I went through the entire India shelf and the *New York Times* archive on microfilm and microfiche. I am also grateful to Sam Abrams, Professor of Creative Writing at RIT for his encouragement.

Lastly, I must thank a man named Hitler (seriously!), a second-hand book dealer near my home. He extended me a hundred-rupee line of credit when I was 11. He refused to sell pirated cheap copies and always got the original stuff. Over the years, I picked up many out-of-print titles from him.

I am also deeply grateful to Ms Mita Kapur for believing in my ability as an author; Hitesh Kanwar for her help in editing and bearing with my impatience; Hanna Lauter and Tini Ruhfus for helping me with the German translations; Rene Chavez for giving me permission to use their pictures. Lastly, thanks to Jesal Bhuta of Click Photography, Mumbai for the author photograph.